THE VAMPIRE'S QUEST

The Realm of the Vampire Council, Book Two

Damian Serbu

A NineStar Press Publication

Published by NineStar Press
P.O. Box 91792,
Albuquerque, New Mexico, 87199 USA.
www.ninestarpress.com

The Vampire's Quest

Printed in the USA
First Edition
February, 2019

Print ISBN: 978-1-950412-05-1

Also available in eBook, ISBN: 978-1-950412-01-3

For Dave Dauberman, a friend always there

Part One

The Archangel Visits

One: St. Michel's First Visit

8 MARCH 1822
London, England

St. Michel stood before Xavier in all his glory, with his sword in one hand and a stern look peering through the golden light flooding from behind. "Listen, Child of God, and obey. Go to Mont St. Michel. Go to the monastery and cathedral built to my legacy and to God's glory. There I shall issue further instructions." As St. Michel parted, his sword lashed across Xavier's forehead.

Xavier cried out in his sleep, waking with blood dripping from his brow. The confines of his coffin never felt so claustrophobic.

He reached up to discover the gash from St. Michel's sword already starting to heal. Why did that surprise him? Vampires healed almost instantly. But how could he imagine their magical healing powers could undo the wrath of an angel rained down in a dream?

The lid to the trunk-cum-coffin lifted and candlelight flooded Xavier's face.

"What's wrong?" Only when he heard Thomas's alarmed voice and looked into his piercing dark brown eyes did Xavier realize his lover had already awakened for the night and no longer lay next to him.

"Nothing," Xavier whispered.

"Nothing?" Thomas almost shouted. "You were screaming. And you bled. There's an injury here." Thomas reached down and touched Xavier's forehead where St. Michel wounded him.

"It's healed now."

Thomas lifted Xavier out of the trunk and moved him to the nearby bed. He held Xavier in his strong arms and rocked back and forth. "What's going on, *abbé*?" Thomas used his affectionate nickname for Xavier, from his human days as a priest. "Tell me."

"You have to believe me. I know you don't have the same faith, but this is real."

"Talk to me." Thomas clutched Xavier harder.

"We have to go to Mont St. Michel in France. Immediately. Tonight. St. Michel, the archangel himself, commanded it."

Thomas frowned. "We arrived here to visit Anthony."

"Anthony will understand." Xavier trusted their closest friend, and the oldest vampire they knew, would accept their explanation for a hasty retreat.

"It was just a dream. Aren't you overreacting?"

Xavier stifled his rising panic. He pointed to his coffin. "The blood. You saw it for yourself, on my forehead. He cut me as a warning. Please, you have to believe me. We have to go." Xavier hated the desperation in his voice. It made him sound unhinged, almost as unstable as the time he disappeared during the French Revolution while human, lost in his drunkenness because he fled from Thomas's love.

"Then we'll go." Thomas petted Xavier on the head, then leaned over and kissed his cheek.

"Do you think me mad?"

Thomas chuckled but squeezed Xavier in his arms. "Always. I never know if your visions are a flight of fancy or real. But they're a part of you. Have I denied you anything since I converted you to a vampire? No. And I never will. So we'll go."

Thomas's skepticism almost convinced Xavier to question what happened, until Xavier stood and saw the blood stain on the silk lining where he slept.

Moments later, Xavier and Thomas said goodbye to Anthony, who as expected, made no protest at their sudden departure. They crossed the English Channel by swimming at vampiric speed and approached Mont St. Michel.

The mere sight of the majestic place awed Xavier. On the northern tip of France sat a small island upon which stood a mystical cathedral, rising out of the clouds and reaching up to the heavens.

Built from the eleventh to fifteenth centuries, legend had it St. Michel visited St. Aubert, the bishop of Avranches, three times in a dream, commanding him to build a tribute to the saint atop the island rock. Enraged, the bishop had not heeded his call; on the third visit, St. Michel hammered the imprint of an anvil into the bishop's head, so when he woke he would believe the saint visited his sleep. Impressed by St. Michel's message, the bishop commenced the project, which took several centuries and various manifestations to complete.

The soaring cathedral built atop the island stretched into the night sky as the two vampires slowed their pace. Xavier and Thomas walked through the fields of grazing sheep toward the water, where they again would need to swim because of the high tide engulfing the island. The small city beneath the castle still acted as a medieval village, with gates and stone walls surrounding it for protection. The one road on the island wound up the steep hill, toward the abbey and monks' quarters. Above the village, overlooking all of

France, the church stood as a legacy to medieval architecture and its grand monuments to God and St. Michel.

St. Michel called Xavier to the shrine, the grandest of all memorials to him. Thomas and Xavier woke an innkeeper and rented an entire floor of his establishment for privacy. They then explored the small island's shops, closed for the night, and last, the grand monastery perched atop. They took a few needed items from sleeping merchants, including an enormous traveling chest they could convert into their temporary coffin, but left behind twice the value of the objects they took.

Xavier and Thomas concealed themselves in their rooms inside the trunk. Xavier braced himself, as the sun rose, for another visit from St. Michel, but woke the next night well rested. With no further divine instructions, the vampires made love and decided to further explore the island.

Inside the cathedral, overlooking the channel, Xavier again talked to Thomas about why they came to Mont St. Michel.

"Did you ever think you're worried about something else?" Thomas pulled Xavier into his arms. Xavier loved the feel of Thomas's long, black hair against his cheek. "Maybe these visions mean something else. Archangels don't *really* visit people."

Xavier looked into Thomas's brown eyes and ran his fingers through his hair. "You saw the blood."

"There are a thousand explanations for that. Why go to ghosts and spirits?"

"Because he came to me." Xavier put his head on Thomas's chest, afraid Thomas thought him insane. Insanity would have been easier to confront than the actual visit from an archangel.

"And so we're here. What now?" Thomas asked.

"We wait." Xavier shrugged and pulled away. "We can tour this magnificent place." Xavier twirled and motioned to the tapestries and view around them. "Here, come back to the courtyard. The view is magical." He reached for Thomas's hand and pulled him outside.

As they admired the water and saw the lambs sleeping on the mainland of France, Thomas came up behind Xavier and wrapped his arms around his waist. Soon, Thomas's tongue lapped at Xavier's ear and his hands wandered across his body. Xavier tensed with sexual passion, leaning into his lover, forgetting about the archangel for a moment.

"Someone will see," Xavier said half-heartedly, at the same time reaching his head back to lock lips with Thomas. "Should we go to our rooms?"

"I can't wait. It's the middle of the night. No one is awake."

They made passionate love to one another, right in the churchyard.

"Blasphemy," Xavier said to his lover as they redressed. "In front of a church. I already have an angry archangel after me." Xavier wondered how much he really meant. Did he think God would disapprove? Xavier felt sure God would dwell more on the power of their love for one another.

But what of St. Michel? Xavier doubted he had the same forgiveness as God. His legacy of violence against those whom he enlisted on his missions told a different story. Then again, Xavier felt certain last night St. Michel would come to him at once, either in their quarters or while Xavier slept through the day. Nothing. No vision. No sign.

"Leave the archangel to me. Nothing will harm you." Thomas smiled at Xavier as they walked down the steep steps toward their inn. "You need to relax."

"I am. I know I worry a lot. But not this time. He came to me. He really did."

"Then we'll wait. For as long as you need and as long as he doesn't prohibit sex."

"He might not want it in front of the sanctuary again." Xavier grinned. Thomas's penchant for blasphemy amused the former priest, despite certain irrational qualms about it. Thomas laughed and pulled Xavier close to him. They spent the remainder of the night in their quarters, with Xavier writing to his aging sister, Catherine, in Paris and Thomas organizing financial affairs.

Before the sun appeared, Xavier retired to their makeshift coffin. Exhausted, he soon fell asleep, before Thomas joined him.

Two: Second Visit

10 MARCH 1822
Mont St. Michel, France

That morning after Xavier drifted to sleep, St. Michel came to him for the second time. With his brow furrowed, he instructed Xavier that someone desperately needed him, and the archangel wanted Xavier to help the person, first by going to Notre Dame Cathedral. Though Xavier flinched at St. Michel's outstretched hand, remembering the tales of pain he inflicted upon others and the gash on his forehead from two days before, nonetheless, he reached out. St. Michel took Xavier's hand in his. It felt warm, human, and Xavier blushed at St. Michel's perfectly formed and sculptured body.

"Come." St. Michel tugged at Xavier's hand to move him.

Though Xavier allowed St. Michel to pull him along, his body stayed behind. Up they went, through the cathedral's steeple, into the clouds, and beyond. "Where are you taking me?" Xavier asked in a whisper, afraid his reluctance to obey the angel's orders might result in his death.

"To what you want from God, perhaps more than anything."

"What do you mean?" Xavier stammered. "What do I want?"

"Forgiveness."

Before Xavier could respond, he stood in a blindingly bright space, with no defined floor, walls, or ceiling. Xavier squinted and spun around, but St. Michel had disappeared. As he began to panic and call out for Thomas, a figure approached. Xavier recognized the tall man at once, with his erect posture, stunning eyes, and French military uniform. It was his brother. "Michel?"

Xavier had envisioned his brother many times since he died during the French Revolution, attacked and killed by an angry mob as he attempted to protect a helpless captured group of priests. His sister's awful lover, Marcel, had poisoned Michel, immobilizing him and allowing the crowd to take over. At the time, Xavier, drunk with despondence over his failed love with Thomas, acted too slowly. He blamed himself for his brother's death. Even after sobering and finding happiness with Thomas, he never forgave himself for allowing Michel to die. Catherine told him a thousand times he was wrong, but he never believed her.

"Yes, it's me." With Xavier's mind back in the clouded reality created by St. Michel, Xavier was snatched into a bear hug by his brother, Michel, who also kissed the top of his head. "A vampire?" Michel chuckled and held Xavier away from his chest. Michel looked radiant and at peace.

Michel read his mind. "And I am at peace. You, on the other hand, suffer too much guilt. Not that it surprises me." Xavier burst into blood tears. All these years of wanting to see his brother came crashing down on him. Michel stood before him, happy. Safe.

"And that's why St. Michel brought you here, little brother." Michel grabbed Xavier by the chin and kissed him again on the forehead. "Forgive yourself." Xavier began to protest, but Michel silenced him with a finger to his lips. "No, listen to me. You live a good life. You care for people.

You're not to blame for all of this world's ills, and your transgressions are no different from those of anyone else. Marcel and the mob killed me. I live here now, with Mother and Father, who send their love. I'm at peace. You should be too. Now, send my love to Catherine. Go to Paris, as St. Michel instructed. There you'll see our sister, and you can give her a kiss from me after you enlist her help."

"I love you." Xavier stepped forward and wrapped his arms around Michel's waist, feeling a cold medal pressed against his cheek as he clutched him.

"And I love you. Now go. To Paris. To Notre Dame Cathedral. And forgive yourself."

"I believe you." And he did. After all these years, Michel's words convinced him of what Thomas and Catherine had spent years trying to convey. He could forgive himself for the loss of his older brother.

Xavier reached out again to hold his brother close and cried out, "I love you."

He opened his eyes and, instead of Michel, saw Thomas standing outside the chest, looking down at him. "You had a nightmare again." Thomas reached down and, without effort, picked Xavier up and carried him to the nearby bed. "What happened to your cheek?"

Xavier reached up to feel his face. He rubbed his fingers across the impression of Michel's medal where it had pressed into his skin. As he massaged his face, the imprint disappeared.

"What's going on?" Thomas looked at Xavier with concern on his wrinkled brow.

"I saw my brother. In heaven."

"Is this about him?" Thomas sat beside Xavier and hugged him. "When will you forgive yourself for what you didn't do?"

"I have." Xavier kissed Thomas on the cheek.

Thomas raised an eyebrow. "So easily?"

Xavier told Thomas about St. Michel taking him to heaven to see his brother. "So yes, with relative ease."

Yet after his visit, he still doubted St. Michel's instructions. Xavier believed he had seen his brother, not a hallucination. Only Michel could forgive him, and so he had. So why did he remain again another night on Mont St. Michel? Why did he believe his brother about his death but not about going to Paris?

Three: Third and Final Visit

11 MARCH 1822
Mont St. Michel, France

Fire came from St. Michel's outstretched palm as he frowned down at Xavier where he lay sleeping. Xavier awoke and tried to rear back as the heat, mere inches away, scorched at his face. Nothing but fire or the sun could kill a vampire, and Xavier—and apparently St. Michel—knew it. Yet Xavier could only whimper and squirm, for in the dream state, St. Michel held all the power. To Xavier's relief, he pulled the fire away once he had Xavier's attention.

"I'm asleep. It's daylight. You're not real." Yet Xavier doubted the truth of his words.

"I've come to you two times, each time offering proof of my reality. Yet you don't believe? Why are you here, at Mont St. Michel, except for my summoning you? Why do you defy my new order to go to Notre Dame Cathedral in Paris?"

Xavier wanted to escape the coffin because St. Michel held the fire in his palm, though not as close to Xavier as before.

"You aren't answering me," St. Michel growled as Xavier lay still. Where was Thomas? Already awake? "Why do you doubt me? Why are you here, instead of on your way to Notre Dame?"

Xavier remembered his first reservations, after they left London to travel here in one night. Nothing had happened. St. Michel stayed away as Xavier slept through the first day.

"But I came to you the second day," St. Michel said, reading Xavier's thoughts. "Despite your blasphemy in front of God's house. I've come to you twice. Yet you defy me. Will you listen? Will you go to Notre Dame?"

Xavier wondered how to respond. Yes, he would listen—anything to remove the threat of fire. He believed the visions both times. Though he wanted to go to Notre Dame after St. Michel came to him on their second night on the island, he convinced himself his mind imagined St. Michel. So he stayed, afraid to leave and go about his life with Thomas, but not yet convinced to go to Paris.

St. Michel reiterated his order to go to Notre Dame Cathedral for further instructions. The fire flared higher in the archangel's hand when Xavier thought of following his command. What was he demanding? An odd quest across Europe? Of course, he ignored these visions in his sleep. "What about the miracles I showed you? Why do you doubt me?" Xavier recalled each miracle, first the lash on his forehead in London, and then the trip to heaven.

"And you wonder what made me angry. You remembered for yourself your utter disobedience." St. Michel pushed the fire again toward Xavier, who cried out in fear. But once again, he pulled the flame back and glared down at Xavier. "You respond only to the threat of annihilation. I tried simpler methods. Twice."

After his visit in heaven with Michel, Xavier spent the night further exploring the island with Thomas and making love on the soft sands of the channel as the tide whirled around, enough to drown any human but exhilarating for the vampires tangled together. The icy March water, capable of killing a person, hardly affected them as Xavier told Thomas the entire story again. Though his lover doubted the truth of it and worried Xavier punished himself, he agreed to wait it out. "I'll do anything to make you feel better again," Thomas told him. At last, they both admitted the first visit from St. Michel spiraled Xavier into a deep melancholy.

Still Xavier resisted St. Michel's call. He grappled between following his heart, which believed the archangel had come to him twice, and listening to Thomas, who protected him beyond all measure and would not risk Xavier's safety if he believed the dream visions were true.

"You know what happens if I must come to you a third time." St. Michel said it matter-of-factly, though the scowl remained. Xavier knew. Violence. Pain. The archangel would not allow any ambiguity about his expectations. "Perhaps this will convince you of my seriousness." St. Michel moved the fire from his palm to his index finger and seared it against the top of Xavier's head.

Xavier lurched awake and shoved open the chest lid, screaming in agony. His head felt aflame. Seconds later, Thomas ran into the room. "Holy shit, what happened?" he asked as he grabbed a shirt from the floor and patted Xavier on the head until the fire went out. "Why did you set yourself on fire? What's wrong? I wake up thirty minutes before you, and you accomplished this?" Thomas grabbed both sides of Xavier's head and stared into his eyes, pleading for an answer.

"I didn't do it to myself." Xavier rubbed his head. It hurt, even as Xavier felt the healing power of his vampiric blood mending the spot. "It's healed now." Xavier looked at his lover to read his emotion and saw a horror on Thomas's face he had not expected. Xavier's heart fell. "What?"

"Bend your head over." Without waiting for another response, Thomas grabbed Xavier by both ears and tilted his head down. Xavier stared at the blankets on the bed as Thomas's finger ran along the top of his head.

"What is it?" The longer Thomas took to react, the more Xavier worried. "Tell me."

"Your head. It healed from the fire but left a small bald spot on the very top."

Xavier looked up and stared into Thomas's eyes. He retraced the wound with his own finger and felt what Thomas described. At the very top, no more than an inch in circumference, Xavier had lost the hair which once grew there. The intense agony of the flame on his head came back to him. If he doubted before, St. Michel left an indelible message about the reality of his visit. They had to go to Paris.

"Tonight." Xavier clutched Thomas with both hands and implored him with his eyes. "We have to go to Notre Dame."

He met no resistance from Thomas, who nodded his head once and pulled Xavier into a hug. Thomas kissed the spot of the wound, and together they prepared to leave.

Four: Notre Dame Cathedral

13 MARCH 1822
Paris, France

By the time Thomas and he left Mont St. Michel and traveled the distance to Paris, even with vampiric speed, they arrived on time to get to their flat before Xavier escaped the rising sun. Thomas often remained outside longer, having a stronger resistance to the sun's approach. He feared taking the day to sleep would allow St. Michel to return, angry Xavier failed again to go to Notre Dame Cathedral.

But nothing happened. The archangel understood, since he read all of Xavier's other thoughts, the abbé had no intention of disobeying again. The transition to Paris, at least, went faster since he and Thomas owned a large apartment near Xavier's childhood home. Because he often visited Catherine and cherished his home city, Xavier convinced Thomas they needed a permanent location, with their own coffin concealed as a trunk, and all the other amenities and staff that otherwise took a couple of weeks to establish.

Pierre, their young butler, had startled at the sudden appearance of his masters. Xavier and Thomas usually sent word well in advance of their approach but didn't have time in the urgency of Xavier's quest. Nonetheless, Pierre had done his job well, with everything in order and prepared for Thomas and Xavier despite their surprise arrival. Thomas kissed the young man on the cheek and doubled his salary for the due diligence and trust.

Xavier woke the next night to find Thomas waiting for him. "How are you? I think you need to feed before we go on this quest." Thomas watched as Xavier pulled himself out of the coffin and went to dress.

Xavier turned around and smiled. "I'm fine." Xavier crossed the distance between them and sat on Thomas's lap. He laughed at Thomas's expression. "Really, I am. These visits scared me at first. I didn't understand them. Now I know they're real, and God is calling me again." Yet something lurked in the back of Xavier's mind, a feeling that more hardship awaited, a challenge greater than facing St. Michel in his sleep. He kept his apprehension from Thomas, however, afraid to worry him further.

"I trust you." Thomas kissed Xavier on the cheek. "But I think you invent these things to cope."

"So I set myself on fire?"

"I didn't say I have all the answers. Just a certain skepticism about your interpretations."

Xavier ruffled Thomas's hair and wrapped his head in a huge embrace. "Good. We need your doubt as much as my belief. Now, come with me."

Xavier jumped up and yanked Thomas along. Before they went out the front door, Thomas pulled Xavier into his arms and drew him into a deep, passionate kiss. He held Xavier for a moment by the chin, then tapped his nose and opened the door. The vampires went into the darkness of the night and sauntered along the Seine, moving toward Notre Dame.

"You're right. I might need all my strength for this. I should feed."

"You don't have to convince me." Thomas wrapped his arm around Xavier and tickled him. "What's on the menu for this evening? Murderers? Rapists?"

"Something fast. I can't ignore St. Michel again."

"You're no fun. I don't know if I like this quest or not. Will we get to have any entertainment on it?" Thomas pretended to pout, but it only made Xavier laugh.

"You're a fool."

"And you're on a fool's errand." Thomas's comment stung a bit, because Xavier couldn't tell if he meant it to tease or as truth. Probably both. "There, how about that?" Thomas pointed to a group of men hiding beneath a bridge. "They can't be doing charity work."

Xavier and Thomas moved into action, separating from one another and sneaking up on the men from two sides. Xavier struck first, snatching the closest victim away without the others knowing. He heard the cries of rage, followed by wails of fear and anguish as Thomas took on the other three men. Xavier grabbed his man's head by the hair while holding his body with the other arm. With his neck exposed, Xavier's fangs descended, and he tore into the flesh and tasted the sweet blood as it moved over his tongue.

In seconds, Xavier knew the man met the vampire ethic's criteria for death. Seeing his life in the blood as Xavier drank it, he saw the robberies, rapes, and other forms of terror inflicted upon the innocent by the idiot. Though after all these years as a vampire part of Xavier still trembled at being judge, jury, and executioner, he believed he saved people by doing so. Finished, he dropped the body to the ground and took the man's knife. He stabbed him in the chest so it looked like a common fight gone bad, then went to see Thomas had done the same with his three dinner guests.

"Three to one. I always have to do more work." Thomas had smashed one over the head with a brick and stabbed the other two.

"You're always hungrier. How many did you feed from, anyway?"

"Two. I got full before the third one died." Thomas came over and linked arms with Xavier. "Do you want any? It's warm."

"I must have fallen in love with your charm. Who else would tempt a lover with such a sumptuous feast of fat men." They both laughed as Xavier turned them back to the quest, toward Notre Dame. Despite his light banter, Xavier felt an incredible weight on his shoulders. What would he learn at the cathedral?

They approached Notre Dame, lit with candles from within, despite the hour's lateness. No one else walked in the middle of the night, even though the cathedral remained secure and safe. It loomed above them, with its gothic towers high above Paris. As they protected the church, the gargoyles adorning it seemed to move at night, watching Thomas and Xavier. Statues of other saints stared them down too. Outside the doors, Xavier stopped and looked up at the cathedral's grandeur.

Thomas came up behind him without making a sound. "Do you want me to go with you?" He held Xavier and kissed him on the cheek.

"I need to go alone. Wait here. Promise?"

"Of course."

Xavier pulled away from his lover and inched toward the entrance. He paused, knowing the huge doors of the main entrance were locked for the night. Instead, he sauntered around the side of the building and looked up high to the top of one tower. He glanced around to make sure no one watched him. Xavier crawled up the side of the building, and in seconds, stood on the walkway between the towers. The gargoyles that looked so tiny from below became life-sized, seeming to glower at Xavier.

As he began to lose his nerve, Xavier almost decided to jump over the side and run into Thomas's arms, until he spotted St. Michel, standing upon the Cathedral's roof with his sword handle raised high above his head but the spear pointing downward, to where he wanted Xavier to go. Yet he lost the fierce expression of his daytime visits, nodding his approval that he was there.

Xavier walked to the tower and went inside. He wound down the stairs without a sound, afraid to alert anyone to his presence. He met nothing but shadow and darkness until he got to the bottom and entered the main sanctuary, lit to God's glory despite being abandoned during the night.

Xavier had loved the grandeur of it as a child, feeling the very presence of God in its ornate architecture, stained glass windows, and religious adornments. It lost its luster after he became a priest and learned of the church hierarchy in control of it, often by exploiting the people of Paris and the hard-toiling priests who never got to step foot in its confines.

Tonight, sent by a prominent saint and perhaps God Himself, Xavier regained his childhood awe as he walked to the altar, unafraid of being caught. Xavier admired the crucifix, intricately carved, with Jesus hanging upon it. He jumped back, however, when Jesus opened his eyes and looked at Xavier.

"Go to Anne, your friend." Christ talked in a soothing voice, with none of the threat employed by St. Michel. "She lives but needs you. Under the bridge, the same one where she returned you to Catherine so long ago. Go help her." Jesus closed his eyes, and the scene before Xavier returned to normal.

Xavier knew better than to question what happened. He paused for a moment, thinking of Anne, as he had so often after they had parted. Xavier became a vampire and had to leave his human life behind, right in the middle of the French Revolution. Xavier met Anne one day during a walk around his parish, launching an intimate friendship. Anne, of mixed ancestry with a white father and slave mother, came from Haiti by way of New Orleans. Her owner freed her and she opened a laundress business in Paris. Seldom would one see a Catholic priest and voodoo priestess mingling, but they respected each other.

When Xavier's life spiraled out of control with the death of his brother, Michel, and then a horrendous fight with Thomas that left him injured, he fled to Anne, drunk with despair. Anne brought him round to understanding himself and convincing him to sober up and come home. Saying goodbye to her as he started his new life with Thomas had been as hard as watching Michel die in his arms, and as difficult as the day he killed his dear friend Maria or risk her suffering humiliation in front of other people. Anne lived, of course, but the pain of being ripped away from her still ached.

Xavier walked out the Notre Dame front entrance, leaving the door ajar. Despite his reverence for the place, he disdained the Catholic officials who governed here. Causing them a slight bit of fear someone invaded their protected space at least amused him.

Xavier found Thomas waiting around the corner, sitting on a ledge overlooking the Seine. "Watching the lovers?" Xavier hopped up next to Thomas, nervous. Another message had come to him inside the cathedral, something he dreaded perhaps more than another visit from St. Michel. He needed to send Thomas away. He could not explain why, but Jesus communicated to him, too, and without verbalizing a word he told him to leave Thomas.

"You mean the whores and their gentlemen clients?" Thomas smiled at Xavier. "How are you?"

"I'm well." Xavier took Thomas's hand and played with it. "It's Anne. She needs me."

"She sent you these messages?"

"I don't know, except I have to go to her, tonight."

Thomas grabbed Xavier's hand. "You would violate the ethic. I don't know if this is a good idea."

"I *have* to go. It's not a choice, ethic or no ethic. It's not like you've always followed the letter of the law."

"Then let's go." Thomas started to jump down but Xavier grabbed his arm and kept him there.

"I need to go alone. Besides, we promised to let Anthony know why we left so soon. Now we know it's about Anne, so we should explain to him."

Xavier hated the subterfuge. True, they promised Thomas's maker and best friend, and also a member of the governing Vampire Council that enforced the vampiric ethic, they would explain their abrupt departure as soon as possible. But Xavier mentioned it to send Thomas away.

"I'll send a letter."

"No." Xavier squirmed a bit. "It's embarrassing. Will you please go see him? I'll see Anne tonight and then Catherine tomorrow. You'll be back before you know it. For me?"

Thomas frowned. "We haven't been apart much. You know I hate it."

"As do I." Xavier nodded. "We also agreed you need time alone with Anthony, and I with Catherine."

Thomas nodded but kept his brow creased. "What do you want me to tell him? The truth?"

"Whatever you feel is best, so he doesn't think I've gone mad."

Thomas stood up and lifted Xavier into his arms. "You won't violate the ethic with whatever Anne wants, will you? Anthony tolerates a lot from me, from us, but I can't allow you to put yourself at risk. You can't interfere with humankind in a way to expose us. I'm not even sure you should go to her."

"I know." Xavier rolled his eyes at Thomas. "You're the one who goes around testing the limits of the ethic all the time, not me."

Thomas set Xavier on the ground in front of him but held to his shoulders. "Are you well? You don't look right."

"I'm worried about Anne. You know what she means to me."

"Then go to her. I'll hurry back. And say hello to Catherine."

Thomas engulfed Xavier in another hug, and Xavier clutched back, trying to hold off the blood tears until Thomas left. Why did he send his lover away, when any other time he hated his absence? Was he going insane? He doubted it, and the bald spot on his head confirmed St. Michel sent him on the quest. But Xavier knew he would be away from his lover for a lot longer than two days, and the journey might very well require he violate the ethic and risk the Council's, and Anthony's, wrath.

Xavier wished he could summon St. Michel for clarification. If an archangel instigated the quest, did his order trump the vampire ethic? It hardly felt like it. His inner being told Xavier such was not the case: beings from heaven may send him on an errand that violated earthly laws without divine protection for doing so on behalf of God. Such had been the reality for much of Xavier's life.

Before he left, Thomas and he kissed again, and their fingers lingered together until Xavier pulled away and insisted he had to get to Anne. He watched Thomas as he ran toward London too fast for a human eye to see. Away from Xavier.

Five: A Dying Friend

14 MARCH 1822
Paris, France

Xavier remembered the scene before him well: the unused bridge on the outskirts of Paris, the no-man's land—created by Anne's magic to ward off intruders—and the bright fire and living quarters underneath it, where he and Anne lived for a time after returning to Paris.

It took Xavier several minutes to compose himself after watching Thomas dart away before he came here. The sight looked as if nothing changed since the French Revolution, when he and Anne spent many good nights after Xavier reformed himself and prepared to return to Catherine and to find Thomas to profess his love.

Despite the warmth he still felt for the place, the atmosphere was disturbed. Anne had never let angry spirits or demons haunt her realm, but Xavier sensed them all around. He headed toward the fire and paused before it when he saw Anne. She lay upon a makeshift bed of straw with blankets piled upon her still form. Her body was not three feet from the fire, which threatened to set her bed ablaze.

"A little cold to be living under a bridge, isn't it?" Xavier walked toward Anne, who grinned when she saw her visitor.

"I sensed your undead self coming my way. The spirits are already up in arms around here, sensing I can't control them like before." Xavier felt comfortable the moment he heard her dialect, a mixture of her Cajun upbringing with a French accent. She had a rhythm all her own.

"I'd retort, but you don't look well. You're awfully close to the fire."

Anne rumbled with laughter under the blankets, which sent her into a fit of coughing. Her thin arm came out from underneath to wipe her mouth. She spoke when she calmed. "Well, then you don't need to ask about my proximity to the fire, do you? A dying, old person needs warmth. Lots of it. Good thing a little spell here and there keeps my fire roaring without much effort."

The vampire ethic forbid interaction with humans a vampire knew in life not only because it threatened exposure, but to remove the temptation to cross them over in order to save them. Xavier wondered today, however, if it also protected their emotion. Other than Catherine, Xavier avoided the misery of seeing his dear and close friends grow old and die. Anthony allowed Xavier to continue seeing Catherine, at Thomas's pleading. Saying the Vampire Council allowed it because of the "unique circumstances," whatever that meant, Xavier continued to see her but no one else. Here Anne lay, too gaunt, freezing under a bridge amidst the winter's snow and coughing because she laughed.

Xavier also knew she would refuse him even if he offered her eternal life. He already had as a last desperate attempt to avoid saying goodbye to her those twenty plus years ago. She had bent over laughing, telling him he already knew the answer, which he had.

"Does the spell keep your bed from catching fire?" Xavier kept a safe distance, always afraid of flames, more so since his visits from St. Michel.

Anne laughed again. "Get around here to the other side where those nasty flames won't get you. Do you think I'd let this fire do any harm to you?"

"Of course not."

"You look well, abbé."

"I am. Or was, until you sent saints and Jesus after me. Did you send them to torture? It was hard enough saying goodbye to you the first time when I knew you were young and had a full life ahead of you."

Anne reached over and patted him on the arm. "What is this talk of Jesus? You think he listens to me? Or that I command St. Michel?"

"Well, you know something. I didn't say anything about the archangel's visits. Or the scar he left atop my head." Xavier bent his head to show Anne, who howled again with laughter.

"Not my doing. I swear. I called for you, but not through him. We can't always control the gods with how we want things done, can we?"

"At least you find it funny."

"I do. Nothing like a good archangel to scare you to death and get you going." Anne coughed again.

"You're dying."

"Yes." Anne nodded and closed her eyes. "And it's about time. I lived a good, full life. Happy, mostly. Not bad for a black woman in a white world chased by the church for what I believed. Don't go around feeling bad or moping because of me. It's time, and I'm ready." She reopened her eyes and wiped at a tear.

"Then why am I here? Or was I right, you couldn't resist torturing me one more time?" Xavier smiled at his friend, whose eyes twinkled despite how she flinched in pain every time she moved.

"It was a way to return the favor of how much I worried about you, when you tried to drink yourself into oblivion, as I dragged you all over France. And for the fact you brought a vampire into my life. Then two, and finally yourself. I owe you a lot for those tricks, you know. You could repay me with the last rites if you're still available as a priest."

"You're dying, and you're in a lot of pain. And you want extreme unction? Even though you never did believe in my church?"

"A church you don't believe in, either. It's complicated, isn't it? Dying, I mean. And faith?"

"It always was." Xavier leaned over and touched his cheek to Anne's. "Perhaps all of our long theological discussions taught me that more than anything else. We have to keep our minds open, don't we? We never know how God will approach us."

"How right you are, abbé. You're a comfort to me."

"But you didn't bring me here to talk about theology. Or to administer the sacrament? What else?"

Anne's eyes grew wide with fear. She clutched at Xavier's hand with a power he thought had long since left her. Then she wept. "I didn't know who else to call, where else to turn. I don't have power anymore, or I could have done this myself. I hate asking this of you. I know you aren't supposed to do it. But I need you."

"What is it?" Xavier petted her hair. "Tell me."

"I'll *show* you." Anne pointed to the fire.

The flames flared to the top of the bridge, causing Xavier to shrink back. Then they died down but left in their place a vision of another land Xavier had never seen. The image appeared as if from a dream. Xavier could tell the event occurred, despite the fact the people and buildings were blurred, not real and solid. The scene engulfed Xavier.

He felt Anne reach over and grab his hand. Her presence and comforting voice surrounded him, though he could not see her. "I'm right here. It's the only way I know to show you. I'll bring you back once you know. You're in New York City. In America."

Buildings huddled close together, and dirt and grime covered everything. The stench of feces and garbage in the muddy streets offended his senses. It was night, with little light illuminating anything, though Xavier could see well because of either his vampiric vision or Anne's magic. A strapping young man in his twenties came meandering around a corner, whistling a tune and tossing an empty bottle in the air, only to catch it again. "My grandson, Duncan," Anne said.

"You have a grandson?" Xavier looked around for Anne in the vision but saw nothing but New York City. "I never knew."

Anne chuckled. "This was my secret. I didn't talk about them because I missed them too much. It was a painful memory. And continues to be. I was raped in New Orleans before we came to Europe. They took my baby away from me and hid her. I never met my child but learned through magic to watch her from afar. I cared for her from a distance the best I could, and then for her husband and son when they came around. Now stop talking to me. We haven't much time and you need to see this. Memorize his face for me."

Xavier glanced back to the young man, who almost caught up to where Xavier stood. Xavier burned the man's image into his mind: the height, around six feet, the short-cropped hair. He was hit by the man's beauty. He had a square jaw and chiseled face with the hint of a smile. His full lips enticed Xavier. Absent Thomas, Xavier thought he could fall in love with the man. Or, at least, lust.

Just as he almost lost himself in the fantasy, two horses came storming from an alley. The white riders snarled as they raced through the streets, then one took out a club and swung it over his head. Xavier ducked before remembering none of it was real. Duncan whipped around in surprise and then terror when he heard the horses behind him. Xavier saw the club smash into the young man's head. Duncan fell to the ground.

The two men reared up their horses and jumped down. As Duncan tried to gain his senses and lurch away, one of the men punched him. Blood poured down Duncan's face as he yelped and tried to get away to no avail. They hit him again and heaved him over one of the horses.

Xavier almost threw up. He had run over to help Duncan, to intervene, screaming at the men to stop. Of course he knew they heard nothing. But he screeched again in anger when both got back on their horses, the one with Duncan again hitting the man over the head with the handle of his revolver. At that, the scene went black and Xavier stumbled back into reality.

Xavier had fallen beside Anne's bed with the blood tears streaming down his face. "That happened?"

"It did." Anne wheezed more than before, Xavier assumed from the exertion of showing him the image. "I can't see him anymore. They took him. I've looked and looked and asked spirits I dare not ask for help. Nothing."

"How long ago did this happen?" Xavier got up, wiped his eyes, and returned to Anne's side.

"Not long. I have one more thing to tell you, and then to ask for my favor." Anne coughed and trembled, barely able to whisper. "I went to dark places after they took him. This body," she motioned down herself, "was fine not one week ago. Healthy as a horse. Until I went to the black magic to find him. I pleaded with the demon to take me and free Duncan, but he laughed in my face. He cackled, saying I was of no use to him. These things happened, he told me. I offered him my soul. But he laughed again, saying no one wanted it. Imagine, a demon telling you your soul's worthless. Then his eyes turned fire red and his nostrils flared. 'I'll tell you what happened. That's it. If you'll release the spirits you captured from me, and then agree to die. Soon.'"

The story sent shivers down Xavier's spine.

"Oh, my friend, was I stupid." Anne coughed. "I should have known a desperate person gets tricked by the demon. Happens every time. I need to save Duncan so badly. I said yes." She shook her head in dismay. "I said yes. The minute I uttered the word, the spirits I saved from the black realm soared away, crying in agony as the demon took possession of them. I screamed at him to uphold his part of the bargain. He stalked back to me, black as night except for those burning eyes, and smirked. 'Slavery. They took him to slavery. He's safe and sound now in the South.'

"And he disappeared. I screamed again at him. I sought to get him back. But we made a bargain, and like a fool I accepted it. All these years, I refused the black magic. In one stupid moment of desperation, I let it all get away from me. Gone were the spirits I protected, and I glanced down to see this emaciated body. He kept his promise to tell me what happened, but it did me no good. It meant nothing." Anne stopped talking as she labored to breathe, sweating from the painful memories.

"So you called for me." Xavier sat beside his friend, who nodded her head.

"I'm so sorry," Anne whispered. "I don't expect you to do it. I don't need repayment for anything I ever did for you, it's not about that. It's..." Anne drifted off, crying.

"You were desperate," Xavier finished for her. Anne nodded her agreement. "And friends never abandon each other. Ever. I'll find him."

As if at last hearing what she needed, Anne's hand went limp in Xavier's. Her open eyes stared into the vacant night, and the fire went out. A chilled breeze blew under the bridge, carrying with it the unsavory smell of death.

"I'll find him," Xavier said again, knowing Anne's spirit hovered nearby.

Numb, Xavier moved into action. Without comprehending how he gained the knowledge, Xavier knew what he had to do. He constructed a funeral pyre and then leaped atop it with Anne in his arms. Setting her on the structure, he kissed her cheek softly and administered the last rites, as she requested. Once on the ground, he rebuilt the fire. Slowly, so as not to burn himself, he reconstructed the roaring conflagration. The priest in him took over as he said a funeral mass while Anne's body burned to nothing.

It embarrassed Xavier he spent so much time with her and never knew about that part of her life. In the vision, he sensed the agony it caused her but also felt the deep bond of love she had for her daughter and grandson. As he gathered Anne's things and heaped them on the fire to follow her into the afterlife, he discovered recent letters between her and Duncan. She had reached out to her grandson, and he rejoiced at finding his grandmother when he always believed he would know nothing more about his family. These, Xavier tucked away in his coat pocket.

So that was the quest St. Michel commanded. Perhaps Anne would never require such a thing of him, but the archangel expected as much. Besides, Xavier did not need the divine command to spur him into action. Anne had saved him. When drunk and despondent, Xavier ran to her for help. She pulled him into her grasp and led him throughout France, letting him decide for himself to become sober, waiting at the seaside while he had a brief romance with the sailor who helped him to understand his sexual longings, and then back to Paris and reconciliation with Catherine. Anne nurtured him until he went to Thomas, his true love, and began eternal life with the man of his dreams. He could never repay her.

But he could save the one thing on earth Anne held dear to her. He could go to America to find and save Duncan. With or without a guarantee of protection from St. Michel for violating vampire laws, Xavier had a moral and spiritual obligation to go on the quest.

Six: Farewell Note

14 MARCH 1822
Paris, France

As Xavier wandered away from the bridge toward their flat in Paris, a soothing presence followed him to the outskirts of town and kissed him on the cheek. Thus Anne gave her thanks. The sorrow hit, even though Xavier always knew death never terrified Anne.

If anything, Xavier felt more determination than grief. He would do anything in his power to bring Duncan to safety for Anne. Only then did he understand the forces at work after their visit to Notre Dame Cathedral. Never in his wildest imagination did he envision a moment when he would want to force Thomas away from him, to deceive his lover. But Anne's request instituted such a drastic measure.

Everything about the mission defied the vampire ethic. Already that evening, Xavier had returned to someone he had known in life despite the code forbidding it. Next, he plotted to go on a quest for her and, worse, to interfere in the lives of humans to change the course of history. True, vampires did as much every night when they interacted with humans, fed on them, or played games and had sex with them. But these were one night, anonymous encounters, not deliberate excursions into their lives. Still more damning, Xavier would expose himself in America by searching for Duncan and interacting with people along the way. Once he found Duncan, he planned to give him the letters from Anne, as well as a few other heirlooms he kept out of the fire.

Which brought him back to Thomas. Since bringing Xavier over, they had never defied a single vampire rule. Thomas disobeyed many of them in his pursuit of Xavier, but once Thomas won Xavier over, they lived a model vampiric life. Protective in his love for Xavier, Thomas forbade Xavier from doing anything that might put them at risk.

Xavier had never imagined rebelling against the ethic. He wanted to spend eternity with Thomas and help as many people as possible by killing evil people when he fed. And Anthony had made an exception for the one thing that might have driven Xavier to defiance when he agreed to allow the continued meetings with Catherine.

But nothing could stop Xavier from doing Anne's task. And Thomas would do anything to stop him. Xavier knew it. So Xavier sat at their desk, quill and parchment in front of him, writing the most difficult letter of his life.

My Dearest Thomas,

I hope someday you will forgive me, for I love you now as always: with an intense passion and longing I could never put into words.

From the day you entered my life, I wanted nothing but to remain by your side day after day. I love you. I am yours, now and forever.

Yet, I write to tell you I must leave without you and without your knowing where I go. I can feel your rage already. Believe me, I have no choice. Forces beyond our understanding demand it of me. It is real, Thomas, despite what you may think. The visions were true. After I left you at the cathedral, I went to Anne, who confirmed what I suspected. She needs me. Remember, she once saved my life. Without her, there would be no us. I must repay her, and only I can accomplish what she asked. She died tonight.

My task requires violating the ethic. No doubt, Anthony and the vampire elders will hunt me down. I will accept my fate, whatever it may be, because a divine calling forces me to defy them.

If I survive this action, I will contact you by getting a note placed upon your pillow inside this flat.

Until such time as I can return, please know my heart remains here, with you. Treat it gently, despite your anger, for it will need much mending when I return from this dreadful absence and once again rest in your loving arms.

Yours forever, Xavier

With his letter written, Xavier went to his coffin and lay inside. His body ached, as in life when he got sick. Not from any illness, from which vampires had complete immunity. It ached for Thomas, whom he wanted by his side. It ached for the gaping wound of plotting to leave in secret, without being able to read his lover's eyes.

As he drifted to sleep, Xavier imagined the trouble already brewing because of his intentions. Knowing Anthony and having heard lecture upon lecture about the ethic, Xavier knew for certain his journey defied the ethic in too many ways to count.

The one solace to leaving Thomas in such haste and mystery rested with the fact Xavier decided on his walk home not to undergo the quest alone. He needed help from someone strong and defiant, who loved him as much as Thomas. He needed to draw power from a person as bold as Thomas. And in order to gain her assistance, he would have to begin the quest with the boldest defiance of the ethic his mission demanded. As soon as the sun set, he would visit Catherine.

Part Two

A New Transformation

Seven: Catherine's Story

14 MARCH 1822
Paris, France

Xavier woke with a shudder when his body sensed the sun's disappearance. With the frantic events of the last few days and his dire decisions, Xavier had needed the rejuvenating energy from sleep. If he intended to get out of France before Thomas returned, he must waste no time.

He hurried from their flat, after dressing, and went to Paris's underbelly in search of a worthy victim to further strengthen his body with fresh blood. Despite continued qualms about killing, the blood thirst demanded his attention. He stalked down a narrow alley, waiting for a murder victim. Thomas always scolded him for preferring such harsh terms, instead of dinner, feeding, or a benign idiom. Or at the worst, hunting. But Xavier insisted on stark terminology to remind himself of the power eternal life imbued in him.

He located a worthy victim, finding it easier in Paris since he knew his home city so well, despite several years away. He prayed for the man's soul as he executed him and left the body in a stream of grime and blood to decay until someone found it rotting underneath the piles of garbage.

Xavier raced through Paris again, using his vampiric speed to run so fast no human could see him, despite feeling the rush of wind as he sprinted by. He slowed on Rue St.

Denis, a block away from the home in which he lived before going to seminary, and where Catherine resided her entire life. The familiar street comforted Xavier as he sauntered along, enjoying the memories of growing up, protected by Catherine, Michel, and his father. He stopped across the street from their mansion, which maintained its grandeur even through all of France's travails since the revolution. How had it escaped the wrath of angry mobs targeting anything stinking of nobility and wealth? How did it still stand in such opulent splendor? Xavier knew, of course, Catherine managed the feat with her careful appeasement and caring for people of all ranks in France.

Catherine and her staff illuminated the entire house, extending a warm glow into the street. No doubt Catherine bustled with activity despite her age and had servants running all over the place to do her bidding.

Xavier paused at the bottom of the stone stairs leading to the front door, wanting to remember things as they were before the revolution, with Michel advancing in rank in the army, Catherine managing the family affairs, and Xavier toiling away in his parish. Part of him longed for those simpler times, before the revolution, before vampires existed in his mind, before age crept up on his beloved sister.

Sixty-four. Catherine was quite old, outliving her husband, Jérémie, and almost all their friends. Xavier visited her at least once a year so they could catch up, talk, and enjoy each other's presence. At first they seldom noticed the way Catherine aged and Xavier remained frozen in his twenties, because his mind and emotions matured despite his youthful appearance. But wrinkles appeared on Catherine's face, framing her bright blue eyes, though they danced with excitement at every advancement in the world Catherine witnessed, or glowed fiercely as she lamented the state of France, and particularly the rights of women. Catherine still talked without taking a breath, commanded a room with her presence, and reveled in ordering men around at her will.

Age, however, would stop for no one but a vampire. She injured herself because she moved too fast and impatiently tried to accomplish the tasks she did when much younger. The last time, she fractured her wrist, which meant Xavier struggled to read her letters because of the trembling script.

With the cold railing under his hand, Xavier closed his eyes and envisioned the Catherine of the Revolution, her long blonde hair pulled up and out of her face, her youthful skin glistening, her smile radiating an excitement at the change in government even as Xavier dreaded the violence and death that came with it.

"Are you meditating about the value of stone? Or perhaps too old to get up the stairs? You don't fool me, you know. You only look young." Xavier smiled when he heard her voice from atop the porch overlooking the street and front door of the house. Catherine grinned down at him as she leaned against the ledge and raised her eyebrow. "Get in here. I may die before you finish contemplating."

Xavier hurried up the stairs and entered the house. "Monsieur! You may not enter here! Guards!" A young footman came storming at Xavier. Two guards charged at him as well. Though unusual for a house to include armed guards, even with vast wealth, the attacks on the Saint-Laurent Estate during the French Revolution continued to shape Catherine's handling of the household. And according to everyone but Catherine, both of her brothers died in the revolution. They "buried" Xavier in the family crypt below the house, thus explaining his sudden disappearance. As Xavier struggled to calm the three gentlemen, Catherine whipped around the corner and extended her arms. "There's no need for alarm. I know him." One guard scrunched his eyebrows together and they all looked skeptical but walked away.

Xavier fell into Catherine's embrace, careful of his vampiric strength so as not to injure his sister. Xavier pushed Catherine away to get a look at her impeccable evening gown and proper posture.

"You look well."

"For an old woman. I see it in your face."

"You saw no such thing." Xavier extended his right arm, which Catherine took as they headed down the hall toward Catherine's study, where they always chatted over a glass or two of wine. She allowed no one into the room without her permission, a rule that stood ever since she commandeered the space after their father died. "I meant what I said about your looking well. I always worry I'll find you gaunt or ill. But once again you defy all odds and refuse to age." Xavier almost said something about the future, about stemming the tide of her advance toward death, but thought it better to wait for such pronouncements.

"You flatter me." Catherine patted his hand, then closed the doors behind them. "No advance announcement? You always send word ahead of your arrival." She poured them each a generous portion of their favorite wine, from the Loire River Valley. "In fact, you *always* announce yourself as if the king of France approached my home. This time, you sneak up on me. It's not wise to startle your elders. I may have fallen right over the balcony wall and—" Catherine clapped her hands together. "—SPLAT! Dead French woman on the sidewalk."

"I'd catch you."

"Don't avoid my point. What brings you here?"

Always his oldest sister, protective despite her advanced age and his being a vampire. And she still read his mind.

"Stop it. We'll get to the point in time. First, tell me about yourself. How are you doing with the loss?" Catherine's husband and longtime friend, Jérémie, died a few months before, and Xavier knew what a gaping wound it left for Catherine. Xavier had come to her at once when it happened, to comfort her during her grieving. Thomas and he stayed for a couple of months, until she healed enough to continue with life.

"I do as well as can be expected. Really, it's true. Don't look at me that way." Catherine sat on a couch and tapped the cushion for him to join her. "I miss him. But in his last year as the cancer took over, I prayed more for the end of his suffering than for his survival. I know it sounds crass."

"Not at all." Xavier held her hand and rubbed it.

"The longer he lived, the more the pain consumed his every waking moment. I did not want to remember him so feeble and sick. In some ways, his death brought peace." Catherine wiped a tear from her eye. "There we go again. I think we covered this ground a million times on your last visit. Did you come just to torment me?"

Xavier laughed. "No. Here, give me that before we start." He grabbed her already empty glass and went to refill it. First, he drank the rest of his wine, enjoying the slight buzz. Vampires had to drink human blood to survive, but food and other liquids did not hurt them. He and Thomas seldom ate or drank because it necessitated going to the water closet or outhouse, a bothersome and grotesque endeavor. Xavier could not resist, however, the occasional bottle of wine and inevitable feeling of euphoria rushing over him.

"Anything else new?" Xavier sat down again and handed Catherine her wine.

"What are you probing for? Oh, I know. Nothing. You're trying to delay what we need to talk about. Let me get this over with. I was born the eldest to a noble family. My mother died giving birth to my youngest brother, who became a priest and later a vampire. It's a long story, don't ask. Father died young of natural causes. My other brother was murdered during the revolution. I run a vast empire of wealth, but this is the end of the line. You see, Jérémie and I never could have children. He blamed me, and I blamed him, but we never stopped trying, even after we knew it was too late and it would never happen. It was too much fun. We lived a happy life together, helping the poor and doing what we could to make this world better. We traveled a bit and had many visits from my brother. You know, the vampire. I told you not to ask. I've taken time to mourn the loss of Jérémie but adjusted as well as can be expected. I'm ready to live the rest of my life until the good Lord calls me home. Oh, did I mention an evil warlock had a spell on me for a time? Dreadful. I almost married him but was saved by loving people around me after I put up quite a fight against them."

Catherine smirked the entire time she let out the litany of facts about her life. She could still say her monologue without taking a breath, despite her age. Her eyes twinkled at teasing him, which made him laugh all the more at her calling him out for procrastinating about his visit.

"Are you finished?" Xavier ran his finger down the stem of his wine glass.

"I could continue. Or go into more detail. Or expound upon the contemporary political situation. Do you realize women have few rights? Unlike men, whose penis bestows upon them magical powers to govern, run finance, and control the church." Catherine set her wine glass down and cupped Xavier's face in her hands. "The question, my dear brother, isn't whether or not I'm done. The pertinent question is whether or not you're ready to talk, or if we're going to ignore this all night and come to it at another time. It's up to you."

Xavier stood and ran his fingers through his hair. "You're not as funny as you think you are." He smiled despite his nervousness.

"That's a matter of opinion. Perhaps I'm going senile, because I amuse myself. Get back here. I'm too old to chase after you. Sit and talk to me. Or are you waiting for Thomas?"

She cut to the chase. Yes, Thomas played a role in the drama about to unfold, but not in the way Catherine expected. Which reminded Xavier of the urgency of his coming. He had to accomplish the task tonight, before Thomas headed back from England, before it was too late to get his quest underway.

Eight: Revelation

14 MARCH 1822
Paris, France

"You know I want to convert you?" Xavier returned to Catherine and looked down at her where she sat on the couch after she called his bluff and asked about Thomas.

"Not this again." She rolled her eyes. "So you *do* think I've gone senile. Otherwise you wouldn't remind me you want to convert me every time you visit. Ever since, oh, you came back the first time after going off with Thomas. How could I forget?"

"We need to talk about it again."

Catherine bent her head and then glanced up at Xavier with a sympathetic expression. "It's not any easier for me, this getting old. But it won't change anything to go over this again and again."

"It's different this time." Xavier sat beside Catherine and grabbed both of her hands in his. "We need to revisit the idea."

"I won't do it. I've told you." Catherine frowned at him.

"You want it, though. You told me yourself. And I know from Anthony you would be young again. Think about it." Xavier tried to sound excited, but he knew his nerves made him sound more frantic than anything.

"Calm down. Be reasonable." Catherine took a deep breath. "I can think of nothing better for myself. It *is* difficult seeing you and Thomas remain young and vibrant while my body falls apart." Catherine held up her bandaged wrist. "I pledged my life to you, though. Remember? To protecting you. I lived for that, perhaps above all else. I won't risk it." Catherine shook her head back and forth.

"I'm willing to take the risk." Xavier clutched her hands tighter, trying to squeeze his will into Catherine.

"I'm not. You asked Anthony, and the Vampire Council forbid it. He said you'd be executed. Do you think I want to live for eternity, knowing it came at the expense of your life? That would be worse than the present death staring me in the face. No." She shook her head back and forth with a violent motion. "And the sooner you put this from your mind, the happier we'll all be."

Xavier searched for a way to get his message across. He had meant to signal the urgency of the matter from the beginning, to let her know right away the difference. He rubbed his hands together and stared into Catherine's bright blue eyes.

"I need to start over." Xavier stood and paced the room. His quest could begin once he got his story out and convinced her. It thrilled and terrified him at the same time. Then he thought of Anne, with her fear and bargain with a demon. He had to get it right for her. He turned to Catherine, who waited patiently, tapping her finger on her knee. "I'm converting you. Tonight." He held up his hand to stop her protest. "I am. I have a mission to undertake, which violates the ethic. I'm doing this with or without your help. I've no choice. What I intend to do will anger the Council and quite risk my life. But my chances of success increase *with* you. So I'm here requesting your assistance. I need you as a vampire, now more than ever. Not because I don't want to lose you. We've established that long ago. But because my mission needs you. I *need* you."

Catherine went still as he spoke, staring at him with an intensity she reserved for serious matters or urgent affairs. "You have my attention. Go on. And what does Thomas think of this?"

"He's part of what I need to tell you. Why I need *you* to come with me. But I want to show you something first. You know our blood heals any wounds, except for fire or the sun's rays? Well, feel this." Xavier knelt in front of Catherine and took one of her fingers in his. He guided it to the top of his head, to the bald spot where St. Michel scalded him with a Divine Fire the vampire blood failed to heal.

"Are you shaving a spot into your skull?" Catherine ran her finger around it a couple more times, then lifted Xavier's head to look him in the eyes.

"That wound came from heaven." His pronouncement caused Catherine's eyes to light with concern, Xavier assumed because she thought he had gone mad. "Don't worry. I'm in full control of my sanity."

"Then you'd better start talking, because this sounds more like the drunk Xavier of the revolution than the happy, rational vampire I've come to know."

Without waiting, knowing he had to get every word correct or risk losing her, Xavier launched into his tale, beginning with St. Michel's visit in London, the archangel's anger on Mont St. Michel, and eventually the visions of Christ at Notre Dame Cathedral. He included seeing Michel in heaven, and every time offered Catherine the proof of what occurred: the blood-stained shirt after St. Michel sliced his forehead, the impression of Michel's medal upon his cheek, which Thomas had also seen, and last, the bald spot. He moved into his visit with Anne, Anne's vision of the past from New York and Duncan's capture, and her bargain with the demon who killed her. At last, he explained to

Catherine Anne's pleading for him to save her grandson in America. "You don't look like you believe me," he ended.

"I've known you longer than anyone else, remember? Longer than Thomas. I can read you, even better than Thomas. I know when you have a flight of fancy or delusions of grandeur. I know when something troubles you and cascades you into religious revelry. So I know this isn't one of those times."

"No, it's not." Xavier shook his head. "Though I believe the saint came to me, that such celestial visits can happen. This wasn't easy to figure out or accept. It's not like I want to risk my life or the wrath of this unknown Vampire Council. I don't have a choice. I have to do this for Anne."

Catherine nodded, deep in contemplation. Xavier allowed the silence to hang in the air as Catherine thought through whatever was on her mind. Xavier took her wine glass again and filled his too. He handed her the glass, and she drank a large swallow.

"I believe you." Catherine nodded her head again. "I wish I didn't. I don't like to think of you going through this. It's so risky. But you haven't convinced me you need me along. What does this have to do with *me*? I assume Thomas understands and will try to protect you from the Council? He has influence with Anthony. Besides, if this angel demanded the mission, won't *he* protect you?"

Xavier got up and sat next to Catherine. She would never accept his theological explanation about St. Michel. And how could he explain to Catherine he tricked Thomas into going to England, avoided telling his lover, and planned to run away from him? Xavier realized she would understand because she trusted him. He was convincing himself, not Catherine, because he knew Thomas would think every one of these awful things when he discovered the letter Xavier had left for him in their apartment.

"It doesn't work that way. St. Michel, or heaven, or whatever, may spur me into action, but none of the divine interference trumps what happens here on earth. Don't try to understand it logically. I don't understand the contradiction." Catherine rolled her eyes, frustrated as usual by his faith convictions, but remaining silent as he continued. "As for Thomas, he knows about the visits from St. Michel and what happened at Notre Dame. But he doesn't know a thing about what happened once I went to see Anne, or about my intentions." Catherine's head shot up. "He can't. He'd forbid it. I know him and how protective he is of me. He can't control the Council, any more than you or I could. He'd stop me because he loves me too much to risk it. I can already hear his argument about how human chance enslaved this poor man, about how Anne insisted I owed her nothing, which is all true. He would understand it means so much to me, but he could never allow me to chance my life this way."

Xavier finished by telling Catherine how he sent Thomas away and left a note at their flat. He then relayed the story of the time he tried to save a few slaves when he and Thomas visited the American South soon after his transformation. He had seen slavery from the moment they got to the New World and, from the very first, despised it. Watching a slave auction in New Orleans pushed him too far when they separated a brother and sister. The screams of agony from the woman reminded him of Catherine and what he would do if someone tried to take her away. Xavier had waited until that night and then snuck in and freed both of them. He carried them, racing far away from New Orleans into the swamps where a band of escaped slaves lived, free of torment. He terrified both of them because he used his vampiric power in front of everyone. He'd left before they asked questions.

Then, he had told Thomas about his actions, sending Thomas into a rage. Not the passionate anger Thomas vanquished when he went through his own conversion experience while he courted Xavier. Nonetheless, Thomas shouted in anger about Xavier risking himself. He made plans to leave America, at once, and refused to think of their ever returning so long as slavery persisted in his homeland. Thomas and Xavier knew it was too much for Xavier to witness and handle, and Thomas wanted to protect Xavier from the Council and any danger to his life.

Indeed, Anthony confronted them about the whole affair soon after they arrived in England. He said he heard of the violation through others on the Council. Thomas explained—Xavier thought him pretty calm—what occurred and what they each agreed to do to remedy the situation: avoid the New World. That explanation appeased Anthony, but not without an admonition to never try such a stunt again.

"So you see why Thomas can't know? And why this is so risky?" Xavier pleaded with Catherine, looking into her eyes and searching to read her thoughts. When she got up and pulled him with her toward the door, he knew her answer without her saying a word.

Nine: Transformation

14 MARCH 1822
Paris, France

Catherine led Xavier through the house and up the stairs. Xavier remembered again sneaking around with her as a child to get a snack, to surprise attack their brother, or to go pester their father until he quit working and played a game with them. He tried to think of anything that would take his mind off the task at hand.

Not because of any doubt whatsoever about converting Catherine. On the contrary, she would handle eternal life better than anyone he could imagine, except perhaps Thomas. She wanted it, from the moment she found out vampires existed and were not an evil force on earth. Nor did it concern Xavier he would enlist her in a mission to disobey the Vampire Council. Catherine reveled in defying authority. In many respects, it fit her perfectly to come over amidst a controversy and assertion of their independence.

No, he avoided thinking about turning her because he remembered he would see her entire life pass through his mind in her blood. While that ability helped vampires differentiate between whom to kill and who deserved to live when they fed, Xavier had never experienced such a thing with anyone so close to him before, aside from Thomas. After he made Xavier, Thomas had seen his entire life and wanted to return the favor. After much prodding and insistence, Thomas convinced Xavier to drink his blood so he could know all about Thomas too. It was so intimate to see someone's anxieties, embarrassments, and darkest fears. To experience with them the triumphs and tragedies of life. It solidified their relationship all the more, that Thomas demanded Xavier see the inner part of himself. But could Xavier see such intimacy from Catherine? They shared much, maybe everything, but it felt like such a violation of her privacy.

Catherine guided Xavier toward her private quarters. No one ever entered here without her strict permission, as even regular servants who needed access had to ask before going inside. She closed and locked the door behind them, before moving into a sitting room and lying back on a fainting couch.

Xavier stood transfixed in the doorway, paralyzed by his latest thoughts.

"I thought the legend a vampire had to be invited into a room wasn't true?" Catherine smiled. "Having second thoughts?"

"No." Xavier shook his head. "Absolutely not. But—" He stopped, not sure how to proceed.

"But what? Does old blood spoil and taste sour?"

Leave it to Catherine to make him laugh and put him at ease. "It has nothing to do with age and everything to do with the bitter attitude of the individual. Yours must be like curdled milk."

"What a charming way to seduce the person whose help you seek. I'm sure my blood is the strongest you'll ever have tasted."

"Strongest and not sweetest?" Xavier knew Catherine's reaction before she said a word and stepped back in mock fear.

"I leave the sweetness to women who float about a house doing nothing but the bidding of men. I've more pressing matters in my life requiring strength." Catherine dismissed him with a wave of her hand. "But here we go again. Shall I give you another miniature version of my life? Or is there another method of avoiding this business you'd prefer? I thought we were in a hurry."

Xavier moved back into the room and glanced out the window overlooking the balcony and street below, where a light rain started to fall. Xavier heard the distant crash of thunder and chuckled to himself. "Fitting, we'd bring you into this life amidst a tempest from the gods. I'm sure they aren't happy about making you any more powerful than you already are."

"No doubt, but I can take them on." Catherine fell silent, as she always had since Xavier was a boy and she waited for him to proceed. Catherine, impatient, in a hurry, and speaking a thousand words per second, always calmed for him. He loved her anew at the memory of it.

"I'll know everything after we do this thing. You understand, right? I'll see every moment of your life pass through my mind in personal detail. You won't be able to hide a thing from me."

"I'm old, not senile. You've told me before." Catherine got up and stood next to him, rubbing his back. "You already know too much. I can't think of a thing I hid from you, and if I did, it was never intentional. This will be fine."

"Did you hear me? Everything?"

"You won't see anything to hurt you, if that's what you're worried about. Or are you too afraid to see sex?" Catherine roared with laughter as she finished her sentence, looking at Xavier's astonished face. "Well, there may be a surprise or two there."

"I hadn't even considered sex. Now I may change my mind." Xavier rubbed both of his hands across his red-hot face. "So, how shall we proceed?"

They stared at each other for a long moment, both deep in thought. Then, at the same time, they fell into hysterics, to the point Catherine sat down and the blood tears streamed down Xavier's face.

"This does feel a bit incestuous." Catherine laughed again. "Let's stop the agony. Explain to me how it works, and then let's be done. There's no reason for a grand ceremony or party. You said we need to get on our way as soon as possible."

"Right. To avoid Thomas."

Catherine looked at him with disapproval. "We still need to talk about him." Then she had them sit side by side on the couch.

"He wouldn't allow it." Xavier worried Catherine would try to talk him out of going. His heart was set, his mind clear that his very soul demanded the calling.

"I can't think of anything that man ever denied you. Maybe he could think of a way to do this without violating the ethic. Maybe he'd understand more than you think."

Xavier had pondered as much himself. Since boyhood, he had a bad habit of sneaking around and doing things for fear someone would disapprove, try to stop him, and give him a lecture about it. He'd learned to do things first and then take the admonitions from people afterward, which gave him what he wanted instead of getting the same disapproval but then being empty-handed. Thomas thought his behavior came from Xavier's upbringing, when his father, brother, and Catherine sheltered him too much and demanded perfection, ironic because of their utter love and devotion.

But with Thomas's last reaction to his involvement with slavery and banishing them from America, Xavier could not gamble it. If Thomas hesitated or disagreed, there would be no way for Xavier to get away. While Xavier despised the deception, at least he never lied to Thomas.

"I know what you're saying." Xavier played with the cross he wore under his shirt. He glanced to gauge Catherine's demeanor. She appeared calm. "I thought through it all. I know he'd forbid this. There's no other way."

"Then I'll trust your judgment." Catherine sounded unconvinced. "Did St. Michel tell you all of this? Or are we into the faith area again?"

Xavier took his turn to roll his eyes. "Don't patronize me."

"Fine. We'll leave it there." Catherine smiled. "Now, what do we do?"

"I have to drink your blood. I'll bite your neck, and then drink until the exact moment I feel your heart stop. Then, I'll bite into my wrist and feed you my blood."

"Oh, just another mundane day, then." Catherine smirked.

"Or maybe I can bite your wrist, so it doesn't seem so sexual."

Catherine laughed harder than she had all night. "You're such a prude. If you can get enough blood out of it, by all means switch to my wrist." Catherine held her wrist up toward him.

Xavier twitched his knee up and down. "You'll feel death, know you died, and reawaken young, strong, and with vampiric senses."

"Will it hurt?"

"Not at all. I promise."

"Then go." Catherine jerked her arm in the air again at Xavier, exposing her wrist to him. "Before either one of us thinks about this any longer."

Knowing she was correct, Xavier leaned forward and latched onto her wrist. He drank the blood, hungering for every last drop, but listening and sensing for the moment he killed his sister. Within a second of her death, he tore open his wrist and pressed it into her mouth, feeling the blood flow into her. After a minute, she sucked at him, then her new fangs descended, and he had to stop her.

Xavier almost fainted with dizziness. True to her word, nothing surprised him or made him feel awful, but it still discomfited him to know all of his sister's life. He also worried she would ask him to return the favor, which he did not want to do. There was so much between Thomas and him he never wanted to share with anyone else.

Then, even more astonishing, Xavier noticed her transformation. As he held his wrist to her mouth, he witnessed the gray hair disappear and grow into the vibrant blonde of her early adulthood. The wrinkles faded, and as the aging process reversed, Catherine became the able-bodied, strong, and self-assured woman of her past.

"Interesting," he said after Catherine finished and spun around, smiling.

"You bring me into eternal life, make me a demon, and all you can say is 'interesting?'" Catherine leaped across the room and into his lap.

"I didn't make you demonic. You brought that with you."

Catherine snapped at him like a dog, letting him see her fangs again. "Do you like my power?"

"Adore it. Like bringing a new kitten into my life."

"So what's interesting?" Catherine played with his hair, feeling his bald spot again.

"Your age. The vampires I know either transformed very young, such as myself, or reverted to their twenty-something appearance upon transformation. You're the spitting image of what you looked like in your late thirties. It's interesting, the reverse aging stopped sooner with you."

"I didn't control any of it on purpose. This was my favorite age, though. With the revolution behind us, living with Jérémie, and having you visit often. I loved it."

Xavier considered what Catherine told him. He suspected the mind controlled when a vampire stopped the process. Most people went for youth and vigor, but Catherine went for strength, tranquility, and happiness.

"Well, this fits you well. But you'd better tie your hair up, before we go out for lessons." Xavier took her hand and brought her into her bedroom. She did her face, her hair, and picked a more suitable dress, and then whirled around again, so fast her hair fell down.

"What kind of lessons?" Catherine fidgeted with her hair and whistled when she wasn't talking.

"First one: quiet can be beautiful." Xavier clapped his hand over her mouth to silence her. "I can't put up with this noise for eternity." She bit him. "Ouch!"

"What *real* lessons?"

"About being a vampire. About how to handle it. Honestly, because you know so much already, we don't have much to do. Besides, we don't have time for all the things Thomas trained me to do. You'll have to learn as we go."

Ten: Family Matters

15 MARCH 1822
Paris, France

Xavier and Catherine spent about an hour running around Paris as he pretended to teach her everything he knew about the life of a vampire. Pretended because she already knew. Every time he wanted to go over a lesson, she had already learned it from one of them or figured it out on her own. Xavier struggled to remember every little thing but kept failing to find anything noteworthy. He gave up.

Next Catherine had to feed but once again needed no assistance from Xavier. She knew all about the ethic, how to lure a worthy victim into her grasp and how to conceal the kill from other people. If anything, she played a game of cat and mouse to perhaps rival Thomas's. Many a man gave more than a passing glance to her stunning beauty as she walked through the streets alone, Xavier having concealed himself high on the rooftops in order to enjoy the show. A few stalked her, others stared holes through her, but all of them monitored the isolated woman, waiting for a chance to pounce.

And so one did, as Catherine turned into a narrow alley. He raced around the corner and grabbed her from behind to pull her deep into the recesses of the darkened part of Paris. Xavier chuckled as Catherine went limp in the guy's arms and allowed him to carry her into a corner. She whimpered and whispered a plea for him to stop. Xavier jumped to the ground in order to get a better view of the show.

"Please, I'll do anything. Don't harm me." Catherine sounded so innocent and afraid as she tried to barter with him, but he went about unbuckling his trousers and pulling them down. "One last chance, please don't. You'll regret it." The man answered by flicking his chubby member, standing at attention.

When he moved toward her, trying to pin Catherine's arms against the wall, she smiled and let him see her fangs descend. In a single motion, she shoved him back across the alley to the other wall and chomped down hard. Standing behind her, Xavier could guess she dismembered the fool when he wailed in anguish and fought to push her away, to no avail.

Catherine jumped off the ground laughing as she pulled Xavier back into the street.

"Lovely." Xavier patted his sister on the hand. "More charm than you had in life." He guided them back toward the Saint-Laurent home for one last thing before embarking to America.

"How many women do you think suffered a similar fate from that brute? I saw. And you don't want to know. Asshole. I need to learn to torture them more."

"I can see between you and Thomas I have no hope of teaching compassion."

"It's not like we go after innocent people. I thought you were a vampire now, not a priest." Catherine rested her head on his shoulder as they continued to walk.

"I'm both." They both laughed at the thought of a vampiric priest. Then they fell into a comfortable silence as they sauntered along the Seine.

"You seem rather serious." Catherine wrapped her arm through his, looking like any other couple, except no respectable people walked about at such a late hour. Catherine pulled away from him and stopped. She looked at the ground and fidgeted, not with her typical uncontrolled energy. "I can't keep this from you." Catherine returned to his side and pulled him along. "How come you didn't see it when you turned me?"

"I tried to ignore as much as possible. There was a lot to take in, despite a vampire's ability to process information."

"I'll tell you at home. Come."

They avoided any servants by climbing an outer wall and entering through a window to Catherine's chambers. They went down a secret stairwell and scurried a short distance into Catherine's office and sat next to one another after she locked the door.

"I deceived you." Catherine clutched Xavier's arm. "I hope you can forgive me, again. This may be worse than when I wandered around under the spell from Marcel."

"What is it?" Xavier grabbed Catherine's shoulders, trying to focus her attention and get her to say it. She never shied away from her feelings or telling him something. That was *his* usual behavior, and coming from her it made him nervous.

She took a deep breath. "I tricked you. Since the first time you offered to make me a vampire, I wanted it. *Desperately.* I so wanted to become a vampire. I feared death. I hated getting old. But I never pressed or wanted to reveal this to you because your safety meant more to me. I knew the Council or whatever you call it would come after you if you turned me. I couldn't bear the responsibility. I studied you and Thomas and probed for everything I could learn about being a vampire, always hoping one day it may happen, always thinking I would be prepared when it did."

"And you were." Xavier pulled Catherine into a hug. "I decided to bring you over, remember? You think it surprises me to know you wanted eternal life? Who wouldn't? It's one of the reasons we can't tell people or remain close to those we loved before our transformation. Because too many vampires would do what we did. It wasn't a trick on your part."

"But instead of talking you out of it, I reveled in the possibility. Even now, I feel a little guilty, but mostly excited."

Xavier laughed. "I guessed all of this." Xavier pushed her away to look into her eyes. "You're not as clever as you like to believe. It's remarkable you held off for so long just to protect me. How could you ever feel guilty when you grew old and watched me enjoy constant youth, without ever begging me for it? I came to you because I need you. I would have turned you sooner, but this gave me the perfect excuse. Do you think I wanted to lose you? That it was fun watching you grow old and fragile?"

Catherine punched Xavier in the arm. "I was a charming old woman."

"Old, yes. Charming? You never accomplished charm, young, old, or now, dead."

Catherine sprang at him and pinned him to the couch, laughing. "I bet I'm a stronger vampire."

"I've no doubt."

Catherine jumped off him and whirled around. "Crap. Now I'm dead, and no one owns all this. What are we going to do?"

"Ah, there *are* things I can teach you." Thomas had trained Xavier in the art of vampiric finance, property ownership, and how to hide it all from prying human eyes. "It's easy to fool people. We need a short-term and long-term plan. Short term: we leave notes and orders around the house, explaining a distant cousin came to visit and took you to his country estate to visit family you haven't seen since childhood. Your staff will remember seeing me and think nothing of it. That gets us on our way to America. If we're so lucky as to survive, then we go to the next stage. While you're visiting these dear relatives, you decide to leave them your empire, seeing how you have no descendants to pass it to. People will marvel how the young cousin looks so much like Catherine before she died, when a short time later we kill you off. Now, eventually we'll have to do something more drastic, but this story should suffice for now."

Catherine rushed to the couch and grabbed both of Xavier's hands, yanking him to his feet. "I've too much energy to sit and do nothing. I thought we had to hurry on a mission. Come on, let's go. Won't the Council be after us soon?"

Xavier pondered the question for a minute. "I'm not sure. Thomas doesn't know much about them either. And Anthony, despite sitting on the Council, or maybe because of it, keeps it very mysterious. They monitor all things vampiric, but I don't know if it's through a network of vampire informants or by magic. Maybe both. So I'm sure they'll find out about turning you and investigate. But it doesn't seem as if they learn these things the minute they happen."

Xavier shrugged. "We'll be off soon enough. I've one more thing for us to do. You decide whether or not to come along for yourself." Xavier walked out of the room, glanced around the hall to see no one approached, and then moved fast. He knew without asking or seeing her that Catherine would follow, too curious to remain by herself. He slipped down a narrow servant's passage and to the basement door.

Heading down, he thought of the awful memories contained in the first lower level: the assault on the nuns during the revolution, how he tried to sneak down to warn them but gave away their hiding place, the rapes, the attack on Xavier, and the trail of blood he followed back up the stairs to the main level, where he found a beaten and raped Maria begging for death. Still he moved on, pushing these things from his mind.

"Is this a vampiric ritual?" Catherine touched his shoulder as they turned to go down yet another set of stone steps, toward the family crypt. "I thought the legends weren't true about coffins and cemeteries and the like?"

Without turning around, Xavier could sense the grin on Catherine's face as she talked, perhaps to hear her own voice. It made him laugh, despite the seriousness of why he wanted to visit their fallen family and friends. "If you continue talking, this will become your final resting place too."

"I'm rigid with fear." Catherine placed both hands on Xavier's shoulders and leapfrogged over him, landing at the end of the stairs in the crypt. Surrounded by cobwebs and a dank, musty smell, she lit a couple of torches and turned back to Xavier. "Why are we here?"

"For strength." Xavier touched the coffin lid of their father, then glanced at the place where they buried Maria and her friends to conceal what occurred in the house. Xavier thought about Maria almost every day: his one friend from within the Catholic Church; their service to the people of his parish; their long talks, and how protective Maria was of him; and that he killed her. As she pleaded with him to end her life, fearing humiliation and having to remain on earth with the horrid memory of watching her friends die and men rape her and them, Xavier had resisted. However, he had come to realize he had to do the terrible deed for his friend. So he went to Catherine's office, got their father's gun, aimed it at Maria, and pulled the trigger.

Funny, how the awful and depressing act of saving his friend propelled him to the greatest event of his life: no longer afraid of killing and coming to terms with the notion it might be necessary, Xavier went to Thomas, ready for his transformation.

"Strength?" Catherine arched her eyebrow at her brother. "It feels very dead to me."

Xavier pulled Catherine next to him and held her there. "This will challenge you, I know. Be still. Be quiet." Xavier let those ideas linger before continuing. "Now, close your eyes." He closed his too. "Do you feel it? They're here. Mom, Dad...Maria... And Michel...especially Michel. They want to protect us, to encourage us on our way."

Catherine leaned into her brother and sighed. "Jérémie too. He's here for me. For us."

Xavier pulled Catherine into his grasp, knowing how painful the memory must be for her. He stayed there motionless for several minutes, remembering the love from each of the people gathered around them with their spirits, giving him the fortitude to launch his quest, once and for all.

Eleven: Departure

15 MARCH 1822
The French Coast

With renewed inner strength from their visit to the family tomb, Catherine and Xavier used their vampiric speed to race to the coast where a cargo ship readied to launch to America. "Here's the boat." Xavier pointed to a large ship set to sail at any minute. The sails billowed out, and the hulking ship creaked as it listed from side to side.

"And we're cargo?" Catherine frowned again at Xavier. He explained to her the safest way to travel was in the hull of the ship, away from prying human eyes or the temptation to feed at sea, where they could be found and murdered during the day. "Did you forget we're rich? I thought we could be glamorous vampires."

"Quit pouting." Xavier puffed out his lower lip, mimicking the expression on Catherine's face and prompting a playful slap on his arm from her. "I explained all of this to you. We could swim, but I hate doing it over the ocean. It creeps me out."

"I bet Thomas doesn't travel this way."

"Thomas *does* travel this way. How do you think I learned it?"

As they snuck aboard, a lump caught again in Xavier's throat. Thomas. Xavier tried so hard to forget about him, to try to pretend all was well with the world. But of course it wasn't. In fact, it was horrendously off-kilter. How could he leave Europe without his lover, without Thomas even knowing his destination? Only the spirit of those he loved gave him the courage to follow through with his calling because he had to save Duncan for Anne. He prayed Thomas could someday forgive him and understand. Xavier grabbed Catherine's hand as they lurked around the cargo boxes, trying to find a cozy place for passage on the sea.

Sensing his mood, Catherine patted his shoulder. "You don't have a choice." Catherine opened a trunk, and whipped out garments and silks bound for New York City. She spread them out on other crates and the ground, transforming their area into a nice home for their journey. Xavier sat on the makeshift carpet, while Catherine jumped onto a bed she made on one crate and looked down at him. "He'll understand."

"What if it makes him angry again?" Thomas had a famous temper, though he kept it under control since transforming Xavier. Their love healed so many of the wounds that generated the intense anger within Thomas because of prejudice and his feeling of being alone in the world. What if Xavier's disappearance brought it back?

"He loves you. And you love him. He'll forgive you." Catherine's soft face glanced down at Xavier, as she had so many times throughout his life when she knew he hurt but could do nothing to stop it. She soothed him with her presence. He loved her for being such a protective older sister. At least this awful calling from St. Michel meant he would never have to say goodbye to her. "How will you contact him when it's over?"

"I arranged it through a trusted servant. I think you've met Pierre. I paid the boy, as we always do, and then bought a small flat for him and his lover. I instructed him I may send a letter, addressed to him at his new flat, and inside would be more payment and a separate note for Thomas. He knows to place the note upon Thomas's pillow at once, when no one else will see him do it. I want to protect him, so this task doesn't place him in the awkward position of having to choose to obey Thomas or me. It allows me to leave on this trip but know with certainty Thomas will get whatever message I send to him." Xavier had gotten out a stack of papers, showing Catherine the address and memorizing it for himself, in case he lost the slip. "I have it memorized. You keep this, just in case." Xavier couldn't continue; he could barely think the rest of his thought: something may happen to him, and Catherine would need to deliver to Thomas the news he died or was sanctioned by the Council.

Catherine took the note. "I understand."

The ship groaned as it moved out to sea. With the coming sun, he and Catherine cleared out a couple of crates on the other side of the ship, in case a sailor ventured down here and found their temporary home, and crawled in to go to sleep. Xavier had slept apart from Thomas a couple of times since his transformation, and then always with the knowledge they would reunite in a short while. The emptiness next to him that morning felt like a gaping pit he may tumble into, at the bottom of which lay a raging inferno conjured from hell.

He prayed for perseverance and strength as he drifted to sleep. He thanked God for Catherine being with him, and for the strong presence of Michel and others to guide his way. Finally, he prayed they would assist Thomas, too, when he found the note and for surviving without Xavier until they came together again. He wanted to pray for Thomas to forgive him and still love him, for him not to lose on the dangerous quest. But thinking it made Xavier cringe he might bring it to fruition, so instead, he allowed exhaustion to once again pull him into a deep sleep.

Part Three

Separation

Twelve: Duplicity

17 MARCH 1822
Paris, France

Thomas seethed.

The rage coursed through his veins, from his heart, through his torso and into the tips of his fingers and toes, invading every inch of his brain. Not since Xavier vanished during the French Revolution had he experienced such intense anger, the time that prompted him to harm the innocent, chase away his dearest friend, Anthony, and to attack anything and everyone around him. It reminded him, too, of his hatred for so much of humanity, the discrimination he faced as a half-Indian always forefront in his mind.

The ire reminded him anew of his weakest moment in life, when he tried to force Xavier to follow his heart and love Thomas. Xavier's refusal hurt Thomas, bringing back to him of all the times others rejected him or dismissed his ideas or company. So he lost complete control and slapped Xavier across the face. Had a human done it, it would have left a red mark and little more, but with his vampiric strength, Thomas shattered every bone on one side of Xavier's face.

He would *never* forgive himself for harming Xavier. Thomas had struggled to gain control of his temper after his violent outburst. Once they found Xavier again, and after Xavier's transformation, Thomas found tranquility and came to terms with the inner demons.

But tonight they returned. He tried to regain composure, to remind himself of all the lessons he'd learned, to list all the reasons for getting his anger under control and resisting the urge to either punch his fist through the wall or fly out the window and kill several people for sport.

He clutched the letter tighter in his fist, wishing his strength could squeeze out all the answers he needed to questions known only by Xavier. Xavier who abandoned him.

Thomas read the letter again. His mind had a hard time latching onto the words of love Xavier crafted and instead alighted on the desertion. Xavier never said or wrote a word he did not mean. Of all the people Thomas ever encountered, Xavier labored in his mind over how to write or say whatever he wanted to communicate. So, on the one hand, Thomas knew Xavier still loved him; he had not forsaken their relationship nor run off with someone else. Those thoughts vanished, though, and his mind dwelled on the rest of the information. And then the anger boiled anew.

Duplicity. Xavier used duplicity to get rid of him. His Xavier. His love! How could Xavier, of all people, ever do that to him? Xavier concocted a ruse to send Thomas to visit Anthony to explain in person their abrupt departure from Anthony's home, all so Xavier could slip away without Thomas knowing.

Thomas crumpled the paper and threw it across the room. Then he smashed his fists on top of his desk, cracking the thick wood down the middle. He spun around, searching for something else to destroy, when he glanced at the portrait hanging over the fireplace.

There stood Xavier, as real as if Thomas could touch him, gazing at Thomas in the portrait. A year ago, Xavier and he found a poor artist searching for work and took him in with the sole duty being to serve as their butler. He did his job well, but they soon discovered his remarkable artistic talent. Xavier took to launching his career, to the point he did well enough to leave them and work full time at his craft. As a parting thank you, he insisted Thomas and Xavier pose for the painting that hung above their fireplace.

Xavier's soft features, his too-trusting eyes, his passion for Thomas—the painting rendered it all. And though the rage remained, Thomas understood it on a much different level than seconds ago when he stood there angry at the world and Xavier for betraying him. Thomas was bitter that society concocted God or Gods who always made Xavier feel guilty. The fury within Thomas returned because of an absolute dread for Xavier's safety. He had written he might violate the ethic and would accept whatever punishment came with it, which Thomas translated as Xavier telling him he *already* violated the ethic.

That damnable Vampire Council Anthony belonged to would sanction Xavier if he violated their precious rules, no matter how much anyone pleaded with them or tried to explain why it happened. Thomas would never forgive himself if they punished Xavier in any way, especially if they sentenced him to death. Thomas would die first, trying to save him.

So the rage came back with a vengeance, but Thomas felt it had a different purpose from previous episodes. He was sure he could control it somewhat so long as he remembered to channel its energy toward saving Xavier and nothing else.

Thomas went across the room and picked up the crumpled letter, smoothing it out on an end table. He read it again and then wiped away the blood tears that had been streaming down his face since he first read Xavier's words.

Thomas struggled for several minutes to compose himself and then called their most trusted servant to come to him. Pierre came into the room with his usual smile and erect posture. Of all the young men they employed over the years, Xavier and Thomas trusted him the most, to the point he probably knew they were vampires, or at least something was amiss. They hired his lover, Andre, too, and the two men became as happy a couple as Thomas and Xavier.

"I need you to listen," Thomas instructed without his usual greeting.

"Of course, monsieur. As always." Pierre went rigid, his concerned face seeming to understand the import of what Thomas said.

"No. Not as always. This is more important. Do you understand?"

"Yes." Pierre nodded.

"Good." Thomas patted Pierre on the shoulder. "I'm leaving but might return from time to time. I won't be able to announce myself as usual. Just keep our rooms at the ready. Now, this is most urgent: a note may appear on the pillows of our bed. If one does, you must contact me at once. This list"—Thomas handed Pierre a note with his financial advisors from around the world—"contains every one of my trusted brokers the world over. It also has several other addresses for my personal mailboxes. If this note appears on the pillow, first—safeguard it with your life. Second—send word to every single one of these places. I need to learn about the note as soon as possible. In fact, I give you permission to copy it, word for word, and send it to each of these places so I'll see it at once. Do you understand? If this happens, drop *everything,* and get André to help you."

Allowing Pierre and André such intimate and dangerous knowledge of their lives risked much, but

Thomas had no choice. If he got a letter, he wanted to go to Xavier without delay.

"I understand."

Thomas saw Pierre trembling. Thomas drew the young man into a hug. He forgot that Pierre, not yet twenty, carried himself with a maturity defying his age. "Thank you. I've never asked something more imperative of you. I hope you know I trust you with my life. And Xavier's."

Thomas turned to leave, wanting to begin his search for Xavier, but Pierre remained, frozen in place. "What else?" Thomas asked.

"Well, I'm not sure." Pierre fidgeted with the list of addresses. "Actually, yes."

"Out with it." Thomas whirled around to the young man and clutched both of his shoulders.

"Is Master Xavier at risk?" Pierre scrunched his brow together and peered into Thomas's eyes.

"What do you know?"

"Monsieur, I'm loyal to both of you. Until tonight, that always came easily enough. But the abbé did something I think you would want to know. He told me not to say anything. I'm torn between obeying him, who trusted me, and you, both stressing the urgency of your point."

Thomas's heart pounded. He guided Pierre to the couch and sat with him, keeping an arm around him to show his understanding and support.

"Listen—" Thomas swept a lock of hair off the young man's forehead. "—You're wise beyond your years and correct. Something is wrong. But it has nothing to do with our relationship. Xavier and I are fine. You must know telling me doesn't risk the trust he placed in you. I have to protect him, and the more I know, the better."

Pierre nodded his head. "A few nights ago, Master Xavier purchased a flat for André and me, right around the corner from here. He said it was a gift for our loyalty. I'd no idea you didn't know." Pierre took a deep breath. "Then he told me he may send a letter addressed to me to our new home. If I got it, I was to place it on your pillow, without you or anyone else knowing. I suppose that doesn't really help, does it?"

Thomas struggled with his inner demons again. Innocent Pierre followed Xavier's instructions, but the subterfuge with Xavier felt like betrayal from both of them. He reminded himself once again the danger Xavier faced made him angry, not the people involved. If anything, Pierre proved his worth by revealing the secret. Thomas calmed himself before he spoke.

"This helps. Good." Thomas stopped himself from saying he had hoped to learn more. "It saves time. There's no need for this nonsense with the note on a pillow. The minute you get the letter, you get to work copying it. Get it to me fast. Now, I must be off."

Pierre stood and straightened his jacket. He breathed deeply again, and his hands shook.

"You did the right thing," Thomas assured him. "Xavier will be fine." Thomas wished he believed the words with the same conviction with which he uttered them. "But I'll need your help."

Thirteen: Global Search

MARCH/APRIL 1822
France/America

Thomas stormed toward the port as he searched for a ship heading out in the middle of the night. He kept his anger in check, though he acknowledged a certain increased volatility in the way he killed his victims. Dismembering them, causing prolonged agony, and frightening them for longer periods of time helped soothe his nerves. He never strayed from the ethic, of course, most of all fearing any lapse in his judgment would bring scrutiny from the Council and thus draw their attention to the fact Xavier disappeared. Still he raged within, frightened for Xavier and lonely without him.

Thomas left, after the discussion with Pierre, to search throughout Paris for Xavier. He did not anticipate finding him at Notre Dame Cathedral again, but he checked to make sure. Nothing. He even paused to see if a divine revelation might come to *him*, but of course the deadened spiritual atmosphere around him confirmed his atheism and fear Xavier's emotional state got the better of him yet again.

Thomas next raced to the Saint-Laurent mansion and interrogated Catherine's servants, where he at least learned more information and figured out a new twist in the plot.

"Madame is gone, monsieur, and we're to have no visitors." Before the butler could slam the door in his face, Thomas pushed it aside and shoved his way into the foyer.

"I know Madame Saint-Laurent." He pulled out a large sum of money, hoping to bribe information out of the man. "We're very close. I need to know where she went."

"I've no need for your money, monsieur. I assure you Madame pays me quite well. In part for her trust." He sealed his lips tightly. But Thomas, never one to give up, concocted a white lie.

"She may be in danger." Thomas crammed the coins back in his pocket. "Let me guess." He lifted his finger to his chin, as if contemplating. "A young gentleman appeared, with short hair, dashing eyes, and rather pale-looking. Madame Catherine locked herself away with him and then left notes to announce she was leaving with an unknown return time. If I'm right, you'd better tell me so we can protect her." As he spoke, the butler's eyes grew wide, and his face went white as a sheet.

"How did you know? We never saw her again. She left notes giving us instructions and telling us to maintain the house but to prohibit anyone from entering until further notice. Did he kidnap her? Is he going to kill her?"

His question gave Thomas pause, but he shook his head to calm the man. "No, he won't." *Not in the way you mean.* "But someone else may. Do you know where they went?"

"No. I swear she left no indication."

"And after this man came here, you never saw your mistress again? She hid in her rooms?"

"And office." The butler nodded. "No one saw her leave or go about the premises. When I went to find her later, she had left detailed instructions and assignments for everyone. She herself disappeared."

If Thomas's instincts were correct, he knew at least the first thing Xavier did to violate the ethic.

Once Thomas left the Saint-Laurent house to a startled butler, he next searched for Anne Hébert. Whatever Xavier experienced at Notre Dame before he sent Thomas to London led Xavier to go see his old friend. Thomas searched under the bridge she called home but found nothing but a pile of ashes and debris lying about. Vagrants wandered nearby, and Anne's boxes and trunks had been ransacked. What happened to the protective magic Anne used to keep people away? He rummaged through the ashes and found a human skeleton, but whose?

An exploration of Xavier's old parish yielded fewer clues, and nothing else in Paris indicated where Thomas's lover had gone. He went to bed that morning worried and trembling. Thomas spent an entire night of searching with little to show for it.

The following night produced less. Thinking he exhausted all possibilities in Paris, Thomas dashed to Mont St. Michel, where it all started, to find it devoid of any vampires. No one had seen Xavier; at least, that's what they said when Thomas quizzed them. Again he teased himself with the notion the archangel St. Michel may come to him for a daytime visit. He stayed on the island, hidden in the bowels of the earth to conceal himself. If a restless slumber indicated signs of the divine, then angels appeared to him. Otherwise Thomas was left with nothing, yet again.

Which led Thomas to the third night without Xavier and a desperate attempt to try to learn where he had gone. What could Thomas do but search every corner of the earth? He had no other options for searching in France for Xavier, so after he awoke he sped to the port he and Xavier always used, thinking Xavier's fear of the unknown would bring him to a familiar launching point, since the rest of the quest would so unnerve him.

He wandered among the ships, wondering how to investigate. Then he thought of at least one desperate idea and put it into action. He gathered a group of young men, paid them well, and sent them to ask anyone and everyone about ships that left port three nights ago, under cover of darkness. Despite a vampire's ability to swim across the ocean, Xavier loathed the idea and insisted upon taking a ship. Perhaps he did so again. A spry redhead came running back an hour later, out of breath.

"Monsieur, I found a ship that meets your needs! It left three nights ago at almost midnight because the captain had been delayed earlier by angry investors. When he got to the ship, he wanted to head out to avoid their following him again."

"Excellent. What else can you tell me?" A feeling deep within Thomas told him Xavier and Catherine stowed aboard that vessel. It had all the hallmarks of what Thomas taught Xavier in terms of finding a ship for transport.

"It sailed for America. New York." Before the boy finished speaking, Thomas handed him a bag of money, more than the young man could otherwise hope to earn in his lifetime.

"You did well. Thank you."

Thomas thanked the boy and sent him on his way. He wanted to leave that second, but such a long journey first required sustenance. Thomas baited a poor fool by winking at him and grabbing his dick. Thomas raced around a corner, and when the man followed, Thomas made another pass at him.

"Fucking sodomite. I'll show you lovin'."

The man grabbed for his knife but Thomas reached out and clutched his arm, cracking the bones within. When the idiot cried out, Thomas shoved a rag in his mouth to silence him. A quick scratch of his arm and taste of the blood told

Thomas everything he needed to know about the sailor-cum-tormentor. He deserved death, and the way he treated people enraged Thomas anew, boiling to the surface all of Thomas's contained anger. He broke the man's other arm, then a foot, before the gent passed out, and Thomas finished him off.

Sadistic. Xavier would have described such a display of wrath as sadistic. When Xavier accused him of such things, Thomas usually found it humorous, which encouraged him the next time. Tonight, however, it saddened him that his inner temper returned and Xavier was lost to him.

Thomas took a huge breath and jumped into the ocean. He knew from past experience he could leave and swim at vampiric speed while the dawn chased him from behind. Unlike Xavier, Thomas had no qualms about swimming the length of the Atlantic, though he disliked getting to the other side wet and scurrying to find shelter. Still, it would help him catch up to whatever lead Xavier and Catherine had as they floated along on a ship.

But Thomas's hope Xavier and Catherine had taken that particular boat to New York faded when he arrived in the New World. Though he located the vessel and paid a few of its sailors for information, he found no sign of Xavier. The defeat left him with no real idea about where to look anymore. Even if Xavier had sailed on the ship, what did it tell Thomas? He could be anywhere in the United States or another godforsaken place. How could Thomas ever find him?

Thomas nonetheless undertook as thorough a search of America as possible. He checked with his advisors on a regular basis to see if any letters arrived, but nothing came for him from Paris. He wrote a letter to Pierre to confirm as much, but knew long before he got a reply there were no communications from Xavier.

After a month of searching, at wit's end and finding it increasingly difficult to focus and obey the ethic, Thomas sat despondent in Charleston, South Carolina. The body of a dead degenerate lay nearby, hacked apart and displayed for a passerby to find. Thomas did not obtain quarters in this city, instead preferring the desolate feel of a cemetery vault to match his mood. Thomas picked himself up and walked back to his cemetery home, settling amidst the bones and spiders for company inside one of the larger crypts.

He had looked everywhere and found nothing. Why had he thought it was possible to find one vampire in a globe of people? Xavier had a head start, wanted to avoid Thomas, and could have gone anywhere in the world. Thomas had but two choices, neither of which appealed to him. He could return to Paris and wait for the note to arrive, which risked everything. Waiting for Xavier's message meant Xavier would elude the Council and return, having completed his secret quest. An unlikely scenario, given everything Thomas knew about the Vampire Council and its informants. Or Thomas could go to Anthony and enlist his help, which risked as much. Telling Anthony meant his best friend, who sat on the Council, could reprimand Xavier and report him for punishment to the secret body. At least he could plead with Anthony to spare Xavier or keep it a secret from the other people on the Council, for Thomas's sake. He had to do something, *anything*, so he posted a letter to his mentor.

> *Dearest Anthony,*
>
> *I could never explain in a letter everything that has occurred since I left you in London. Suffice it to say I need your assistance, more than when I called for your help during the French Revolution, and even more than after Xavier disappeared into the*

underbelly of Paris with Anne. He's missing again. He ran away on a religious quest. Do you remember my explaining why we left your place, because this archangel visited Xavier in his sleep? Xavier sent me alone to you in London so he could slip away. I can't find him anywhere. Please, you and the Council can locate others of our kind. I know you can help. I'm desperate, as you must realize from the mere fact I contacted you with this embarrassing, and dangerous, situation. I'll await your reply here in Charleston. You'll find me in one of the bars, stalking my next victim and thereby trying to keep my anger in check. Merely a warning: it's returned.

Love forever, Thomas.

Anthony's quick reply shocked Thomas. His friend often took weeks or months to get back to Thomas, even when he indicated the urgency of the moment. Thomas spent but two weeks meandering about the South, hoping to find Xavier and murdering for food as many people as he could, when Anthony's letter arrived.

The note was short and simple:

Thomas,

I will follow this note by no more than two days.

Love, Anthony.

Fourteen: Vampire Purgatory

19 APRIL 1822
The Rocky Mountains

Thomas pondered again how he got here so soon after reading Anthony's note. He sat in a frozen bank of snow, high atop the Rocky Mountains, annoyed and bored. He screamed at the top of his lungs for Anthony to return, but stopped when an avalanche of snow came crashing down on a mountain opposite him. Where had Anthony gone, and why did Thomas have to wait for him in the godforsaken cold? Why would anyone ever come here in the first place?

He had bitched to Anthony about it the minute they arrived. "I despise the cold. This place feels worse than purgatory."

Anthony had laughed at him, tilting back on his tall frame, his long blond hair flowing almost to the ground. "You sound like a petite damsel in distress, taken by an evil villain from her comfortable country estate. You're a vampire: you can't feel the heat and cold. And you've never been to purgatory, though you deserve it for all the consternation you give me. And remember, you chose to follow me. I shouldn't have brought you. So sit there, give me a moment, and I'll come to retrieve your precious ass from the snow before a wolf decides to eat you for dinner." With that, his friend ran away. Thomas could have followed, with the tracks in the snow and his being as fast as Anthony, but he obeyed and sat here alone, thinking back on the events that brought him to this point.

TRUE TO HIS word, Anthony had appeared in Charleston one day after Thomas received his note. Thomas spied the tall man with striking blue eyes and long hair from afar as he exited a bar and courted a young Southern aristocrat. Anthony always did like to mix business with pleasure.

Thomas hurried over to the two men. "He'll take your heart and smash it in his fist after he deflowers your nice ass." Thomas whispered in the young man's ear when he got up behind him, causing the poor gent to scramble away and bringing a frown to Anthony's face.

"Why do you always have to chase away my fun?"

"This trip isn't about fun, is it?" Thomas only half teased. "Come."

He pulled Anthony through town to his crypt and locked them inside.

"Charming." Anthony scanned the tomb, then lit several candles and cleared a spot to sit. "At least the rest of the company in here matches your demeanor. I like it better when you're with Xavier to civilize you."

"I like that better too," Thomas snapped.

Anthony put his hands up. "All right. All right. Tell me, what's going on?"

Against his better judgment, because he worried about Xavier's safety from the Vampire Council, Thomas explained to Anthony what happened since he left London and found Xavier's letter at their Paris flat. He attempted to truncate the story and keep out certain details, lest Anthony decide to inform the rest of the Council to watch for a rogue priest-cum-vampire. He left out his suspicion that Xavier transformed Catherine, and said nothing about the way Xavier promised to communicate with him. Anthony sat like a statue the entire time.

"And you think he may be violating the ethic?" Anthony asked after an agonizing pause when Thomas finished his tale.

"I trusted you with this." Thomas pointed at Anthony. "Remember. This isn't about penalizing him, or a hunt for him to send him to the wolves on the Council."

"I understand. But I can't protect him or help you find him if you keep things from me."

Thomas took his turn to pause. "This Vampire Council is full of cowards and fools. They follow arbitrary rules without thinking about the context. They threaten us who disobey without a hearing. I know you're one of them, which is often difficult for me to explain."

"And yet *I've* explained it to you a million times." Anthony rolled his eyes and kicked a skull across the floor. "I appreciate your point of view. Events from long ago, during the war which almost destroyed all vampires, save a sadistic one who wanted to become pure evil, led to its more vigilant enforcement of the rules. He killed my lover. So the rules exist to protect all of us, including you, from such a repeat fate. Got it?"

Thomas smirked. "You'll protect Xavier? Promise me. We're friends. This isn't about those rules."

Anthony stood and came over to Thomas, picking him off the floor and hugging him. "I have no closer friend on earth than you. I'll do what I can. Now, come with me to a more civilized location and dispense with *everything* you know."

They retired to a more luxurious hotel, where Thomas revealed he thought the quest demanded Xavier violate the ethic, though he had no idea how. Still, he said nothing about his suspicions regarding Catherine. After sleeping the next day there, Thomas awoke to find Anthony preparing for a journey. He hoped it was to find Xavier.

"When you wrote, I was already in America." Anthony tugged a bag closed. "The Council sent me on an errand. I'll help you. I'll devote all my energy to what you need and to helping you find Xavier, but first I have to complete this task. I want you to come with me. We can discuss strategy along the way. I've already started the process to search for Xavier." Thomas's heart sank, which Anthony must have read on his face. "It's safe. Come."

And so they set out westward in the New World, past all signs of civilization, save for a few fools or lone individuals wandering around among the wild animals and Indians just east of the Mississippi River. Thomas made the mistake one evening of wandering into an Indian settlement, at first being welcomed because of his overall look. But upon closer inspection, some of them recognized Thomas for what he really was and sent him away, lest they feel compelled to kill him.

Anthony and he fed on the stray bandits who fled so far away from authorities on the East Coast, or the Indian here and there who murdered or deceived his own people. It frustrated Thomas they took their time, a few days' worth, before they arrived at the base of the Rocky Mountains. Thomas wanted to hurry, but Anthony implored him to slow down, explaining it would take time before his methods discovered anything, and searching before then would be futile. Thomas heard Anthony's words but had a difficult time accepting them. He needed Anthony, however, and so endured the journey and tried to enjoy the majestic scenery, though without Xavier it was difficult. He had never seen such wide-open expanses.

On a foothill near the entrance to a canyon going into the Rocky Mountains, inside a cave Anthony occupied before along with resident bats, they slept through one more cold day before awaking, with Anthony explaining they had to climb to the highest peaks, where snow still had everything in its grip despite the spring thaw down where they were.

"Snow? This late?" Thomas thought Anthony had gone mad.

"Snow, at times year round."

"And why do we want to go there?" Thomas tired of the games.

"Not want, but *need* to go there. I told you, the Council sent me." Anthony became uncharacteristically silent, leaving the banter behind and coming over to sit on an uncomfortable log next to Thomas. "I'm taking you to a secret Council location. I've their permission, because I trust you. When I told them I didn't want to do this alone again, they agreed to allow me to take you with me. I'm not tricking you. I think we need to wait. In the meantime, you're keeping me company while I do this distasteful job." Anthony put his arm around Thomas and squeezed him. "We'll find him."

Anthony's warmth comforted Thomas, and his words piqued his interest. If he had to wait, at least Anthony added intrigue to the situation. Thomas got to go on a secret mission for the Council he despised? Interesting. "You have something unpleasant to do?"

"Yes, though this is better than last time I came here." Thomas's head spun because Anthony was not making sense. "You'll see. Come on, let's be done with it."

He and Anthony left their few packages behind, save one small bundle he carried, and hurried up the mountain. Hurrying for a vampire, of course, meant they traveled up and down several mountains, through a stream or two, and to the highest, snow-filled peaks in a matter of minutes. Thomas felt like a mountain goat, leaping from rock to rock with no apparent purpose or destination. Before they arrived at a point where the tree line stopped and the water would flow the other way, Anthony halted and planted Thomas in the snow bank, where he now sat alone.

THOMAS SENSED A presence and sat motionless, waiting for it to approach. Out of the corner of his eye, Thomas saw it slink along, close to the ground, spying on its prey and waiting to pounce. Before it did, Thomas launched himself off the ground high into a pine tree. The mountain lion landed where Thomas had sat, looking perplexed and letting out a roar. Defeated, it sauntered away to find new prey.

Just as Thomas became bored with the cold scenery again, he heard Anthony hurrying back to him. When his friend stood below, spinning around and searching for him, Thomas leaned forward on his branch and dropped on top of Anthony. He laughed hard for the first time in days when he saw Anthony, covered in snow, scowling from beneath him.

"At least I can amuse you." Anthony pushed Thomas off. "Why do you act like the teenager I met on the 1600s Massachusetts frontier? You're an ass."

"Thank you. And before you say anything else snide, I'll warn you I have a new friend who would like nothing better than to eat you for dinner."

Anthony froze, using his senses to find out if Thomas had found an enemy. His response made Thomas laugh harder than a minute ago. "There." Thomas pointed several yards away. "See her? She wants to eat us."

"Are you teasing the poor animal?" Anthony slapped Thomas on the back of the head. "Stop it. Are you ready?"

"I've been sitting here alone on a desolate mountain, with a mountain lion for company, waiting for you *once again*, and you're going to ask if I'm ready?"

Anthony became serious and pulled Thomas close to him. "One more thing. You must promise to keep everything you see a secret. I'd prefer if you even kept it from Xavier, though I know that's a flight of fancy. It means much the Council allowed me to bring you here. Please don't betray my trust."

"Of course not. I never would."

Anthony nodded, then grabbed Thomas's hand and pulled him along, over another peak into a drift of snow on the other side. Then he began digging into it. "Hold on to me," Anthony instructed, so Thomas grabbed his pants and followed along as they dug deeper into the snow, to the point it covered them. Thomas became almost claustrophobic despite knowing he could spin around and get out of the snow in mere seconds. They got to an enormous boulder Anthony pushed aside and squeezed behind, pulling Thomas with him. A tunnel extended for a long way before them, until Thomas saw a tiny dot of light at the other end. As Anthony started down the tunnel, torches flared to life in front of them, illuminating the way.

"How did that happen?" Thomas asked Anthony, who walked in front of him.

"Magic."

Thomas yanked Anthony to a stop and spun him around. "You bring me all the way to an underworld cave, start pyrotechnics, and then think all you need to explain is that magic lit these torches? What's going on?" Fear welled inside Thomas at the revelation. What exact powers did the Vampire Council possess?

Thomas expected a scolding or dark secret, but Anthony chuckled and put both his hands on Thomas's shoulders. "You're going to be the first vampire to have a heart attack if you don't settle down. There's nothing here that threatens you. We're fine. I'm going to explain everything." Anthony linked his arm through Thomas's and started them down the tunnel. "Yes, it's magic. I know magic, or at least certain kinds the Council taught me in order to assist with keeping our laws. Lighting these torches is nothing."

"All these years, you kept this from me?" Thomas was hurt at discovering a hidden part of his friend's life.

"Not really. You knew I belonged to the Vampire Council and had certain duties and pieces of knowledge I couldn't share with you. I never use any of this magic outside of my official duties. And you knew the Council could do mysterious things, such as put the book of laws in front of your face, out of nowhere."

"So you're a witch?" Thomas turned from hurt to amusement, continuing with his emotional ups and downs. "Do I need to burn you at the stake?"

"Please do. If it gets me away from you." Anthony stopped them before they entered a large space carved out of the middle of the mountain that glowed orange and red all around. "I'll need to do a lot more explaining when you see this." Anthony ushered them into the space, which nearly took Thomas's breath away.

They stood at the entrance to a cavernous room the size of the sanctuary at Notre Dame Cathedral. Solid rock made up the walls and ceiling, that someone—or magic? — polished until it became as smooth as marble. High atop, a line of torches lit up the highest points. Despite all the fire, no smoke filled the air.

But what lay at the center of the grand scene drew Thomas's attention most of all. A gigantic rectangular pit sat in the middle of the room with no railing or other impediment to falling right into it. Fire arose, with dancing orange, red, and yellow flames flickering about and creating shadows off the shining rock walls. Several iron boxes hovered above the flames, suspended by nothing.

"Prison." Anthony glanced at Thomas. "Now you'll thank me for all of those times I protected you from the Council's wrath at your willful disobedience."

Thinking of Xavier and his quest and seeing the awful place panicked Thomas. He fought to maintain his decorum, however, lest he signal a secret to Anthony. "Prison? What do you mean, prison?"

"Vampire prison. How hard is it to understand? The Council has three options when someone violates the ethic. It can reprimand them and issue a warning. The least punishment. Or, in the most extreme cases, it can sentence them to death and immolate them on the spot. But for those offenses serious enough for punishment, but not worthy of death, we bring them here, to prison."

"How? Don't they fight back?"

"Magic." Anthony lifted his eyebrows at Thomas and smiled, seeming to miss the anxiety building within Thomas. "We have spells to incapacitate a vampire's power long enough for us to capture them. That's how we can execute vampires too. Once we get them here, we lock them in one of those boxes, tell them their sentence and the reason behind it, and then keep them here until they've served their time. They can't get out of the box because the enchanted fire would engulf them in flames."

Thomas stared in terror at the boxes before him. Blackened tombs, with no source of light or comfort. "You put people in there? For how long?"

"It depends on the violation. We don't take this lightly, and it's not arbitrary. Without this ethic, the vampire world would descend into chaos. Even with it, one vampire almost destroyed all of our kind except for the few who followed his diabolical aims. I've told you the story, remember? Do you understand? He almost wiped us all out. He entrapped the Council after they made the stupid mistake of putting him on it. He started an all-out war, which we barely won. Many, many of us died, on and off the Council, before we subdued him. He was a powerful sorcerer before he became a vampire, and when he was transformed and then learned vampire magic, it made him all the more powerful. We almost lost the battle. That's why we monitor the transformations and restrict our numbers now. There are very few vampires. You wouldn't believe me if I told you how few."

"Try me. How many? And how many do you have trapped in this awful place?"

"Prison is supposed to be awful or it wouldn't be prison. Right now, in all the world, no more than about one hundred vampires roam."

Thomas whipped his head to look at Anthony. "That's it? You can control the population so exactly?"

Anthony nodded. "We want the other vampires, those not on the Council, to think more exist because it makes everyone believe other vampires lurk around to help us monitor all of them."

"And in those boxes?" Thomas jerked his head toward the iron jails floating above the wicked fire.

"Placing vampires in those boxes is the distasteful part of my duty. Just one resides there currently, whom we came to release tonight. Her time was up, which is why I had to come here at once. Stand back and watch."

Anthony pushed Thomas to the side and closed his eyes as Thomas stared in disbelief. He began a low chant that sounded like an ancient language. Anthony waved his arms in the air, and the torches above blazed brighter but the fire in the pit ceased altogether. One box, with its darkened iron and strong bolts moved toward them, until it hovered above the ground at Anthony's feet. He opened his eyes and clapped his hands, opening the lid.

A slight woman, with bright-red hair and dazzling green eyes, peered out. Thomas expected her to rant and rave about being in the terrible place, but instead she jumped out and stood before Anthony, as if expecting him to further scold her. Her hesitance turned to a slight smile when she greeted Anthony.

"Am I free?"

"Soon." Anthony tugged her into a hug. "I'm sorry for what you suffered. It was necessary. You know what comes next: I'll enchant you one more time to conceal the location of this place and take you to a port. Then you're free again."

"Thank you so much for saving me." When she reached out and embraced Anthony again, she saw Thomas for the first time and drew back, afraid.

"Don't worry. He's safe. I told you, you're free now."

She nodded but never took her eyes off Thomas. Then Anthony had her lie down and chanted over her. She went limp. Anthony sent the iron crate back over the pit and then restarted the fire before lifting her into his arms.

"Come." Anthony started back down the tunnel, carrying her.

"Will you quit giving me commands like I'm a dog?" Thomas lifted his arms in the air, exasperated. "That's it? You show me a prison from hell, reveal you know magic, free this poor woman, she thanks you, you knock her out with a supernatural spell, and I'm supposed to follow you back to the surface like we shared a drink at a saloon?"

"Yes." Anthony grabbed Thomas's arm with a free hand and pulled him along.

Thomas followed reluctantly but slowed Anthony's pace. "What did she do?"

"Tried to make another vampire without permission, after telling the man she could do it. He ended up exposing her and wanted to hunt down and kill her and any others she knew. This could have blown our cover everywhere."

"Why did she do it?"

"She loved him. She wanted a partner."

"That doesn't seem so evil. How long did you imprison her?"

"Ten years, which is nothing for a vampire." Anthony reached over and grabbed Thomas's arm, speeding them up. "And you missed the point: she was going to transform him, with no permission and no idea he would freak out."

Thomas contemplated, feeling part revulsion at the whole thing and part understanding for its necessity. He remained silent as they dug back through the snow and headed down the mountain.

"Are you going to carry her all night? And why did she thank you? Seems odd, to thank your jailor."

Anthony stopped and set her down when they reached their cave-cum-campsite. "You're full of questions tonight. Like an annoying five-year-old."

"You're the one who wanted to show me this grand spectacle." Thomas waved his arm at the mountains to emphasize his point.

"Fine. But remember, I wanted company because going to the prison makes me sad. That's why I brought you along."

"*You're* sad?" Thomas arched his eyebrow. "Think of the poor fools in those boxes. She was in there for ten years, no doubt awake for more than half the time. And hungry, feeling like she'd starve to death."

"True. But she had a very light sentence and would never starve to death. The Council has compassion and knows what limits a vampire can endure. Some have been imprisoned for much, much longer. The magic allows them to survive without blood."

Thomas had no desire to know how long the horrendous Council would cage a vampire in that terrible place. The mere thought chilled him to the bone. "You didn't answer my questions."

Anthony gathered his things and prepared to leave. "I'm carrying her to New Orleans, where she'll get on a boat to go home to Ireland. We have to get there tonight, so we can't delay any longer." Anthony picked up his belongings and the woman, throwing one crate to Thomas and moving them along, racing across America at a dizzying speed. As they went, he answered Thomas's other question.

"She thanked me because the Council had to decide the length of her imprisonment. I argued for a short term because she's a good soul and meant no harm. I then entreated them to make it a light sentence, because the rules stipulated to send her away for a century."

"A century?" In shock, Thomas almost stopped running but kept moving because Anthony did not pause.

"The Council takes the ethic very seriously."

Anthony then remained silent until they arrived in New Orleans. Thomas stepped back as Anthony concealed them in an alley and reversed the spell on the former prisoner. The young woman jumped up, hugged him again, and ran off. She and Anthony promised to rendezvous when next Anthony returned to his estate near London, and Anthony introduced her to Thomas. All the while, Thomas's stomach turned in knots at Anthony having once again reminded him about the Council and its serious enforcement of the ethic. He could never stand to know if they trapped Xavier alone in one of those awful boxed prisons.

Fifteen: Long Nights of Nothing

30 APRIL 1822
New York City

A month passed since Anthony came to Thomas. Once they had released the vampire in New Orleans and allowed her to return to Ireland, he and Thomas discussed what to do about finding Xavier.

To Thomas's dismay, Anthony recommended very little. They sat in a sidewalk café, sipping god-awful British beer Anthony loved, after feeding on vagrants. Thomas, antsy to get started after enduring the trip in the snow, pleaded for them to act.

"And what would you propose we do?" Anthony ran his finger along the top of his glass. His cavalier attitude annoyed Thomas. "You already searched. We could go about the world, searching in every city, on every farm, at every port, and never find him. We've no idea where he went. We've no idea *why* he went. You can't tell me a thing, other than he might have boarded a ship to New York. So what good does it do to stumble about looking for him?"

"Then what?" Thomas spat the words at Anthony.

"We wait. Until I hear from my people, there's not much else that makes sense to do."

Thomas slung back the last of the bitter beer, hoping for a vampiric buzz to calm his rising anger. "Brilliant strategy. What about this magic you revealed? Why not use it?"

Anthony sighed. "It doesn't work that way. And I can't reveal it to you."

"Thank god I came to you for help."

Anthony launched out of his chair, seized Thomas by an arm, and pulled him out of sight. He did not let go until he rented rooms in an awful pub and got them upstairs. Despite his rage, Thomas followed. Anthony tried to push him onto the bed, but Thomas refused after seeing the bugs scramble out of the way.

"You will *not* degenerate into the vile beast stalking Paris during the revolution." Anthony stood inches from Thomas, his jaw clenched, a vein in his forehead pulsating. "That will get you, or Xavier, *nowhere*. Don't think I don't see it in you. I can smell it coming out of your pores. You conquered those demons—don't let them seize you again."

Thomas agreed with every word Anthony uttered. Yet Thomas struggled between his rational response and his inner demons, the ones Anthony had so astutely pointed out. On the one hand, Anthony and he had little other recourse. Thomas acknowledged as much when he reached out to Anthony for help. Yet rather than addressing a small issue or passing fancy, they worked on something to do with Xavier. They had to find him, to protect him from whatever led him away and from the damnable Council and its iron boxes. Doing nothing seemed so irresponsible to the man he loved.

Seeing Anthony's soft face and sparkling blue eyes staring at him as he fought these emotions, Thomas collapsed. The blood tears burst forth as he fell into Anthony's arms and clung to him.

"I can't lose him."

Anthony kissed the top of Thomas's head. "I know."

They stayed that way until the morning sun approached. Anthony led him out of the pub, where they had no place to conceal themselves, into the nearby swamps, where they found an abandoned cabin and created a makeshift tomb within it. Even the fish, vermin, and alligators in the remote spot felt cleaner to Thomas than the dirty pub of moments before.

The next evening, without prompting from Thomas, Anthony explained his strategy. "We'll stay in New York. I've lots of informants there and can get any message sent to me. I know it's not ideal, but we can search around for Xavier, too, because you said he may have sailed for New York. If I know anything about the network, it won't take them long to get word to us. I know it's not ideal. I know it's not what you wanted to hear. But it's best for Xavier and us. Anything else leaves us wandering for no apparent reason."

Thomas agreed to the plan after Anthony ascertained they had no other options other than to wander the world as vagabonds, which risked missing an important communication. In fact, Thomas thought of the ultimate message he awaited from Xavier through Pierre. He never told Anthony, lest the note from Xavier reveal too much about how he violated the ethic and thereby put him at risk.

In New York, Thomas could get all of *his* people to deliver his messages too. He sent a dispatch from New Orleans before they left, in fact, telling Pierre to first send any letter to Thomas's person in New York, and only then finish copying the rest of the letters to send around the world.

Comforted they at least had a plan, he and Anthony bought a large house in New York and went about setting up their staff in a matter of three days. The thought of Xavier, his precious Xavier, kept him going and muted the fury building within him.

Part Four

The American South

Sixteen: Slavery

1 APRIL 1822
Alexandria, VA

Xavier's blood boiled as Catherine hauled him along, her strength surprising him. At first he resisted her efforts to return them to their quarters, but she grabbed him around the waist and carried him an entire block despite his struggling to get away. By that point, he resigned himself to following her orders and slumped over in her arms, allowing his sister to lug him the rest of the way. But he was still upset.

Xavier understood the anger that could envelop Thomas, overtaking him to the point he saw nothing but the source of his ire. How often he had scolded Thomas, bewildered at the way his love could become so focused on items making him so unhappy? Yet Xavier bobbed along in Catherine's arms, unable to contain the fury. He wanted to kill every human he saw, maim them in unspeakable ways, and force them to experience the evil they inflicted upon others.

Moments ago, he and Catherine meandered about their latest Southern town, Alexandria, Virginia, searching for Anne's grandson. Instead, they bumbled right into the end of a slave auction. Xavier despaired at seeing these poor souls ripped from their loved ones and auctioned like cattle or beasts of burden. The Southerners sickened him, with their disregard for humanity and the joking way they went about the business of selling human beings. He thought of Anne, had she not escaped to France with her family, or the black people he and Catherine met in New York, who assisted them in starting their search for Duncan by providing secret information about networks of people established to free slaves. How could anyone buy human cargo when they saw the humanity in their eyes? What devilish reality haunted such a vile place that allowed others to use people as nothing but work animals?

Xavier first reacted by running around a corner and emptying his stomach of bile and little else since he and Catherine had yet to feed. Then he returned to the spectacle, determined to watch and learn something about these Southerners who called themselves civilized. He never saw such Southern "cultural" displays because these events ended before Catherine and Xavier awoke for the night. But they got up a bit earlier than usual, and the crowd set up torches to illuminate their business into the night. After purging, Xavier watched for but a minute before the anger welled within him. He mumbled curses to Catherine and almost ripped the head off a gentleman who brushed into him.

"Calm yourself," Catherine whispered. She placed her hand on his arm. "It's dreadful, but remember our purpose here. We're already in danger and can't risk the ethic too much more."

Catherine's words worked for a little while, until a weeping young woman screamed in agony as her captor dragged her onto the wooden platform and slapped her across the face when she refused to stop crying. When Xavier lunged forward intent on stealing the woman from them and freeing her, Catherine snatched him from behind.

In their rooms at a small inn, Catherine tossed him unceremoniously onto a bed. "Are you well?" she asked in a soft voice.

"Yes." Xavier sat up and brushed off his clothes. "Maybe not my emotions. This is very difficult."

"I understand why Thomas forbade your coming to America. You can't handle it."

"And you can?" Xavier tossed his arms in the air and slammed them down onto his thighs.

"No. But I respect the fact we can't change all of this by going on a mad rampage. You know I love to defy authority, but maybe the ethic is right this time. We can't do anything as vampires that will reverse all of this." Catherine swept her hand toward the window for emphasis. "This is sick. You're right! I'm trying to approach this realistically."

Catherine already calmed him. She *was* right, of course. Two rogue vampires running around the South had little chance of ending an institution so embedded in the fabric of a society. Yet he had a hard time rationalizing that fact as the scene from tonight tore at his inner being like none before. In removing Xavier from the Americas, Thomas had read the situation correctly too. He knew the depravity would overwhelm Xavier.

Xavier glanced about their quarters, full of luxury with all the refinements a human, or vampire, could ever want. Catherine picked the finest lodging and the largest rooms within it, where she concealed their sleeping quarters in large trunks and set out a small painting of the Saint-Laurents, done right before their father died. To think, blocks away, people slept in mud and their own filth, waiting for an aristocrat to purchase them the next day and take them into fields for countless hours of toil and misery. Distraught, he turned to the one thing that still had the power to calm his nerves. He prayed.

Xavier bowed his head and took in the silence around him. He searched his mind for a sign of the divine, finding it in the cool breeze blowing through the room, in the solid presence of his sister's love, in the will of the slaves for living despite their desperation. Comforted that he could call God forth even here, he contemplated the appropriate prayer.

"Are you praying again?" Catherine interrupted with a chuckle.

"Shush," Xavier whispered, not wanting to break the spell. He couldn't stop a slight grin from turning up at the corners of his mouth.

"Say hello from me." Catherine sat on the bed and leaned into him. Xavier opened one eye and looked at her. "Go ahead." Catherine motioned him on with her hand.

Despite Catherine making him laugh, Xavier recovered the sense of peace and God's presence. God never answered, nor did Xavier expect such a thing. He wanted to avoid any commands from heaven if they came in the form of St. Michel. His state of mind nonetheless gave him answers and a sense of purpose. It empowered him to continue, despite the impossible odds. The trees swaying outside reminded Xavier of the greater presence that surrounded them. He understood what he needed in a flash: not divine intervention to explode the South and its institution altogether, not a grand answer as to why God could allow such a thing as slavery to exist, not a specific directive for what Xavier should do at the moment. Instead, he asked God to help his confidence, to focus on their task and know if he could succeed at his endeavor, then in a small way he changed the world. He wanted to work within himself without feeling the guilt at not having done more, at not having carried the weight of the world on his shoulders and altered it by himself.

His prayer centered him. Not that he forgot the auction of humans, but rather his spiritual life condoned his moving forward without insisting he alone end the evil practice. It gave him hope his small actions would make a difference, though they felt inadequate to him much of the time. He ended his prayer, feeling much better, when Catherine knocked on his head.

"Are you in there?" Catherine asked.

Xavier burst into laughter. "Will you stop?"

"I was getting bored. I tried to give you and God time together, but after a while it gets too quiet."

"Yes, heaven forbid we had a moment of peace and quiet."

Catherine smiled. "Did God say anything about me?"

"Yes," Xavier nodded. "He said you're a childish imp, and you should stop pestering Xavier so much."

Catherine slugged Xavier in the arm. "God must fear assertive women. At least, that's what I learned from all those Catholic priests back in France."

Xavier pulled the cross out from underneath his shirt and dangled it in Catherine's face. "I'm one of those French Catholic priests."

"Hardly."

"What *do* you believe these days?"

"I'm not sure." Catherine pushed herself off Xavier, leaning against the wall. When he furrowed his brow, Catherine lifted her eyebrows and threw her arms in the air. "I'm not playing coy, this time. I wish I had a better answer. I think we both know I don't have the same faith as you. It never made sense to me. The church hurts too many people. And how could I embrace all of these religious traditions that insist on keeping men in power, telling women what and how to believe different things? How could they ever speak to me?" Catherine paused. "But I'm not like Thomas either. He doesn't believe anything."

Xavier chuckled. Catherine described Thomas's atheism in a way Xavier found endearing. Of course, Thomas came to mind once again. Not that he ever left it. But Xavier could immerse himself in his time with Catherine and focus on his mission so it dulled the anxiety rumbling within at having used deception to abandon his lover. He thought about sending a dispatch to Pierre to at least indicate to Thomas he was all right, but that might give Thomas hope or give away what Xavier was doing and where. He had to wait.

"Well, we'd best get going or we'll lose a night." Xavier got up and straightened his clothing. He tucked in his shirt and wiped off his boot.

"Can you handle it?" Catherine came over and put her hand on Xavier's back.

"Yes. I don't have much choice, do I?"

"I suppose you're right." Catherine walked to a small desk and leaned over it, examining their map they used to guide them on their search for Anne's grandson, Duncan. They traveled from one place to the other, searching for him, enlisting the underground railroad for help, and hiring bounty hunters to hunt for him too. Though they had a few solid leads to indicate Duncan was in Virginia, they had yet to find him in over a month.

Once they had arrived in New York City, they explored in vain for a couple of days for information. A young black man asked them to follow him home. Why he trusted them Xavier would never know, but he had overheard them asking about Duncan and showing a drawing of him. The youth told them he befriended Duncan and wanted to see him returned to New York. He described to them the underground railroad, a group of ex-slaves and free blacks secretly working to get people out of slavery to the North. Once connected, Xavier and Catherine followed the network in reverse, tracing the men who captured Duncan to their usual selling points, learning Duncan ended up in Virginia. They had little else to go on, but at least it gave them something.

Seventeen: A Slave Woman

1 APRIL 1822
The Virginian Countryside

Xavier looked over Catherine's shoulder at the map, folded to focus on Virginia. They *X*'ed out a number of towns, having explored there but finding no sign of Duncan. They thought he had been sold in Washington, DC, and moved to Virginia, based on the intelligence they gathered. But where did Duncan go from there? Catherine picked Alexandria, thinking perhaps someone resold Duncan at auction.

Xavier took deep breaths as he glanced at the *X*'s on the page before him, each representing one place where countless slaves lived. The small shacks as living quarters, the cornmeal mush they ate meal after meal, the fear in their eyes when they saw a white man, Xavier, approaching them. At these moments he struggled against hating all humankind, becoming like Thomas, who thought people evil and therefore hardly caring about any of them. Xavier set his chin on Catherine's shoulder to once again feel her grounding presence.

"If we go here—" She pointed to a spot on the map. "—then we can circle this area, and come back here. If we come up with nothing, then we begin here tomorrow, and then head out." Catherine looked at Xavier for approval.

"Sounds good."

Later, after Xavier followed Catherine around in the dark for a couple hours, Xavier slipped away from Catherine for a moment and fed on an overseer whom he found alone in the woods, dragging a little girl along behind him. She had run away the minute Xavier grabbed hold of the man, before Xavier could bite into his neck and drain his blood. Once sated, Xavier reunited with Catherine.

They came upon a strange area where nothing moved or made a sound. The eerie quiet began to unnerve Xavier. He had just mentioned the strange stillness of the countryside when Catherine froze and motioned for him to hold steady. She put her finger to her mouth. Then Xavier heard it, too, with his vampiric senses. Someone breathing nearby. Xavier peered toward a growth of bushes and, too late, saw the figure leap out and run.

Catherine and he gave chase and caught up with the woman. She struggled against them to no avail, her torn dress and gaunt figure looking ill, even more sick than other slaves in poor condition. Catherine soothed her and convinced the woman to stop struggling against them. The three stood in the middle of a tobacco field, silhouetted by the full moon.

"You're like *him*," the woman spat, as her eyes darted all around, afraid.

"Like whom?" Xavier asked.

She laughed. "You don't know? You're in trouble, and now so am I."

"What are you talking about?" Catherine moved toward her, but the woman jumped back.

"We're not here to harm you," Xavier said. "We need assistance in finding someone."

"This place isn't safe for you."

Catherine shot a concerned look at Xavier. "What do you mean?"

"The one who controls me—he doesn't like others in his territory. He freed me, saying the sweetest things, making all these promises, and instead, made my life worse than when I was nothing but a slave in the field. Took me out of spite, he did, because he took a liking to me. So he freed me from master but enslaved me to him, promising not to hurt my children if I stayed in the area and saw him once in a while. But he didn't free them. I don't have a place to live. And you two"—she pointed first at Catherine and then at Xavier—"he won't like you at all."

"Who are you talking about? What is he doing to you?" Xavier suspected before she explained a thing they had run into another vampire.

"He's one of you. Dead. Sucks my blood while he rapes me."

Xavier was shocked, not at finding another vampire or at the information he took such liberties with another slave, but everything pointed to one who violated the vampire ethic in the open. How did the Vampire Council allow such a thing? Xavier thought it ironic, a violation of the ethic made him indignant. He wondered where the mysterious Vampire Council had gone.

"Where is he? What else does he do?" The woman allowed Catherine to approach her.

"He came all the way from Africa because he could have power over my people. Get out. Before he finds you."

"I can't leave. I have to find someone." Xavier reached his hand out to Catherine, who handed him the drawing of Duncan they had a street artist make, based on Xavier's description from the vision Anne gave him. "His name is Duncan. Have you seen him?"

Her eyes widened with recognition, and too late, she tried to act nonchalant. "Could be any boy working the fields around here. They all look alike, don't they?" She smirked at her last comment.

"You've seen him." Xavier grabbed her arm, desperate for information, but she yanked it away and reared back. Xavier let go and put his hands up in surrender.

"Please." Catherine stepped between them. "You're protecting your family. We're trying to protect ours."

"You have a black family?" The woman laughed.

"Not in the sense you mean." Catherine was allowed to approach the woman, but Xavier stayed behind. "But yes, Duncan is our family. He was stolen from us. Please."

"He'll kill me if he finds out. And everyone I love. Go to the fire. It's the one burning brightest. There you'll find him, and your Duncan. And then he'll kill you."

With those words she sprinted in the other direction. Xavier thought to pursue her again but Catherine grabbed his arm and stopped him. "Let her go. She's afraid. We've got what we need."

"What are we getting into?"

Catherine shrugged. "We'll find out."

Xavier and Catherine walked toward the location the woman indicated but saw no fire or any other sign of life. The night had gone black again when Xavier lurched to a stop.

"We need to go find her again. I can't leave it."

Catherine tilted her head at her brother. "What do you mean?"

"She's afraid. Alone. Under attack. We have to help her escape. We have to get her out of here."

"We can't, and you know it."

Xavier ignored Catherine and turned around, retracing their steps to the middle of the field and then following the woman's tracks and smell into a nearby wooded area. She had climbed a tree to hide from them, but they spotted her.

"I told you everything. Please, leave me alone." She hugged the tree, though no more than a few feet off the ground.

Xavier climbed the branch of a neighboring tree, bringing himself to her height, and sat on it. He dangled his legs over the limb and swung them back and forth. He saw Catherine, standing several yards away, watching.

"I can free you. Tonight."

"How are you going to do that?" The woman peered at him, a small bit of hope revealed in her face.

"You already know about us, right? We can do anything he can do. You've seen him move fast, too fast for any human?" She nodded. "We can too. You've seen his strength and cunning? Ours matches his. But there are two of us. If he's threatening you, he's violating the laws that govern our kind."

The woman let out a derisive laugh. "Laws, for the undead? He controls everything and everyone."

Xavier jumped from his branch to hers and put his hand on her shoulder. "Laws do exist. And even if they don't, we can get you out of here before he knows you're gone."

She stared at Xavier for a long time, the wheels in her head turning. A couple of times she almost spoke but then backed away from it. Her eyes welled with tears, and she shook her head back and forth. "Can't. My babies. I won't leave my babies."

"Where are they? We'll take them with us."

Again she fell quiet, deep in contemplation. "Where can you take me? How far? Will I really be safe?"

"We'll take you out of the South, to the North. To people who help slaves escape to freedom all the time. We can get you all the way to Canada. A safe place for you to raise your children. *Free* children."

Without saying a word, she jumped down and Xavier followed her. She walked to the edge of a clearing and pointed to a row of shacks across the field, darkened except for the moonlight shining down.

"Third one in. An old woman lives there, with two little babies and a few teenagers. The babies are mine. If you can get them and bring them back, I'll go with you."

Xavier dashed forward, leaving Catherine with the woman to wait. He crept along the edge of the buildings and then froze. The hair on the back of his neck stood straight up. Without seeing it, without smelling it, without any other indication at all, Xavier knew a vampire lurked nearby. Knowing his chances were better with Catherine if a fight ensued, he sped into action. He raced inside the building and grabbed the babies from the sleeping old woman's arms, sprinting out with vampiric speed, as the old woman screamed an alarm, and the babies wailed in fear. It took mere seconds to cross the field and put them in their mother's arms.

"Quiet them. Now!"

"We have to go." Catherine touched Xavier's arms and pointed back across the field to the gathering slaves who looked at them.

The babies quieted to a murmur in their mother's arms, but Xavier had no more time to waste. "Follow behind, and keep watch," Xavier instructed Catherine, who nodded. Xavier grabbed the woman from behind. "Trust me. Close your eyes and hold your children very, very tightly." He picked her up and ran faster than he had ever run as a vampire. He spotted a darkened figure approaching the other slaves too smoothly and boldly for a human. He hurried on, past the plantations, speeding over bridges and rivers, out of the South and to a rural home in Delaware he and Catherine visited on their way south. The pattern in the quilt signaled a safe house hung on a nearby tree, as if airing out but a beacon of hope. Xavier stopped and set the mother and her children down, both again screaming in agony and fear.

Xavier did not know if Catherine made it or followed him until she stopped next to him a few seconds later. Despite their vampiric agility and bodies, they both breathed heavily from the exertion. Catherine strode to the door and knocked.

The free black woman who instructed them on where to go in Washington, DC, opened the door and motioned them inside when she saw the woman and her children.

"We can't stay," Catherine said. "We can't explain. Can you protect them?"

"Of course. What's going on?" She wiped her hand on the apron around her waist.

"Get them to Canada." Xavier ignored her question and moved to the door, motioning for Catherine to follow. He opened the door, when the woman whom they freed stopped him.

"Wait. One more thing. Your man. Your family. He's there. With the other one. I know it."

They had just enough time to leave and get back to Alexandria and their rooms before the sun rose. Xavier nodded his thanks and went out the door.

In no time, he and Catherine slammed the door shut on their rented apartment and flung themselves into their respective trunks. As the dawn approached and he drifted to sleep, Xavier said a quick prayer of thanks for the direction that had come to him.

Eighteen: A Dark Prince

2 APRIL 1822
Alexandria, Virginia

Xavier pushed open the lid of his trunk, at last able to consider everything from the night before.

Feeling confident they saved the woman and her children—Xavier never asked her name—he turned his attention to everything else they learned. First, she recognized Duncan and told them for certain they found him. Then, she warned about a vampire who lived in the area. But even without her claims, Xavier had *felt* his presence. He was sure he saw the vampire emerging from the darkness as the slaves gathered and shouted at them after he stole the babies.

But why had he not followed? Xavier fretted the entire way the other one would come up behind Catherine and attack. Thankfully, she materialized next to him, and the vampire never pursued them.

Xavier found Catherine tonight already awake and picking through his clothes. "I already fed, on a drunken louse beating his wife." She said it as if she sauntered down a Parisian street for bread. Like Thomas, vampirism became her. Catherine held up a pair of Xavier's trousers and considered them.

"Do you often dress in men's clothing?" he asked.

"Why should only men wear pants? These dresses are rather impractical, especially when we have to sneak around in the dark *and* face a vampire. I'm wearing something of yours tonight."

Xavier sat beside her on the floor. "What about your hair?"

"I'll tie it up. Do you have a problem with this?"

"Of course not." Xavier shook his head to emphasize his point before Catherine launched into a tirade about women's rights. "I'm trying to learn from you."

Catherine tossed the pants aside and next snatched up a shirt. "I hope these go over my bosom."

"It'll be tight. Might snap a button right off." Xavier laughed when he made his sister smile. "Are you sure you don't have anything else to tell me?"

Catherine wrinkled her brow. "What are you talking about?"

"It's just, since I transformed you, we haven't had time to talk. We had to hurry on this mission without discussing what I did to you, and what I learned."

"You made me a vampire. What on earth should we discuss? I told you I had nothing to hide, and you saw as much in the blood." Then Catherine's eyes lit with recognition.

"Men's clothing?" Xavier smiled back. "Not that the two go hand in hand. But I suppose if you want to kiss any more women, you may find them more readily dressed as a man."

Catherine roared with laughter, tilting her head back and laying back on the oriental rug. "Oh, that? You remembered, did you? An occasional kiss never hurt anyone. Forget you ever saw it."

"You spent an inordinate amount of time to make me deal with my sexual secrets, but you held the same ones."

"Not the same." Catherine shook her finger at him. "I like both. A little taste of each, thank you. I had Jérémie for one flavor, but a few fondles here and there with the ladies never hurt him, or me. He liked to watch."

Xavier crinkled his nose but grinned. "Enough. I already know too much. Are you ready?"

"Should we strategize? This is more than we predicted we'd face. A human captor, white Southerners, and a bunch of slaves are one thing. A rogue vampire? That's quite another."

Xavier thought for a minute. Thomas had schooled Xavier again and again on how to combat another vampire because he feared a fellow vampire threatened Xavier more than anything else. Xavier had to practice against Anthony and Thomas pretending to come after him at the same time, so he became adept at fighting vampires, if he did say so himself.

He and Catherine discussed the situation for a few minutes, agreeing on the best way to proceed and then hurrying to where they found the woman the night before. The eerie quiet remained, absorbed into the plants and trees. Even the bugs failed to fly around. Unlike other areas where slaves moved about at night from plantation to plantation or reveled around a fire, nothing moved here. They rounded a bend when at last Xavier saw the fire roaring in front of them a few hundred yards ahead.

Not a small fire over which to cook food, but a raging inferno, spiraling into the night sky, almost touching the top of short trees. About twenty feet behind it, sitting high atop a chair built on stilts and surrounded by slave guards sat a dark figure, staring straight at them.

He wore a bright-red cloak and yellow pants that contrasted with his dark skin. His lips curled in a snarl, revealing the fangs beneath. The slaves surrounding the fire began a ferocious beating of drums and singing, dancing in circles and chanting over and over.

"This doesn't look good," Catherine whispered to Xavier.

"No, it doesn't." Xavier wondered at a vampire so unafraid of fire. Had he staged the scene to ward off Catherine and Xavier? It was a bold statement.

Catherine held him back. "Are you sure you know enough to combat a vampire?"

"He has Duncan. We don't have any choice. Do we?"

"Promise you'll be careful. This is dangerous."

Xavier wanted to thank Catherine for the obvious but thought better of any humor, given the situation. Instead, he walked forward, his head held high, right to the edge of the circle. The slaves came to a halt when they saw Catherine and Xavier standing before them. One of them broke rank and approached them.

"You dare approach His Excellency? Without an invitation? White people aren't welcome. We'll feed you to him for lunch."

"Joseph, stand down." From atop his perch, the vampire's deep baritone ordered the man, so the slave went back to the others. "Go." With but a word, the vampire dismissed all the slaves, who filed back toward their shacks and the big house behind them. Only then did Xavier recognize the place as back to normal, where he had come to the night before to save the babies.

The vampire rose, standing atop the platform in front of his chair, towering above them. He hovered there for a moment before leaning forward and jumping down to stand a few feet in front of them. He stood a foot taller than Xavier as he looked back and forth from Catherine to Xavier with a sneer. He rolled his neck around as if stretching, then grabbed a nearby long spike and twirled it in the air.

"You should be afraid of fire, shouldn't you?" He jerked his head at the pyre roaring behind him.

"Shouldn't you?" Catherine shot back.

"It's *my* fire." His eyes grew wide and he smiled, his white teeth and fangs glowing in the night. Xavier took a step back, not knowing what he meant by claiming the fire as his own. Catherine remained in her spot, so Xavier stepped forward again. His hope they could settle things amicably faded like one of the sparks flying up into the night from the fire. "You stole from me." The vampire jabbed the spike into the ground and folded his arms across his powerful chest. Under other circumstances, Xavier would have thought him beautiful. Instead, he just looked imposing.

Xavier shook his head. "No, we didn't. You can't own people. You don't. You don't possess them. We've but one thing to ask of you, and we'll leave."

The vampire squinted his eyes as the fire reflected off his bald head. "For a vampire, you don't hear very well. You sneak into my territory. You see the signs, you felt my presence, and *still* you came. Then you take up with one of my people and steal her away, right from under my nose. Now you return, presuming to instruct me on what I can and cannot do with these humans? I should toss you in the fire right now."

"You can't do that either." Xavier's lips trembled, seeing the vampire get angrier and bolder with each word. He forced himself to continue. "The ethic. The vampire ethic. You know about it. You violate it. You're interfering with all of these people, with all of these human affairs. You can't do that. And, and—you can't kill another of our kind without cause."

Xavier's words hung in the air as their nemesis glared at them.

Catherine moved closer. "What kind of soul lurks inside you?" She spat her defiance in his face. Xavier and she had not planned such a scene, and he wondered if she acted in calculation or because of one of her unpredictable mood swings. "You of all people should know what you're doing to them."

"Because I'm black?" The vampire strode two steps forward and stopped, mere inches from Catherine's face. "All the black folk stick together?"

Catherine spit in his face. Xavier's heart leaped into his throat, and he surged forward, moving to protect her. But the vampire laughed and wiped off his face, then smeared it from his hand onto Catherine's shirt, brushing across her breasts. She slapped his hand away. He walked back to his fire and turned in front of it to face them.

"The ethic, here? I assure you, it's of little consequence."

"You rape the women. You control these slaves. Everything you do violates the ethic. You're immersed in their lives." Xavier spoke but kept his distance, calculating whether or not he could shove the vampire into the fire.

"I protect them." The vampire waved his hand toward the shacks. "By arrangement with the owner. I control them, and then he doesn't beat them."

"Nonetheless, it violates the ethic." Catherine was unfazed. "And raping women is a strange way of protecting them."

"You two think you know an awful lot about this here ethic. How old are you? A couple of years? I've lived for centuries. There is magic to protect against the ethic, or at least I created it. Beyond my little invention, it's the profile you keep that matters, not the letter of the law. I stay here on my one little plantation, except when I go outside the territory to feed. I live right in the big house with the master, working with him. If what I do doesn't risk exposure, then my magic conceals me from their prying eyes. They're not as all powerful as everyone thinks."

Xavier contemplated what he said, baffled. Thomas and Anthony talked of the Council as an all-knowing, all-powerful entity. He had met very few vampires, but they all acted the same way—as if the Council could appear and sanction them at any minute and never missed a thing a vampire did. That was the truth as told to Xavier. But this one violated a number of the laws, as Xavier understood them, without impunity. What did it all mean?

"Even if that were all true, though I doubt it, you rape them." Xavier tested the vampire further. "You use them as your personal toys. The Council would never stand for it."

The vampire chuckled. "You're listening to the ravings of a madwoman. She was raped all right, by her own father. She claims the master raped her, too, after she undressed and seduced him in the shed. She'd tell anyone anything to get them to free her. She saw her chance when you two idiots appeared. Sure, she knew your power because of me and then took advantage of it to get what she wanted from you."

Xavier didn't know what to believe anymore. Nothing made sense. His head spun with trying to understand everything.

"If you're so noble, why not free all of them?" Catherine spoke with an edge in her voice.

"Where do you think I could take a gaggle of black folk in the new world? I told you, I have an arrangement. The master and his wife let me be to take care of them and control them as my little kingdom, so long as no one gets hurt or disappears."

"It violates the ethic," Xavier repeated, less sure of himself.

The vampire came back to them. "What do you want?" He poked Xavier in the chest. "I'm a lot older than you, so don't go lecturing me about the damn ethic. I told you I countered it. I keep a low profile. The Council acts all high and mighty, making sure all the little people in their vampire world think they see everything everyone does, like omnipotent gods. Like Zeus and his crew on Mount Olympus, ready to strike with a bolt of lightning should anyone dare defy them. But they don't know everything. Their magic can be limited. It can be countered." He folded his arms on his chest again. "I make my own rules. Trust me, they either don't care or don't have a clue. Whichever. I've been doing it for centuries. Ever since that one tried to wipe us all out. So, you tell me, what do you want? Tell me, and then get the hell out."

Xavier assumed he referred to the battle that Anthony had told him about, where a single vampire tried to kill the entire Council and anyone who crossed him so he could transform all vampires into a legion of Satanists, or was it devout Christians? Either way, Anthony said he was a zealot. Still Xavier had no idea what to think because he violated the ethic, but the Council *did* seem to overlook him. And what was all the talk about magic, with the Council and his own magic? Whatever, the tact had gotten them nowhere so Xavier changed the subject.

"You stole a slave." Xavier tried to sound bold but heard the quiver in his voice. "Duncan. We want him back."

Again the vampire grinned and then snarled at them. Catherine moved between them, as if to protect Xavier.

"I didn't steal anyone. *Bought* him at the market. The master did, not me. I just like him."

"So you admit he's here?" Catherine asked.

"I never denied it. But you can't have him. He's mine now. It makes no matter to me how he got here."

"Let us see him." Catherine walked right up to him, apparently unafraid. "Never mind any of this chatter about ethics and councils. Let us see he's safe, and we'll go."

Again Xavier had no idea what Catherine planned. They got away from their original plan long ago, and all of the talk confused Xavier. Why did the vampire get to violate the ethic without retribution? Because of his sorcery? Or was he lying? Bluffing? Xavier knew he should concentrate on the task in front of them, but his head spun from everything. Thankfully, as she had his entire life, Catherine took control.

"Be my guest." The vampire mock bowed and motioned his hand toward the slave quarters. Without telling them where to go, or following, the vampire allowed Catherine and Xavier to proceed.

Still bold, Catherine nodded and walked around the fire, toward the encampment. The slaves had retreated to their homes but stood looking toward their vampiric god, watching the interaction take place.

Xavier spotted Duncan, remembering his beautiful body and dazzling eyes. He stood by himself, behind everyone, but watching. He seemed well, at least from a quick glance. Xavier started to approach him when the vampire grabbed his shoulder from behind. "Enough."

Xavier spun out of his grasp and jumped over the vampire, pushing Catherine along with him in a move Thomas taught him to get distance between an attacker.

"Go." The vampire pointed away and started toward them again. "Go, or you'll find out who the Vampire Council will back in this matter."

Xavier started to speak, thinking of beginning the fight he was sure would come right then, but Catherine tugged him back. "It's not the time," she whispered.

"Yes, it's not the time." Of course, he heard Catherine speak to Xavier.

Not knowing what else to do, Xavier acquiesced to Catherine's recommendation and whipped around to leave. But he first seized the spike from the ground and hurled it toward the vampire, aiming to land in front of him. The vampire stood his ground, not flinching when the spear jabbed into the dirt mere inches from his foot.

Nineteen: Assassination

5 APRIL 1822
Alexandria, Virginia

Xavier hatched the plan as he slept the day after their confrontation, reminding him of the days he spent as a priest when something troubled or confounded him. In order to find a solution, he studied the problem until it hurt. Often, in his dreams or half-awake state in the middle of sleep, the answer came out of thin air. It always seemed so simple then, making Xavier wonder what took so long to come up with it in the first place.

While the plot for tonight came in the same manner, nothing about it seemed simple. Despite all the questions last night raised about the Vampire Council, and without knowing what connections the vampire may or may not have to it, Xavier's determination to kill him risked a lot.

The vampire would expect them to come the very next night, to challenge him or attempt a bargain. Thomas had drilled into Xavier any surprise, no matter how simple, gave him the advantage. So he and Catherine pretended to have left or gone about other business. Whether the vampire watched them or not, he and Catherine pretended to move forward, going about their lives as if they had never gone to the vampire or looked for one of his captives. They went to the length of moving out of their accommodations and hiding several towns away in an abandoned farm house.

Tonight, having waited a few days to act, Xavier knew they had to time everything with perfection. Catherine and he waited until minutes before the sun would appear on the horizon, keeping their distance and then running to the vampire's plantation.

Despite all the scheming and attempts at surprise, they arrived to find him standing in front of the fire, hunched over and ready for an attack.

With their ploy undone, the fight commenced too soon, and their enemy was as at least as powerful as Thomas and maybe as much as Anthony. Despite their two to one advantage and all of those practice sessions against Anthony, they struggled against the vampire and battled for several minutes with no one gaining the advantage.

The vampire ripped their clothing, scratched them, and whirled around to avoid their counterattacks. Xavier got him once, clawing through his shirt and ripping open the skin on his back. He roared and lashed out, charging Xavier and pushing him into a tree. Catherine countered by taking an iron spike and ramming it into his eye.

The vampire let go of Xavier and rushed backward, toward the fire. His wound healed, but Xavier wanted to vomit at the sight because the spike remained planted in the middle of his eye. As Xavier knew from his training, the split second taken to remove the spike could create a disadvantage.

The sun barely appeared on the horizon, but Xavier already felt weakened and tired. They had no place to go, and the vampire would kill them if they let down their guard. Catherine and he stood again, crouched and waiting for the assault to recommence.

Too late to protect him, Xavier saw the fool boy come racing out of the darkness with a scythe. He raced toward the vampire, who swung his arm and batted the child twenty feet through the air. The boy, no more than ten, slammed onto the ground in the tall grass. What Xavier failed to notice were the children coming from the opposite direction, at least twenty of them. Even with their numbers, they were no match for their vampire captor. Xavier felt nauseous about what he would do to them.

Except Xavier was already engaged in a battle to the death, making it impossible to worry for too long or do anything to stop them. A split second before Xavier knew what to do, Catherine went into action. At the moment the vampire thrust the first three little girls away from him toward the fire, Catherine launched herself at the vampire's head and jumped on top of him. Xavier first pushed the girls away from the fire, then shouted with pain as he grabbed a burning stick. With all the force he could muster, he flung himself at the vampire and forced the stake through the vampire's lower back and into his intestines. Knowing the body would heal from the wound, Xavier counted on the fire to immobilize their enemy.

The vampire cried out in desperation, but Catherine shoved him into the fire, keeping her foot on him until the flames consumed him. He struggled out of the conflagration and rolled on the ground to put it out, but Catherine, Xavier, and then the children grabbed anything burning and tossed it on him. Xavier almost threw up again when the young man who started the children's assault lifted his scythe high in the air and whacked off the vampire's head. Xavier tossed it in the fire and watched it burn before he collapsed, the sun having defeated him too. A strange tingling sensation consumed him, as if a magical spell evaporated around them as the vampire's remains were engulfed by fire.

Xavier drifted into an unknown reality, with light flashing in his eyes and a feeling of floating upward. Stars danced on his eyelids.

He expected pain or suffering but felt nothing but peace and contentment. Xavier dreamed of Thomas, wishing him farewell and hoping beyond hope Thomas knew how much he loved him. He felt sorry at not having said goodbye, and at having dragged Catherine into the whole mess. Then he remembered Duncan and said a small prayer to Anne to forgive him for having failed.

It shocked Xavier the next evening when he awoke as he had every night since becoming a vampire. He glanced around his surroundings—a cellar full of wine. Someone had lain him out in the open with nothing protecting or concealing him. Where was he? And how had he gotten here?

Only when he looked over and saw Catherine reading a book did he relax.

"We're not dead?" He knew it sounded stupid.

Catherine laughed. "I guess not. Although someone has a terrible intolerance for the sun." She walked over to him and sat on the ground.

"What happened?" he asked.

"Two fool vampires attacked a much older and wiser vampire. They did well enough, but had quite a conundrum as the sun approached, when a group of small children saved their sorry lives."

"I know. But we died. Or at least I did."

"Then how are you here with me right now? Or are you undead undead?"

"Stop it. Tell me what's going on."

Catherine brushed hair out of his face and ran her finger along his cheek. "I have good news and bad news."

"What's good?" He didn't want to hear anything bad, not yet.

"He's dead. We burned him. And you passed out, unable to withstand the first rays of sun. I was getting weak but had enough left in me to make sure we completed the job. The children had me carry you here, promising to safeguard us through the day. They wanted to kill him, for everything he did to them and their families. Their parents forbade it, afraid of what would happen to their community, but the children slinked away and insisted on trying something. That's why they came to our rescue. I've been talking to a couple of them this evening, waiting for you to awake. You're later than usual. We're in the wine cellar underneath the big house. If you look over there, you can see where he slept."

Xavier got up and brushed himself off. He inspected the casket that had housed their nemesis, then walked around the room, looking at the opulent bed in one corner, so out of place. He perused the wine, taking out an appealing bottle.

"French." He took a corkscrew and uncorked it. "Sorry. No glasses." He took a swig and handed it to Catherine.

She drank too. "Good French, no less."

"Is there any bad French wine?" Xavier drank again, the buzz already calming him. "So, the bad news. You know, the Vampire Council will come after us now. Regardless of what he said, we've gone beyond the pale. The humans know about us, we murdered one of our own, and all because of a mission the Vampire Council would never approve."

Catherine nodded as she opened another bottle. "True. We knew from the beginning, though."

"What's the bad news?"

"He's gone." Catherine set the bottle down and looked at Xavier with a face that always made him melancholy.

"I know. We killed him."

"Not the vampire. Duncan."

"What do you mean?" Xavier jerked his head to stare into his sister's eyes for an answer. "He's with the other slaves."

"No, he's not." Catherine shook her head. "I woke before you. The kids were all huddled outside the door waiting for us. The master and mistress fled a couple days ago. The children said they left without the usual preparations and instructions for the slaves. They raced around the house, packing a bunch of items. The vampire helped them go with a few possessions and about three or four slaves, including Duncan. The children have no idea where they went."

Xavier sat still, not knowing how to respond. He and Catherine were alive. Thankfully. And they had gotten rid of the vile vampire. Whatever the reason, whether he violated the ethic or not, he caused a lot of harm and pain for the people around him. Xavier marveled they defeated a much older vampire, though it took human interference.

Yet he had so hoped to end their quest last night. Once he realized he lived and saw Catherine sitting there, he allowed himself to wish they could walk away with Duncan, take him to New York, and send a dispatch at once to Thomas.

With a sentence, Catherine deflated him. The war raged on. He and Catherine thought for a while about what to do and where to go, then went outside to greet the children. They stayed a safe distance away but chatted until the adult slaves came around and ordered the kids back with a wary look toward the vampires.

Catherine and Xavier quizzed the kids about where the family might have fled or if they owned any other property. They learned nothing to help them. It took time to assure all of them they were safe and Catherine and he meant them no harm.

And so their search continued with little new information. Except the name and description of the master and mistress might help them. Xavier had to keep his painful distance from Thomas, whom he missed every waking moment. But his soul drove him forward, and he recalled his prayers that pacified him with doing the small things, one tiny act at a time to change a small part of the world.

Catherine and Xavier spent the next couple of nights freeing all of these slaves, almost one hundred in total. With all the white people on the plantation gone, it took little to spirit them away one at a time until they all resided in a small town in Canada, with a number of other escaped slaves. Some of the children even hugged Xavier goodbye when he and Catherine got the last of them to freedom.

If he had to violate the ethic, if he doomed himself and Catherine to an unpredictable fate, he would do anything in his power to help people along the way. Maybe one day the future generations of these slaves could assist others or keep the underground railroad alive and well.

Catherine surprised Xavier by joining him on the task, opening a new account in each slave's name and depositing thousands of dollars from the Saint-Laurent fortune.

When they returned to America and slept for the day in a cave in the middle of Kentucky, Xavier reclaimed a small sense of peace. He remained on edge, of course, knowing his nervousness would remain until he returned to Thomas and found out what the Vampire Council intended to do to him. Yet God answered his prayers and gave him a purpose. Catherine remained with him, seeming to enjoy their adventure despite the danger. At least he had her presence, and the smiles on those faces as he departed the group of freed people who for the first time in their lives had hope for the future.

Part Five

Searching in Vain

Twenty: Loneliness

11 MAY 1822
New York City

The farther Thomas got from last seeing Xavier, the more difficult his mood swings became to control. Thomas hardly believed almost two months had passed since he discovered the dreadful note from Xavier reporting he went on a quest as instructed by a divine vision.

Thomas seethed at religion's effect on Xavier. He worried that Xavier, a sensitive and delicate soul still as a vampire, searched too hard for divine inspiration and meaning for life. Why did society so plague Xavier that he fretted about being a good soul, of doing the right thing, even when it came naturally to him? Courting Xavier during the French Revolution, Thomas grew to despise the Roman Catholic Church, and Xavier's past with it, because they combined to inculcate in him a feeling of inferiority, a sense he had to behave and act to perfection for acceptance. Thomas long suspected Xavier's inner demons led to his pensiveness and constant worry. Whether or not an archangel visited Xavier, these concerns haunted Xavier and played into his actions once again. Thomas hated anything troubling his Xavier.

Of course, Thomas had fallen in love with that very trait when he first met Xavier. His sensitivity lured Thomas with its need for reassurance and belief in people. True, Xavier lost his *blind* innocence when he watched his brother's assassination and then assassinated his best friend out of mercy. Xavier killed the destitute to eat without remorse as a vampire. But the philosophy he existed to make the world more palatable remained imbedded in his person. Xavier exuded a warmth and goodness Thomas loved.

In fact, Thomas loved everything about Xavier. His sensitivity. His passion, his caring. His sense of humor and the way he could tease Thomas like no one else and make Thomas laugh about it. His slender body and those beautiful eyes that could bore right into Thomas's soul. It maddened him since Xavier fled, that Thomas thought about him *more* than ever before.

Xavier's absence created his current conundrum: as his search for Xavier kept Thomas going, it inspired the anger dancing under the surface of Thomas's every waking moment. Stupid people infuriated him. He wanted to murder people for the smallest of slights, no matter if unintended. He tortured his victims longer because he could. That was the ugly side of Thomas lurking within, bitter at the isolation and judgment he received on the Massachusetts frontier so long ago as a half-breed: the son of a white father and Indian mother. Xavier and Anthony taught him so much about why the rage rumbled within, and in doing so, Thomas came to cope with it. Without Xavier his life was empty, his soul hollow, and the anger controlled him.

Anthony still worked with him to control it, as he had almost since the day they met. Usually, Anthony's calm demeanor and knowledge about Thomas helped and could soothe his ire until Thomas regained control of it. Anthony represented part of the problem. But over the last few weeks, Thomas had a difficult time hiding certain pieces of knowledge from Anthony as he tried to shelter Xavier and relied on Anthony's help to find him. And he suspected Anthony knew much more and had more at his disposal to help than he admitted to Thomas. Something about the Vampire Council lurked under everything in a suspicious way.

Stranding himself in New York City did nothing to help either. It made sense to stay here to wait for Anthony's network to bring word to them. Anthony assured him every day it would accomplish the job, but the longer it took, the more Thomas worried about what Xavier and Catherine had done to doom them in front of the Vampire Council. In the past, he witnessed Anthony learn Council business within seconds and then zoom away, so why was he taking days upon days? Thomas waited in New York City because no other choice presented itself.

He ventured out of the flat intent on two things: feeding and checking with his sources to see if a note had arrived from Paris. He accomplished the latter, when his contact here shook his head and grimaced at having to tell Thomas no, nothing had come from Europe.

Feeding took a little longer because Thomas dragged out the process. It made the night pass more quickly, without the longing for Xavier taking up every waking minute.

Thomas moved into the underside of New York to seek his prey. He had not fed in a couple of nights, which heightened his hunger and passion. He strode by a couple of unsavory types but their dirty appearance and lackadaisical attitude failed to entice him. He wanted a feistier combatant. He hardly expected to meet the cute lad who came up to him, asking if he could give directions to the nearest saloon.

Thomas chuckled at the request. How difficult was it in a large city to find a place to drink? "Not a very good approach. Only an imbecile couldn't find a pub around here." Thomas smiled and noticed the man, who at first glance appeared to be in his midteens, was closer to his midtwenties. He was beautiful, with brown eyes, soft cheeks, and the slight stature Thomas desired. In a different era, Thomas would have had him in bed already.

The young man smiled. "Well then, do you need a companion to take you to a saloon?"

Thomas cusped him under his chin. "You're bold, adorable, and my type. I'm afraid I'm taken."

"So? I just want an hour or two." He leaned closer to Thomas, grabbing Thomas's crotch and feeling his growing excitement. "It feels like you're game."

Thomas pulled away. "I can't. But thank you. Be careful down here."

Thomas walked away, miserable with himself. He could never betray Xavier, but the long absence made it so difficult sexually for Thomas, who missed holding Xavier, making love to him, sliding in and out of his lover as Thomas peered down on him from above. Without sex for so long, Thomas almost lost control. If he had Xavier, even if they separated for a couple of nights, the young man would never have so aroused Thomas. What was he becoming?

He hunted again, searching the corners and alleys for his victim. He found one in a surprising source. Not concealed well at all, he found the beautiful man from moments ago holding down a poor boy with his hand clamped over the boy's mouth.

"This won't hurt long. You'll like it." He sweated and struggled to undo his pants and contain the innocent child at the same time.

Thomas sprang upon him in one quick motion, grabbing him from behind by his shirt and leaping onto the roof of the building. Hidden there, Thomas slammed him down, cracking bones and causing him to scream out in pain.

"This won't hurt for long either." Thomas leered over him as the man tried to scramble to his feet but fell when Thomas's foot planted on his chest. Thomas wanted to degrade him. Releasing his inner fury felt good. Standing atop him so he could not move, Thomas peed on him, glad he had a beer with Anthony the night before so he was able to function now as necessary.

Then Thomas sat and toyed with the man. First be broke a finger, then he undressed him and scratched various surfaces of his body. He broke an arm and then a leg. The man whimpered and cried the entire time, begging Thomas to end it.

"I thought you liked me." He cringed at Thomas through tears of pain.

"I liked your looks." Thomas tilted his head and winked at him. "Not you. How could you do that to him?" Thomas ran his nails down the man's cheeks.

"Just kill me, please."

Thomas had enough too. He leaned over and bit into the victim's neck and enjoyed the savory taste of his blood. He blocked out the visions of his life, not wanting to bother with what it taught, instead focusing on the bitter tang of blood as it flowed down his throat. He tossed the body aside when finished and started home.

Thomas was still miserable. More miserable than when he awoke. First, he'd wanted to have sex with another man. Well, not really, he resisted that urge. But the absence of Xavier and their sex life was getting to Thomas in ways he never predicted.

One thought rolled over and over in Thomas's mind: *Xavier, dear Xavier, how I need you.*

He got back to their home to find Anthony waiting for him in the parlor. "I want to speak with you."

Thomas feared another lecture or that he did something wrong to inspire the latest request for conversation. Had Anthony spied on him again, as he did during the French Revolution, waiting to reprimand Thomas for the slightest of misdeeds? He lost the patience for it. "Spare me. I don't have time."

"Will you listen to me?" Anthony got up and stood in front of Thomas. "We *should* talk about you. But another matter demands our attention."

Twenty-One: Rogue Vampires

11 MAY 1822
New York City

Thomas settled into a chair opposite Anthony once he realized he'd overreacted to Anthony's request to talk. In his foul mood, he expected Anthony to scold him for his temper or rebuke him for having tortured another victim for too long. Instead, Anthony had news of his own to address. Thomas had to get himself under control.

Anthony returned to the couch and played with a letter in his hands. "I tried to ignore it, but this is the second time a report came to me. I have to act."

"What do you mean?" Thomas leaned forward, curious and apprehensive.

"In April, the Council got word about two vampires who ventured into another one's territory. He confessed to having violated certain aspects of the ethic and concealing it by magic, but he insisted these two new ones intended to do worse, and he feared for his life. He wanted us to help him."

Thomas's stomach turned in knots. He could not escape a dread at what he was hearing. "What came of it?"

"Nothing. He sent the message through emergency channels, which employs magic to get word to the Council. I returned his inquiry. He wanted assurances we would at least be lenient on what he had done if he told us everything, including how he hid for so long from the Council. I informed him the Council would take his confession into account, as well as his future cooperation." Anthony shrugged. "He never replied. I thought nothing of it until this came today." Anthony waved the letter in the air. But again Thomas was suspicious, because Anthony tried to conceal the contents that looked from afar a lot like his own handwriting. "The Council requires I investigate this immediately."

"What is it?" Thomas almost hesitated to ask. "And why do *you* always have to investigate everything?"

"I'm the closest to Virginia. It makes sense they want me to take care of it. I'm certain it's the two vampires that worried this one into exposing himself. The Council received news a vampire was killed near Alexandria."

"Who's the informant?" Thomas interrupted Anthony.

Anthony shrugged, again irritating Thomas with his attempt to feign an ignorance Thomas hardly believed. Though he wanted to know more, Thomas decided he could not press the issue further without giving himself away in return.

"I'm guessing," Anthony continued without making eye contact. "I think these two vampires followed through and murdered the other one before the Council got involved. He might have been killed, anyway, for what he did. But these two need to be investigated now."

Thomas searched for an innocuous way to gain more information. "If he violated the ethic and would have died anyway, so be it. Maybe he provoked them."

"If they need a good defense attorney in front of the Council, I'll enlist your assistance. Do you want me to explain this or not? It affects you."

"Me? How?"

"That's what I'm trying to explain." Anthony threw his arms in the air and rolled his eyes, but grinned. "They killed him, right in full view of humans. Since then, they've taken to wandering the South, freeing slaves as they go by helping them escape. It's gotten bold enough around Virginia the slaves talk amongst themselves about the white gods who come at night and take them away. If that doesn't sound like a vampire, I don't know what does."

If Thomas had doubts at first or hoped for other news, Anthony's words confirmed it: they were talking about Catherine and Xavier, though Anthony seemed unaware. Thomas wracked his brain to figure out something to compel Xavier to leave him. He felt confident enough in their devotion to one another to think Xavier would never get up and leave without a profound reason pushing him away.

The possibility of coming to America to free slaves made sense, because Xavier always fretted over American slavery since he first saw it. Thomas took him back to Europe and forbade them from visiting the Americas, so long as the peculiar institution remained, because Xavier could not control himself. He violated the ethic right in front of Thomas to free a slave and talked of wreaking havoc throughout the South to free people. It took all of the persuasion Thomas could muster to pull Xavier away to safety, lest Anthony and the Council discover Xavier's deeds and intentions and sanction him for them. Only back in Europe, after several years, did Xavier move on with their lives.

Then Xavier disappeared with Catherine, after Thomas assumed he transformed her into a vampire. Then Anthony gets word two rogue vampires wander the South, killing a vampire and freeing slaves, so involved in human affairs the slaves started a legend about the mysterious figures roaming their land, trying to free them.

The whole story fit Xavier perfectly.

It also confirmed Thomas's worst fears: Xavier violated the ethic because St. Michel sent him on a damnable quest. Cursed angel. Only in Xavier's world could an angel send him on a mission that imperiled his life without also guaranteeing to protect him. Thomas hated religion all over again. And Xavier converted Catherine against protocol, though Thomas thought he could talk Anthony out of sanctioning Xavier. Then he might have killed another vampire. Thomas thought the vampire violated the ethic or perpetrated a profound evil, because it was out of character for Xavier to have gone after him. Perhaps Thomas could mount a defense against the infraction to protect Xavier. But freeing slaves so openly was another story. And combining all three things: if Thomas was correct and Xavier did it, then he had to get to Catherine and him first, before Anthony, because the Vampire Council would come down hard on both of them.

"Are you listening?" Anthony asked. "Or are you already mad at me?"

"I was trying to imagine who would do these stupid things. What did you say?"

Anthony laughed and came over to give Thomas a big hug. "I know you're preoccupied with Xavier. Forgive my carrying on about this."

"I understand." Thomas pulled away and ran his hand through his long, black hair. "What were you saying?"

"I have to leave. I know we intended to stay here until we got word about Xavier, but I have to go investigate this incident before it goes any further. Now. Tonight. I'm sorry, because I don't want you to think I'm abandoning you when you need me. You stay here, and if you hear anything about Xavier, go on without me. Otherwise, I'll return as soon as possible. I'm certain by then we'll have heard something."

Anthony went to his desk and started to shuffle papers around and pack them into a satchel. Thomas considered how to proceed before answering Anthony.

"I want to go with you."

Anthony spun his head around, surprise written on his face. "What about Xavier? Don't you want to wait here? I can have my people in New York send word to you instead of me."

"I appreciate it. But can't we have them send word wherever we're going?"

"Yes." Anthony nodded his head, pretending confusion. Thomas witnessed such an act before from Anthony, which alarmed him all the more. He wanted Thomas to stay behind and knew or suspected more than he let on.

Thomas launched ahead before Anthony could put the pieces together. "I can't be alone right now. I know I should stay in case we hear anything. Let's have them send a dispatch to us so I can stay with you. It's my anger." Thomas took his turn at acting, pretending to feel remorse.

Anthony turned around and straightened up. He came over and put his arm around Thomas. "You're afraid of your temper again?"

"I never violated the ethic. But it gets harder and harder without Xavier. I need you." Thomas figured a little white lie never hurt anyone. Truth be told, he *did* need Anthony, and Anthony grounded him and got him that far without incident. He just exaggerated how much he needed Anthony so he could go along and intercept the rogue vampires before Anthony found them. Besides, he would bet his life on Anthony knowing a lot more than he admitted.

"I already took you to the prison. I can't imagine it would hurt anything to bring you along." Anthony stared hard at Thomas, scrutinizing him until Thomas fidgeted and turned away. "Promise again not to reveal anything to anyone. I may need to use magic to subdue whomever I find. You might see or experience things you aren't meant to know."

"Of course, I promise." The mere thought of Anthony casting a spell on Xavier made his blood boil. He wanted to spit the words at Anthony and mock all of his power. Giving in to his anger, of course, would alert Anthony to the fact something was afoot. He got enough control of himself to say the words without inflection. "But I'd like to talk to you more about that before we go."

Anthony tidied up and headed for the door, as if ready to leave. "We need to go. Tonight, I said."

"I know." Thomas pulled Anthony back into the room. "We'll be out the door and there before the sun rises, ready to move into action tomorrow. I promise."

"What is this about?" Anthony stood before Thomas but set his bag down.

"Sit." Thomas jerked his head toward the couch. "Please?" Anthony obeyed. "In all my worry about Xavier, I never got to talk to you about this magic thing. I know, you told me it had to do with the Council, and you kept a lot of things from me involving them. I understand. I do." Thomas struggled again to find the right words. "It bothers me, though, that you have this other power you hid from me for so long."

"It has nothing to do with our friendship. I tell you more than anyone else in the entire world. You know you're my closest friend?" Anthony reached out and took Thomas's hand.

"Of course, I know. But we were lovers for a time."

Anthony raised his eyebrows. "If we want to talk about betrayal as lovers, we could start with the one who played a passive role to become a vampire and then reversed course. Whose lie crushed the other one that time?"

"I know, I know. But still, magic? You're a witch? You could have used it to help us find Xavier. Or to help Catherine get away from Marcel. How many times did we need those skills in the past, and you hid them? I'm hurt."

Anthony clutched Thomas's hands. "I have to follow the ethic too. Just because I'm on the Council doesn't give me free reign to do as I please. They can sanction me too. We conceal the magic because it's to be used in extreme emergencies. I've never used it for myself, only in service to the Council. You can't know how many times I've been tempted, here and there, to do a spell for my benefit. But I can't. You know how much the ethic and its enforcement means to me. I would never violate it. It would go against my nature. I shouldn't have revealed as much to you as I already did. Please forgive me?"

Thomas leaned over and hugged Anthony. He believed the explanation, with Anthony's absurd sense of duty and worship of the Council. That personified Anthony. But he failed to trust he learned the entire story.

But Thomas's real reason for even bringing up the sorcery had little to do with their friendship and a lot more to do with Xavier. How much power did Anthony really have? How and when did he use it? And what would he do to Xavier, if Anthony caught him first?

Twenty-Two: Investigation

12 MAY 1822
Alexandria, Virginia

Thomas fidgeted with a throw pillow as he waited for Anthony to return. The night before, after Thomas tried to learn more information from Anthony about what he could and could not do with the magic, to no avail, the two vampires hurried southward, arriving in Alexandria with enough time to feed before retiring to their coffins. Thomas tossed the pillow in the air and then caught it.

Anthony sought out a choice establishment, where they concealed themselves in the largest and most opulent of rooms. The pillow went into the air again and back to Thomas's hands. Thomas did love the luxury afforded vampires because of their wealth. True, he had hidden himself in crypts and other decrepit places to match his mood. But typically the finest places suited him best. Growing up on the Massachusetts frontier when the western part of the state served as a wilderness in the eyes of many European settlers, Thomas knew nothing of silk or satin, nothing of ornate furniture and servants to clean one's quarters.

Where had Anthony gone? He said he wanted to ask a couple of questions around town and would then return to take Thomas with him. The pillow launched into the air but veered away from Thomas. He reached to grab it but sent it shooting across the room, where it slid under an armoire.

Thomas jumped over the love seat and lowered himself to the floor to get the pillow. Reaching beneath the armoire, his hand hit a glass bottle and then felt the pillow. Curious, he pulled both out.

Thomas got off the floor with the items in his hands and walked to a chair. He threw the pillow back onto the couch but clung to the wine bottle. To find a discarded bottle in a rented establishment hardly called for an inquiry, unless it was a French one. A very expensive French wine, no less. Thomas lifted the bottle to his nose, hoping to catch at least a slight odor of the owner's essence. He smelled nothing but wine.

Anthony claimed the two vampires were in Alexandria. The habits of a vampire would seek out the finest of establishments, which were few and far between in the town. It meant they would stay here. And who in the Americas knew the best French wines? Who else would ask for them, or perhaps bring them along? Thomas clutched the bottle to himself, thinking of Xavier's gentle hand upon it, perhaps his lips tasting the mouth of it.

When he heard footsteps in the hall, Thomas hid the bottle and jumped back to the couch before Anthony entered.

"How did it go?" Thomas asked, trying for nonchalant but thinking he landed somewhere closer to suspicious.

"Interesting." Anthony sat beside Thomas and patted his knee. "Very interesting. These two seem careless, or they're amateurs."

Thomas winced at the characterization. And why did Anthony gaze at him, as if watching his response. "Maybe the Council should hire me to investigate these things too."

"We can't afford your price." Anthony laughed. "I'm surprised you aren't charging me."

"So what did you find out?" Thomas grew impatient, once again fighting to control his rising anxiety and anger.

"I looked around town but found nothing unusual. Typical southern town, though this one thrives on the slave trade. A rather disgusting habit but it makes it easy to find victims for feeding. So nothing helped me out until I talked to the owner of this place. He said about a month ago a couple rented this very space," Anthony swept his arm through the air, indicating their quarters. "A husband and wife, he supposed, who kept odd hours and to themselves. His slaves refused to enter here even after he ordered them to do it. Told him something unnatural was in here."

"And what does this tell us?" Thomas asked.

"The vampires stayed right here." Anthony pointed to the floor for emphasis. "We're close. I have someone for you to meet in an hour, and then we should know a lot more."

While waiting for the person, Anthony and Thomas toured Alexandria. Thomas marveled at how the Southerners tried to conceal from themselves the reality of their lives. Blocks from the slave trade, a person could turn down a street and see fancy houses that made it seem as if one alighted upon the most cultured of places imaginable, although small slave quarters lurked in the back of every yard. And not very far from all the refinement, one came upon the free black community where people struggled to live respectable lives despite confronting prejudice and danger at every turn.

From time to time, Thomas worried his mixed race heritage and long, black hair might give him away to the Southerners and cause a stir. He therefore learned to carry himself as an aristocrat with a haughty attitude to warn away any questioning. He often spoke in a foreign language, giving him an exotic aura to further insulate him from their prejudice.

"It's time." Anthony glanced around and then jerked his head, indicating for Thomas to follow.

Thomas assumed they would meet the mysterious figure in a bar or perhaps back in their rooms, but instead, they headed out of town into the Southern countryside. Away from all humanity, with not an animal nearby and no sign of people, they stopped beneath an enormous magnolia tree.

"Why are we meeting out here? This is desolate." Another oddity brought about by Anthony. They had taken to meeting and going to strange, out-of-the-way places ever since Anthony took Thomas to the mountain jail for vampires.

"You'll see. She can't mingle with a typical crowd around here." Thomas hated Anthony's vagueness but learned long ago the more he questioned, the more Anthony would keep from him. "She'll be here soon." Anthony pulled a plant from the ground and sniffed it. "You look nervous. Does our investigation scare you?"

Thomas snorted a laugh. "Scare me? No. Bore me? A little."

"You wanted to come along."

Before Thomas could think of a snappy retort, a woman came walking down the road, whistling a song Thomas recognized as a tune the slaves sang in the fields. A smiling black woman came into the moonlight. She was stunning, with big brown eyes, her hair tied up behind her, and a dress more like what Thomas saw on the aristocratic Southern white women. A vampire.

"Who is this?" she glanced to Thomas and then back to Anthony.

"A friend. Thomas, meet Harriet. Harriet, Thomas." Anthony motioned his hands between the two of them.

She held her hand out to Thomas, so he kissed it. "A pleasure," he said.

"Likewise. You're beautiful. Anthony keeps all the attractive ones hidden for himself."

Anthony laughed, and her carefully crafted façade cracked as she broke into a smile.

"He's very taken, I assure you." Anthony gave her a hug, which she returned with a tight embrace.

"And not by you?"

"Not by me." Anthony shook his head. Thomas feared Anthony would launch into their sordid history, but he left it there. "You're still single?"

She nodded. "I have much to do. I'll worry about companionship when this ends." She waved her hands at the fields, which seemed to explain everything.

"This angel of darkness lives in the South despite everything it stands for." Anthony moved them off the road to below the tree. "She prefers to hunt here."

"It's my duty until divine intervention ends this deplorable institution."

Thomas thought perhaps the woman could provide a defense for Xavier's actions. "You hunt here? Do you help the slaves?"

Harriet's demeanor changed from nonchalant to rigid in seconds. "No. That would violate the ethic." She darted a look to Anthony. "I asked for special permission from the Council, through Anthony. They denied it. They do allow me to stay in the South as long as I want. I prey on the ones who deserve it, feeding on those who kill their slaves and mistreat people. I like the good taste of a foul bounty hunter more than anything. Otherwise I stick to the ethic. It's awful. These are my people."

Thomas felt for her. How she could stand to remain here and watch it night after night impressed him. Even his Xavier, with much less of a tie to the slaves, could not handle it. "I've encountered the same thing with my people." Thomas never felt the same affinity for the Indians as she expressed about the slaves, but he deplored the white man's treatment of them, nonetheless. He explained as much, which softened her demeanor anew.

"I wish we had more time for the two of you to get acquainted." Anthony embraced them both by putting one arm around each of their shoulders.

Harriet nodded. "You want to know what I learned. I never saw them. But about two months ago, I met another vampire around here. I stick to the lower South most of the time, where things are much worse. But I had ventured to Washington, to see how things progressed in the nation's capital. On my way back, I stopped near here, and there he was. He regarded me with suspicion, asking all sorts of questions about why I came here and who knew about it. He wanted to know if the Council sent me. I got a little scared of him, with all those questions. He said he lived on a plantation with the slaves, which I found curious. I did not want to challenge him, though.

"So I assured him I was passing through and didn't mean him any harm. He said he'd prefer if I stayed out of his territory, so I did. Then, about a month later, here he comes into Alexandria, saying he's hunting vampires. He stalked right through town, an action which stands out in these parts. A big, angry black man storming around in bright clothing gets attention here.

"He quizzed me over and over about what I had seen and who I was with. I got scared, so I ran away again. Figured I better stay out of his way. About three nights later, however, slaves down the road started talking about a plantation where gods freed all the slaves. I go among my people now and then to stay attuned to their reality. Slaves talk different from whites; they knew I was dead and said a vampire had those slaves held captive by working with their master. But these other two killed him and freed them all." Harriet shook her head back and forth.

"If we could have a moment?" Anthony looked at Thomas, dismissing him, so Thomas walked down the road a bit. Harriet abided by the ethic, though her face betrayed a turmoil about it when she spoke. Thomas focused, however, on what she said about the executed vampire. He violated the ethic, so perhaps Xavier and Catherine could get away with it? Thomas hoped as much, though he doubted things could end with such ease.

When Anthony caught up to him, Harriet had disappeared.

"Where did she go?" Thomas looked around to see if she followed.

"I've no idea. She wanders the South, doing her thing."

"How do you know her?"

"I knew the one who transformed her and condoned it on behalf of the Council."

"Knew?"

"Yes, knew. It's a depressing story." Anthony surged ahead, walking at a human pace but faster than before. "You know how Xavier detests the South and slavery? I quite agree with him. An older vampire came from Africa when he heard reports of what was happening here. This was almost one hundred years ago. He lived among his people, doing as she does now, his small part to alleviate their suffering without violating the ethic."

Anthony stopped and wiped a blood tear from his cheek. "I met with him a number of times and tried to talk him out of it. He decided to immolate himself because he couldn't take it anymore. He either had to free slaves all over the place and thus face execution by the Council or commit suicide. To save me from having to report a friend, he decided to take his own life. But first he wanted permission to transform Harriet to carry on his work. He had studied her for a long time and thought her up to the task. How could I deny it?" Anthony's voice cracked. "So he transformed Harriet, and we spent a few weeks training her before he went off by himself. That's how I know her, and that's why she does what she does. She's still a slave."

They walked in silence the rest of the way. Thomas marveled at Harriet's fortitude, to continue her calling despite the ability either to flee or lash out. He never experienced the despair of the other vampire, either, who solved his angst by ending his eternal life. At his darkest moments, when he thought he lost Xavier forever, Thomas never contemplated suicide.

Thomas worked his way out of an emotional lethargy and almost asked Anthony where he led them when they came upon an abandoned plantation.

"Is this the place?" Thomas thought it felt eerie. It was too quiet and forsaken, void of even a passing rodent.

"Yes." Anthony searched around, finding an obvious vampire's quarters under the house, and motioned Thomas over to show him. Hidden in the dungeon's recesses they located a pile of decaying human bodies. They next inspected a bed set in the back corner and found blood stains all over it.

Then they went outside, searching the area and coming upon an enormous fire pit. "Stand back," Anthony told

Thomas. Anthony closed his eyes and enchanted a spell, then remained quiet for several minutes.

"This is the place," he said.

"What place? What's going on?" Thomas began to panic that Anthony saw Xavier in a vision or knew what happened.

"Strange. The first vampire, the one who lived here, violated all sorts of our laws. The Council never learned of it. I sense a powerful magic concealed him, but I never knew any such thing was possible. The Council knows and sees all. And then, he was killed. I can see his death by fire, or I suppose I should say I could feel it." Again Anthony peered at him, almost as if he thought Thomas murdered the vampire.

Thomas blew out a huge breath. "Well, he deserved it. If he violated the ethic, then the other two did nothing wrong."

Anthony halted and stared at Thomas. "What do you know? Why do you keep defending these two? Whether or not this first one did anything wrong, no other vampire has the right to do what they did. I would know if the Council sanctioned his death."

"Maybe someone else on the Council ordered it. You can't always know everything the Council does."

"I would know." There Anthony went again, with his secrecy about the Omnipotent Council. How could he know everything? Thankfully, Anthony continued before Thomas said something stupid. "Yes, this vampire earned his death. But these other two are acting another way altogether. What's gotten you so interested?"

Thomas was sure Anthony knew or at least suspected Thomas hid information from him that would implicate Xavier in these matters. However, Anthony danced around the issue as if testing Thomas. Thomas would never give Xavier up.

"I hate the Council." Thomas shrugged. "You know that. I'm trying to understand their arbitrary ways." Standing in front of the fire pit, it unnerved Thomas how Anthony went silent so he looked into his eyes. His face had gone bright red with anger. "What?" Thomas asked.

Thomas heard Anthony's teeth grind together. "Your attitude makes me sick."

Thomas arched his eyebrow, unsure why an idea he repeated over and over during his vampire life made Anthony so angry.

Anthony erupted, causing Thomas to step back. "The laws you defy protect you." Anthony stalked over to Thomas and poked him in the chest. "You think everything's a big game, don't you? Well, let me tell you something. The Council hates what it has to do, as much as you hate it. These laws protect all of us. They allow us to survive. Can you understand? No! You're Thomas, the vampire who does as he pleases. This task. These investigations. That prison, they all weigh on me. I don't get to live the carefree happy life you do." Anthony jabbed him in the chest again. "Why is this so impossible for you to understand? It's not arbitrary. And it's not meant to inflict punishment upon vampires at the whim of those who enforce the ethic. The Council and its ethic save us." Anthony pounded on his own chest two times with both fists.

Anthony grew quiet and pulled away from Thomas, who stood still. Anthony had yelled at him previously, but this time it was more pointed. Again, Thomas wondered if the secret he held from Anthony about Xavier prompted the unusual reaction.

"If you don't like it, you can leave." Anthony turned back to Thomas, speaking more softly but with his jaw set. "No one made you come along."

Thomas struggled to find an appropriate response to both pacify his friend and hold true to his own convictions. He loved Anthony and always respected his devotion to the Council and his utter reliance on the ethic. He also understood the reason it existed. He never got, though, why it had become so rigid, so black and white. But, to question that might send Anthony into a renewed fury.

"I've never understood." Thomas held his hands up in surrender. "You know I try. It's not in my nature to obey rules, nor do I think it's a good thing no one can question the Council or even know who sits on it." Thomas walked over to Anthony. "I've always respected your sense of duty to it. *Always*. I know you do what you think is right, for all of us. That doesn't change either. I'm sorry I got under your skin."

Anthony nodded his head and put his hand on Thomas's arm. "Being a part of the Council can be so difficult for me. This case troubles me." Anthony stared hard into Thomas's eyes, as if waiting for information Thomas would die to keep hidden. "These two vampires killed another without authorization. It seems like they're terrorizing the South. We can't allow this to continue."

"What will happen to them if they're caught?" Thomas didn't want to know, but the question came out anyway.

"In the least, a very long prison sentence. *Long*. And that would be a bare minimum in order to teach them the danger of their ways. Maybe death, depending on their attitude and exactly how far they've gone."

Thomas stepped away from Anthony, his eyes narrowed. He loved Anthony. If any of these punishments came to pass, however, if Xavier and Catherine were these two they hunted, and if Anthony attempted any of those penalties, Thomas and his friend would fight to the death. Thomas was certain.

"Tell me one more thing." Anthony nodded at Thomas's request. "How is it decided? Any time I accuse the Council of arbitrary action you insist more goes into their decisions. But you never explain it. You tell me to trust the system. All this vagueness sounds random."

"How many times and in how many different ways do I have to explain this to you?" Anthony clenched his fists at his side. "I can't tell you anymore. It's forbidden. I assure you, nothing random happens. Would I participate in a system that punishes people for no reason? I thought you knew me better."

"I do." Thomas nodded. "I trust you. With my life, and everything important to me." Thomas meant the words, but he also stared back hard at his friend to let him know the weight of what he said.

Over the course of the next couple hours, things moved toward normal in their relationship. They failed to find anything else at the plantation and soon had to go to their hotel before the sun rose. They chatted and actually laughed a couple of times.

Yet a distinct chilling of their relationship hung in the air. Neither quite trusted the other as much, probably with good reason. They hugged as they retired to their crates, the tight embrace of dear friends. At the same time, each held his body back a little farther than usual. Each remained a little guarded from the other.

Twenty-Three: Correspondence

14 MAY 1822
Richmond, Virginia

Thomas hurried through the Richmond streets toward a financial office his point person in New York City recommended they use for correspondence. At long last, Thomas got word when he awoke that Pierre sent news from Paris.

He dodged an old slave pulling a heavy cart down the middle of the street and stepped in front of a lady in fancy attire. "Excuse me," he whispered but pushed past her at the same time. She grunted and her companion yelled at Thomas, who forged ahead without looking back.

Inside the financier's office, Thomas stiffened. With vampire speed, he read papers strewn across a desk to discover the man did most of his business in the slave trade. Thomas trusted his New York advisor, but such evil work gave him pause. Perhaps he needed to find someone else.

"Pardon me. I have a dispatch to collect," Thomas told the clerk sitting behind a desk, dispensing with any formal greetings.

"If you could give me a moment." The man glanced above his small wire glasses and held up a finger. He then returned to making notations in a ledger.

Thomas stepped back, tapping his foot. His rage started to well within him. To calm himself, his mind wandered to everything that had transpired in the last two days, hoping against hope Pierre's letter would resolve all the turmoil and reveal Xavier's location.

After the tense night in which Anthony and he searched the abandoned plantation and Anthony grew to suspect Thomas hid information, the next night proceeded on the surface as if nothing unusual had happened between them. They woke at almost the same time, grabbed their cloaks, and headed into the Southern landscape to search for these "rogue vampires." They talked pleasantly enough as they wandered along, looking for clues but finding nothing. But something gnawed at Thomas, as if Anthony played a charade of searching for clues he already knew. They ended a bit early and hunted for worthy victims together, finding them in a couple of men sneaking around with whips and chains and dragging two black men along with them, whom they released. Fed, they retired before dawn and agreed to continue looking the next night.

Throughout their time together, a tension neither would acknowledge hung in the air. Thomas wanted to know more about what Anthony thought and knew regarding these mysterious vampires-cum-killers but refused to bring it up for fear it would further arouse Anthony's suspicion. For his part, Anthony seemed aloof, sticking to trivial topics and not wanting to discuss what they searched for as they plodded their way from plantation to plantation. The conversation in front of the firepit had changed their friendship.

After several minutes of waiting, Thomas could not stand it any longer. "Will you be long?" he asked the clerk. "My people assured me you did the utmost to respect business associates. I can't stand here all night waiting to learn if it's true."

The man dropped his pencil on the desk and took a huge breath. "We do a lot of business here for very important people. I can't stop everything for every Injun who walks through the door. You'll need to wait."

Thomas moved to stand over the man and scowled down at him. His head throbbed with the intensity of his anger. "If you know what's good for you, you'll tell me whether or not you received a communication for Thomas Lord." He enunciated each word with force.

The man drew back and popped out of his seat. "I apologize, Mr. Lord. I had no idea." He turned around and went to another desk and grabbed a stack of letters. He handed one to Thomas and waited for his pay.

"You'll get nothing from me. An Injun's money isn't worth much anyway." Thomas slammed the door behind him, making sure to shatter the glass in it, and rushed down the street.

He had to find a quiet place to open the letter, and fast. Thomas thought of going to their rooms, but if Anthony saw it or suspected a thing, it could ruin Xavier. Instead, Thomas walked into a saloon, full of half-clad women, loud men, and flowing with drink all around. He took a chair against a wall and tipped back onto two of its legs.

He tore at the envelope and took out two letters, recognizing Pierre's dignified scroll at once.

Master Lord,

Enclosed you will find a letter sent to my address and dispatched to you. While it did not come from Monsieur Xavier as we anticipated, it utilized the channels he established. I thought it best, therefore, to forward it to you at once.

Your faithful servant, Pierre

As Thomas read Pierre's note, his heart sank. Why would someone else write to him, and not Xavier? He scanned to the bottom of the second letter and saw Catherine's signature. He almost became ill, fearing only the worst could induce her to write to Thomas.

My dearest Thomas,

I write this to you without Xavier's knowledge. He informed me about how to contact you in the event the worst happened to him. We're both doing well, so you needn't worry. At the same time, I am worried about his actions and what may happen to him as a result.

I wish I had time to summarize the entire story for you, but he will return at any minute and always wants me by his side. To ensure I can dispatch this tonight, I give you an abbreviated version.

Xavier came to me in Paris with news the Archangel St. Michel had visited him. Mind you, I tend toward the same skepticism as you, regarding his typical religious sentiments. But I am convinced, from his story, this indeed happened. Whether from divine inspiration, another magical source, or perhaps from the deep recesses of his own mind, the vision is true to Xavier. He knew you would stop him from the mission the angel sent him on and therefore transformed me as his partner.

A vision Xavier had at Notre Dame Cathedral sent him to Anne Hébert as she lay dying. Her grandson, Duncan, was stolen into slavery. He was a free black in New York but taken by bounty hunters. She pleaded on her death bed for Xavier to go save him. As you know, he credits her with saving his life, and that, combined with the holy revelation, propelled Xavier forward.

We were close to finding Duncan but failed. Now, we search all over the South for him, to no avail. I wish I could tell you where to find us, but I've no idea where we will be from day to day, and Xavier told me we would be heading out tomorrow.

We need your help. Xavier will listen to you. He not only searches for Duncan but has taken to freeing slaves and upsetting the system here in the South. He violates the ethic all the time. Thomas, I'm worried sick about what the Vampire Council will do to him. He'll stop if you tell him to. Come, find Duncan with us, and then get him out of here, please.

I am having a hard time guessing your mood. I know Xavier enraged you with what he did. But Thomas, he loves you as much as he always did. It terrifies him to think about what you now think of him. Don't abandon him. Come for us.

Yours in love, Catherine

Thomas crunched the note in his hands, not from anger, but from agony. Despite his increased rage since Xavier disappeared, nothing made him cross with Xavier. Nothing. Yet Catherine suspected he might become so irate he would abandon Xavier.

He had hoped Pierre's correspondence would tell him more, but at least Xavier was safe. Thomas also knew he and Anthony hunted in the most logical areas; they roamed through the South, as did Catherine and Xavier. Thomas got back to their flat and concealed Catherine's letter seconds before Anthony returned. They had several hours yet before dawn, and Thomas wanted to search.

"What invigorated you all of a sudden?" Anthony asked when Thomas urged them to leave at once. "I thought you hated the Council's business?"

"I can't sit around doing nothing." Thomas knew his explanation made no sense and saw the distrust in Anthony's eyes. He ignored it and pulled them out the door.

Twenty-Four: Hunting

15 MAY 1822
Atlanta, Georgia

After receiving Catherine's letter the night before, Thomas hunted with Anthony with a renewed passion. He suspected all along Xavier and Catherine were the vampires who defied the ethic and sent Anthony on his investigation, but she confirmed for him that he searched for Xavier in the right locations. Having exhausted their exploration of Virginia for the time being, Anthony relocated them to Atlanta to scour Georgia, yet he went on two other missions to meet with vampires, almost as if the other search were a ruse. Thomas mistrusted the situation more and more.

As they walked between plantations, they came upon a group of slaves sneaking about, hiding in the bushes when they saw the two vampires approach. When Anthony stepped forward, three men and one woman slunk back into a cotton field, but another woman stood firm and waited for them. She squinted her eyes and ordered them to stop several feet from her.

"Are you good or bad?" Her heavy dialect sounded Caribbean, not the typical rhythm and sound of an American slave.

Anthony held his hands in the air. "We mean you no harm. We want information."

"You stay right there"—she pointed at them—"and maybe you'll get what you're seeking."

Thomas moved behind Anthony and peered over his shoulder as he continued the conversation. "We're seeking two people. We want to know if you know anything about them."

She smirked. "People? Or two of your kind? The white gods, perhaps? What do you want with them?"

"What do you mean, 'gods'?" Thomas leaned over Anthony's shoulder with anticipation as he asked the question.

"The ones who save us. That's who *we're* looking for." She indicated the people behind her with a flick of her head in their direction. "Talk came all the way from the coast about those two who only come at night. Like you two." She narrowed her eyes at them again. "Saving us. Taking us to freedom."

"Do you know this? Or is this a myth?" Thomas wondered at the harshness of Anthony's words, but once she spoke, he knew Anthony baited her into giving up the information he wanted.

"Myth? Do you think the stupid black folk go around with delusions in their head, searching for the unknown?" She straightened her posture. "You don't frighten me like you do the rest. Oh, my people fear you and your nature. I know better. And if I was wrong, we'd already be dead. So don't go belittling me. The white folk know something is wrong this time too. They're looking for them, too, just like us, but for different reasons. No, this is real. Instead of haunting places, your kind are trying to do good."

"And are they here?" Anthony asked.

She shook her head. "No. We've been told to head toward the coast. Maybe Charleston."

"Thank you." Anthony bowed and turned around, pulling Thomas with him. They hurried away and left the band of runaways behind.

"Should we help them?" Thomas asked, stunned the conversation ended so abruptly.

"No."

"No? That's it? Are you going to tell me what's going on?" Anthony didn't say a word and started running at vampiric speed. They arrived back in Atlanta, Thomas following Anthony with no idea about their plans. Inside their rooms, Anthony began packing until Thomas grabbed his arm and spun him around. "What?" Thomas knew his face reddened, and he had spit the question at Anthony.

"There's been enough 'helping of them' going on. Those runaways chose their fate. They must live with it. Vampires interfering with such circumstances is what we're trying to stop. Did you hear her? These stories travel up and down the East Coast, into the interior and throughout every slave state. And now the white people know. Do you understand?" Anthony jerked his arm away from Thomas and continued packing.

"Understand what?"

Anthony slammed a book into his trunk. "What these vampires are doing," he shouted. "They endanger all of us. They killed a vampire, violating the ethic. Now they run around freeing slaves, creating these myths and hopes, inciting the slaves and getting the Southerners to hunt for them too. They've exposed all of us. I'm trying to decide what to do."

"Don't you mean we're trying to find them?" Thomas asked.

Anthony glared back at him. "I had no idea it had become this urgent. This"—Anthony pointed out the window, as if indicating something tangible—"goes beyond anything I imagined." He slammed the trunk lid and scribbled instructions about where to send it.

After his outburst, Thomas followed Anthony's lead and packed his belongings too. Anthony would take care of arrangements for what to do with all of it, as he always did.

Anthony stormed toward the door but halted before he opened it. He turned and looked at Thomas. After taking a deep breath, he reached out and pulled Thomas into an embrace. "I love you." He started to say more, and Thomas wanted to hear it. Instead, the stoic, reserved Anthony took over. He pushed Thomas away and took a deep breath.

With one expression, Anthony conveyed a world of meaning to Thomas. Their friendship had withstood a number of tests in the last month, and in the last two days even more so—they still cared for one another. Yet both also knew the strain on their friendship had just begun. Both had secrets. Both pulled in opposite directions.

Part Six

The South

Twenty-Five: Abolitionists

12 MAY 1822
Somewhere in Tennessee

"We need to reconsider our plans." Catherine blew an exasperated breath and collapsed onto the ground. "Look at us." She raised her hands in the air and motioned around them.

Xavier glanced at the trees, the earth, the dense bushes nearby. They abandoned their refined quarters a month ago to help escape detection, and it wore on Catherine.

"We *have* reconsidered." Xavier hardly wanted to revisit the conversation but sat next to her and grabbed her hand. "This is awful. I know it." She laughed. "'Miss I Live in a Mansion and Have People Serve Me' doesn't like living in sheds and cemeteries in the wild. We'll take a break from it soon."

"You're a smart-ass." Catherine fell backward onto the ground. "I'm not talking about creature comforts. Not that I couldn't use a sofa or chair from time to time. Or a clean landing spot. Our clothes are still in Richmond. I'm talking about the danger."

"We can't dwell on it." Xavier stood up, afraid of what Catherine would say next.

"Are we going to keep at it until they come for us?" She sat up and looked at her brother. "This can't last forever."

Xavier felt the world slipping out of control again, causing his head to spin. How had it gotten to that point? They'd arrived in America on a very specific mission: find Duncan and return him to New York. Along the way, Xavier had also become a crusader against slavery. They searched for Duncan first and foremost but filled the rest of their hours with helping the slaves escape. They set out to defy the ethic as little as possible and instead threw it away like a piece of trash.

Most of all, Xavier hated how it endangered Catherine, though she always brushed it aside when mentioned. He knew, even as vampires, she worried more about his safety than her own.

"You're just tired. You need a task to enliven you." Xavier reached down and pulled Catherine to her feet.

"It's more, and you know it." She pulled back when he tried to urge her on. "I'm talking about your safety. If I knew they'd reprimand you and send us back to France with a firm scolding, none of this would bother me. But you said the Council has executed people before. Dead. I can't live with that. I've already lost you once. I won't do it again." A blood tear trickled down her face.

Xavier stared at her, not sure how far to go. He went for the blunt truth. "We passed the point of worrying about that long ago. We're doing the *right* thing." He wanted to add St. Michel would protect them, but the last time he used religion Catherine almost killed him herself. Besides, Xavier accepted St. Michel's command came without a legal dispensation from the vampire ethic.

"I'm worried." Catherine moved into an embrace when Xavier held out his arms. They hugged. "We could stop."

"What about Duncan? I can't give up until I find him." Again he bit his tongue, thinking in addition to promising

Anne he would do something, St. Michel would not take kindly to his abandonment of the quest.

"I think we should contact Thomas, at least. For help. Or let—" Catherine cut herself off.

"What?"

"Nothing." Xavier knew his sister too well, though. She hid information from him and had for several weeks. Whenever Thomas's name came up, she became nervous and cut off their conversation.

Catherine pulled away and nodded. "I'm emotional today. I know what we can do."

Typical Catherine, she snapped out of her funk. Or faked doing so in order to avoid more talk of Thomas. Xavier dismissed the subject because he cried almost every time they talked about Thomas anyway. He missed Thomas with his entire soul. The more they did, and the longer they did it, the more Xavier worried he would never see Thomas again. The Council could swoop in any day and execute both of them, without any warning. Did he believe an angel would come soaring in to save him?

Catherine and he both had their moments of despair, knowing they crossed several impossible lines on their insane mission from God. Part of Xavier wished they could stop too. How many times had he started a letter to Thomas? Or the one he almost sent to Anthony, confessing all and pleading with his friend to represent him before the Vampire Council in order to spare his life? Each time, he remembered the visions and Anne's dying appeal. He had no choice but to continue, alone except for Catherine, who insisted she would never leave his side, no matter how much she disagreed with his actions.

As they neared a small town, Catherine spun around and grabbed Xavier by the shoulders, lurching them to a stop. "This is a grand adventure," she said.

As in life, Xavier could never keep up with his sister's mood swings. "A minute ago you wanted to quit."

"Still do." She nodded and walked forward again, so he followed. "You're in danger, and I can't stand that. But being on a mission like this, knowing we're in danger, *does* excite me. Wait until you see what I've done." Catherine sprinted ahead to the outskirts of town in mere seconds. She collected herself while Xavier waited, knowing she loved theatrics and a good surprise.

They approached a small lawyer's office, where she knocked.

"Ah, my lady." A slight man in a suit answered the door. He peered each way down the street, then hurried them inside with a motion. "Please, sit." He indicated two chairs opposite his desk. He remained standing during the formal introductions. "I never thought I'd be involved in such a transaction. Mind you, not that I don't revel in it. I support this organization and pray all the time they succeed. But, well, my clients might not feel the same way."

"You never told me how you came to oppose slavery." Catherine's flirtatious tone always lured victims to her bidding, Xavier thought to himself. "A Southern-born-and-bred boy does not fit the model of a future abolitionist."

"No abolitionist, I assure you. Nothing of the sort. My grandmother, who was from the North, hated slavery. *Hated* it. I can't say I share her passion."

"But you said you don't own slaves?"

He shook his head. "Complicated, isn't it? I disapprove of the entire institution. It's my home, though. And these are my friends. So I stay. In agreeing to help you, at great risk I might add, I found a way to honor my grandmother."

Catherine stood and walked over to him. She touched his arm with her fingertips. "And uphold your convictions." Xavier smiled when the man's face turned crimson.

"At any rate," he said, stepping away from Catherine. "You brought the paperwork?"

Catherine fumbled inside her dress for a second, causing the poor guy to turn his head in embarrassment. "Here you go."

He whistled when he looked at the paperwork. "One hundred thousand dollars? Are you sure? That's an exorbitant sum."

"I know my business." Catherine straightened her dress and turned to Xavier. "Will you escort me to dinner?"

"Of course." What in the hell was she talking about? He held out his arm.

At the door, she turned back and nodded. "Thank you." She smiled at the peculiar little man.

"I'm honored." He bowed as they headed out the door.

They walked through town until they hit its edge, then sprinted into the countryside, stopping when Catherine laughed too hard to continue. Xavier laughed, too, though only she knew the joke.

"What was that little charade about? What dinner?"

Catherine laughed harder. "I've no idea. I was ready to go. As for the rest, I found him the other night, taking a walk while you were out. Anyway, we struck up a conversation. I tried to seduce him because I was bored, but he rebuffed me. So instead, I got him to help me send money."

"To whom?"

"Did you see his shock at the amount?" Catherine chuckled again. "He thinks me a ridiculous little woman being careless with her money."

"Who did you send money to?"

Catherine slapped her forehead. "Didn't I answer you? I sent it, in honor of you, to the American Colonization Society. It's a group in the North fighting to end slavery. They want to create a nation in Africa for all the slaves."

Xavier wondered at the notion of sending random people to Africa. Yet he knew the organization worked hard to combat the peculiar institution, as the Southerners called their enslavement of fellow humans. "You scolded me earlier, saying we needed to stop this and return to Thomas. But you deepened our involvement?"

Catherine chuckled. She had gone from morose when they woke to giddy. She jumped toward him and grabbed him around the waist, then spun him in circles.

"I love you. I did it for you." She set him down. "If we're going on this mission, hell-bent on wherever it takes us, then we should go all out."

Xavier smiled, ever thankful for his sister.

Twenty-Six: Harriet

13 MAY 1822
The Mountains of North Carolina

Having found nothing in Tennessee, Xavier and Catherine moved to their next destination. Xavier decided he wanted to cover as much territory as quickly as possible. Catherine agreed, thinking their constant movement better protected them from the threat of the Vampire Council finding them. Last night Tennessee, tonight North Carolina.

A light breeze blew through the trees as Catherine and he spied for prey. While Xavier argued to look for Duncan and free a couple of slaves, Catherine insisted she needed sustenance first. So they sat in a large oak tree, watching a road beneath them, waiting for a suitable victim. Xavier almost protested they wasted too much time, when Catherine elbowed him.

"Look." Catherine pointed to a figure weaving along coming toward them. As he got closer, Xavier could hear him singing to himself, a vile song about the slaves. "There's just one. We'll have to share." Catherine jumped off the tree and landed a few feet from the man.

"Whoa. Dear lady, what kind of gentlewoman jumps from trees?" He stumbled back, almost falling but gaining his balance before swaying back and forth in front of her.

"What kind of drunkard walks alone on a dark night?" Catherine stepped toward him.

The man lurched his head up and creased his brow. "I thought perhaps you were a lady. But such talk—"

"You thought wrong."

As the banter continued, Xavier felt confident the idiot deserved death. The man scolded Catherine before launching into a tirade after she mentioned impotence. "I've shown many a woman the meaning of being with a man." He rushed toward Catherine and grabbed her by both arms. Instead of falling, she stood as solid as a rock and, opening her mouth, descended her fangs. The man shook and then passed out in her arms.

"Get down here and help me drink."

Xavier obeyed, and they feasted together. After arranging his body to resemble a drunk who died from the alcohol, they headed down the road again.

"We had a trail on Duncan in Virginia and lost him." It frustrated Xavier, because the longer it took, the more threat Duncan might die or disappear before they found him. What if the Council swooped in? Then they would never fulfill his obligation to Anne.

"We'll find him. We found you, didn't we? You could have hidden during that awful revolution almost anywhere in France. We kept at it until Denys found you and Anne under the bridge. Don't give up. We'll figure it out."

Xavier wondered what, however. They had searched every property owned by the family who was aligned with the vampire and found nothing. He and Catherine wandered with no idea of what to do to locate Duncan. Freeing slaves or at least protecting them helped, because it gave Xavier a purpose. But all of the delays and directionless searching kept him from Thomas, which became more difficult with each passing day. He cried himself to sleep every morning.

Lost in his thoughts, Xavier started when Catherine blocked him from moving forward. She put her finger to her mouth. "Shh." Xavier listened and heard the rustle of cloth against leaves. Only a vampire could hear that sound. He nodded. Catherine motioned with her head for him to follow into the underbrush, where they crouched. "It has to be a vampire," she whispered.

Xavier nodded again, his heart racing at the thought. A Council member come for them? Another vampire nemesis?

After several minutes, a figure approached, walking down the road and whistling a slave spiritual. She stopped right in front of them and came forward. A woman's shoes crunched a few feet from where they hid.

"I can see both of you, as well as you can see me," a woman's voice said in a commanding tone. "You might as well come out."

Xavier looked to Catherine for direction. She tilted her head and raised her eyebrows. Then she nodded and stood up. Again Xavier found himself following her lead. They stepped out of the bushes and onto the road, a couple of feet in front of the vampire.

She was beautiful. Despite her brown skin in the South, her dress looked aristocratic and refined. It clung to the contour of her body, pushing out her breasts and clinging to her sides until it swooped out at the bottom.

"Hiding from another vampire signals hostile intentions," she said.

"No. We didn't mean anything by it." Xavier worried they fell into another fight with a vampire. "We were frightened of you."

Catherine shot her head toward Xavier, looking at him with disapproval.

"Frightened vampires? Of what?" The woman's face lit with recognition. "You think you're being hunted? You're the two freeing the slaves. And you killed one of our kind, no?" Catherine crouched down, readying herself for a fight, but the woman put her hand in the air. "You'll get no quarrel from me."

"Are you with the Council, searching for us?" Xavier felt more secure after she called Catherine off.

His question made her laugh. "Lord, no."

Catherine stood rigid. "Then how do you know about us?"

"Because there *are* people searching for you. I met two of them. They told me all about you, and to watch out. They wanted to know what I knew."

"You happened upon two members of the Council and they revealed all this news to you? I doubt it." Catherine squinted at the woman, still bracing for a fight, but got more laughter in return.

"My name is Harriet. And if you'll stop threatening me, I'll tell you everything. I'm on your side."

Xavier stepped between Harriet and Catherine and put his hand on Catherine's shoulder. "Let her speak." They turned back to Harriet.

"I was a slave once. Used to pray someone like you two would come along and take us all away. We knew nothing but miracles would save us, and so I waited for one. Mine came in the form of another vampire, from Africa. He hated slavery and wandered through the South, killing masters and overseers who deserved it but never violating the ethic. It drove him mad he could do so little. He wanted to create an uprising, but the Council refused it. He did what he could, until he killed himself. But not before making me to take his place.

"Before he died, he worked with one from the Council who trained me and allows me to continue the work, so long as I adhere to the ethic. Which doesn't mean I like it. I struggle everyday not to defy it, and I do little things to spit in its face. In the end, though, I worry too much. Not about me, mind you. I'd die a million deaths to get rid of this vile practice. I worry because I try to protect them. Without me, who would kill the most seditious? Who would kill those who make Satan look kind?"

Xavier melted in her presence. She had a charisma he could not resist. Catherine, on the other hand, continued to frown.

"None of that explains how you knew about us," Catherine said through clenched teeth.

"No. It doesn't." Harriet stepped forward and tapped both of them on the arm. "Believe me, I mean you no harm." She kept her hand on Xavier's forearm but removed the other from Catherine. "I want you to succeed. You're doing everything I ever dreamed of doing. When I first discovered you, though, it was right as you got into an argument with the vampire who manipulated and controlled the other slaves.

"It frightened me to have two of our kind moving about and killing other vampires. Then the one who trained me, the one who sits on the Vampire Council, he appeared with another of our kind. Asking questions about you two. Pretending to search for you. I'm sorry I told him anything, but then again, something's off. Because the Council seems like it could figure all this out without the theatrical hunt."

Before Xavier could probe her confusing statement further, all three jumped when a scream filled the night. They raced toward the sound, coming from a way down the road and around the bend. They came upon a slave woman, hiding behind a shed, giving birth. Catherine and Harriet went into action, helping the woman and delivering a screaming baby girl. Xavier stayed away, frightened by the scene and lost as to what to do. When Catherine and Harriet carried the woman away at vampiric speed, Xavier followed until they placed her in a safe house.

With the woman safe, they headed back down the road. "Come with me." Harriet led them to a small house, abandoned deep in the mountains of North Carolina. "I'm staying in the cellar here. It's safe. Join me."

"Thank you," Catherine answered.

The tension between the two women had evaporated, much to Xavier's surprise. As they settled in before dawn, they chatted about nothing in particular, until Xavier asked the question haunting him since she told her story. "The member of the Council you know. Who was it? And what did you mean, something's off?"

"Don't think ill of him because he's hunting you. He's a good person. There were two, but I just knew one. Anthony allowed me to be made and lets me do what I do to help the slaves. I've known him since my creation and trust him with my life. But you should know he'll find you. That's what I meant. From what I understand of the Council, they already know where you are. It would take nothing for them to appear out of nowhere." She looked into the clouds, as if watching for them to descend.

Xavier's heart pounded at the news. "And the other one with Anthony, what did he look like?" Despite the alarming news she shared, he only heard Anthony was with someone else.

"Indian. Long, black hair. Muscular and confident. Not what I expected from a Council member because he seemed annoyed with them."

Thomas. She had seen Thomas with Anthony. Xavier's dream for a resolution to everything soared with the thought Thomas was looking for him, too, even as he laughed at her thinking Thomas belonged to the Council.

Twenty-Seven: Charleston's Witch Doctor

14 MAY 1822
North Carolina

They woke the next evening to Harriet asking Xavier and Catherine about how they decided what to do from night to night, which prompted Xavier to tell her about their actual quest to find Duncan. Harriet said it sounded impossible without other assistance and told them about a witch doctor she knew in Charleston. She gave Xavier an address and sent him on his way, without his giving a second thought to their remaining together until he came upon the outskirts of Charleston. Why had Catherine, who disdained Harriet at first, taken a liking to her? His face turned bright red when he realized the attraction between them had escaped him the entire time.

Focused on his mission, however, he went to the address and discovered a rather plain-looking house in the middle of the free black community and knocked. An elderly black woman answered the door and reared back when she saw Xavier. She made a sign with her hands and called out for "Malcolm" as Xavier tried to convince her not to worry.

"A white one?" An old black man shuffled into the room using a cane and pointed it at Xavier. "We know of a black one whom we trust. But a white one? What do you want?"

"Harriet sent me."

The man nodded and then looked at the woman, who left the room. "Come. Sit." He pointed to a wooden chair in the corner and sat opposite it on a bench. "A friend of Harriet's is a friend of mine. My wife doesn't like the undead. Harriet did my family a great favor, and I owe her. What do you need from me?" He tapped his cane against his boot and stared into Xavier's eyes.

"To find someone."

The man nodded. "It will cost you."

"I can pay anything."

"No." He shook his head. "Not money. I don't need it. Wouldn't have anything to buy with it, anyway. I need action. You promise to go to Denmark Vesey, as if you came from heaven on a mission to free the slaves, and then you'll get your information from me."

"I don't understand."

"He's got ideas. Visions of great things to inspire us to throw off the yoke of slavery. But he's afraid, like we all are, and needs inspiration. A visit from your kind might do the trick. You promise to go to him, give him courage, and I'll help you."

Desperate to find Duncan, Xavier agreed, though he did not understand what the man meant. "I need you to tell me the location of a captured man."

Malcolm pushed himself up with his cane and, once steadied, pointed it at Xavier. "First, you go. Come back, and no matter the outcome, I'll help you find your person."

Xavier got up without saying anything and headed toward the door. The man then whispered a scheme and directions to Vesey's house and patted Xavier on the back as he escorted him outside. Still wondering at the complete lunacy of it, Xavier soon stood outside the home of Denmark Vesey.

He glanced around the deserted street before jumping to the roof and then stomping across it. He could hear people scrambling about inside and took that as his cue to swing over the overhang and crash through a window. He landed in a bedroom, with nothing but a small bed of hay and dresser in the corner. It was abandoned for but a moment when two men brandishing weapons stormed into the room. Without a word, they rushed at Xavier and stabbed him multiple times.

As Malcolm requested, Xavier stood straight up and allowed the attack, despite the stinging pain. After several seconds, he shoved the men away with vampiric power and removed his coat. He tore off his shirt so they could see his body heal itself. Impressed, the two men lay where they had fallen and watched in shock.

"Speak to me," Xavier said. "Which of you is Denmark Vesey?" One of them raised a shaking hand. Xavier looked to the other one. "You must be Gullah Jack?" He nodded but did not move.

Xavier picked up his coat and put it on, feeling a bit awkward without a shirt underneath. "Go sit on the bed." Xavier leaned over and grabbed Denmark's arm, pricking him with a fingernail as he helped him to his feet. When both men turned toward the bed, Xavier licked the little bit of blood on his finger to see Vesey's life pass through his mind.

Denmark went to sit on the bed, with Gullah Jack crawling across the floor to join him. As he waited for the two men to settle down, Xavier said a silent prayer, asking forgiveness for impersonating God. Until then, he thought of the entire plot as a fool's errand but not of the extreme danger these two men would face, and anyone who followed them, if they failed. He needed forgiveness of this, too, but hoped its necessity along the way of his quest for Duncan would give divine amnesty. Never mind the vampiric ethic, because everything Xavier had done tonight disobeyed it.

"I know of your plans. And your fear. I come to encourage you to act them out. Tell me of your faith. Tell me of this plot."

Denmark grabbed a Bible from a dresser drawer and stood before Xavier, shaking. He flipped a couple of pages and pointed to a story with his finger. "The Exodus. It tells us God will free our people."

Xavier nodded. "You must lead them as Moses did his people."

"And I want to. But how? The white man has weapons and power."

"Trust yourself. Organize the people. You already know how to bring Christians and Africans together." Xavier turned to Gullah Jack. "You can conjure for those who don't believe in Christ." Back to Denmark. "And you can report of visions and stories from God for the Christians. Combine your efforts. You've planned it out. You know where to get weapons. You know whom to trust. I'm here to encourage you to *act*." Xavier walked over and held Denmark's hands in his own.

Denmark Vesey turned to Gullah Jack. "This is the sign we've been waiting for. Ever since I saw Haiti, I knew we could do it. Do you see it?"

"I do. I do." Gullah Jack nodded.

Xavier turned to leave but Denmark called him back. "When? We need to know more. How will we know the right time?"

Xavier went to the familiar for his answer. "July 14th. Do it in honor of those who stormed the Bastille in 1789 to forever change France. Reenact their bravery here in America." Xavier turned to leave, nodding once at the two men and leaping to the ground.

Hoping they could succeed but feeling Malcolm and he sentenced these men to death, Xavier hurried back to Malcolm's and pounded on the door.

"They'll fail. You must know. I just executed them."

Malcolm closed the door behind Xavier and plodded over to his bench. He waited until Xavier took the chair opposite, then pulled a small end table between them. He picked a crystal ball off the floor and dusted it. "What's our business is our business. Let us worry about our own deaths."

"You implicated me in the plot."

"I exploited you, but so they would hurry and do that which they planned. Don't make yourself bigger in this than you are. One step along the way. You helped me to do what I would have done in time anyway. You sped it up. And as payment, I'll find this Duncan for you. Gullah Jack and I go way back, and he introduced me to Denmark. They've a sound plan, and it's worth the risk. What's done is done. It was our agreement. Wipe it from your mind."

Malcolm fell silent and hunched over the table in front of him. Soon, the whites of his eyes showed as he chanted and rubbed against the crystal ball. In little more than a few minutes, the man took powders out and clapped them into the air. Coming out of the crystal and appearing in the smoky haze, Xavier saw a vision of Duncan right here in Charleston.

Malcolm collapsed to the floor, and all the magic disappeared. Xavier rushed over to help him, but Malcolm already sat up. He reached for his cane and allowed Xavier to help him to his feet. Malcolm wiped off his pants and shuffled toward the door. He turned back to Xavier before he opened it. "You did nothing wrong. We made an agreement, that's all. Go on your mission."

Xavier paused. "God's speed," he said to Malcolm and rushed out the door and into the night.

Twenty-Eight: Death to a Tyrant

15 MAY 1822
Charleston, South Carolina

Outside the home Malcolm revealed as housing Duncan, Xavier stood, thinking about how to crash into it and free Duncan when a sudden wave of nausea overcame him. Vampires didn't get sick, yet it felt as in life when he threw up and had to retire to bed for a week to recover. As he stumbled away, he looked up at a second story window and saw a white woman staring down at him, wiggling her fingers in his direction. A few blocks away, his mind began to clear, and his senses returned to normal. He hurried out of Charleston and back to North Carolina, where Catherine greeted him at the door.

"You were gone too long. I should never have let you go alone. Where have you been? What—" She grabbed his jacket and whipped it open. "Where's your shirt? Get in here." She pulled him into the room by the arm and pushed him onto a chair, then knelt in front of him. "Explain this to me," she said and waved her hand in the air, up and down his body.

"I will, if you'll give me a chance to speak." Xavier heard Harriet laugh from the other room. "Not that you don't have explaining to do too."

The corner of Catherine's mouth turned up but she tapped him on the knee and wound her finger in the air. "Explain."

"I went to the sorcerer. After a brief negotiation, he traded with me. I did a quick favor for him, and he returned it by showing me Duncan's location. He's in Charleston, and I know where. But it's complicated."

"What did you have to do, bugger him? Where's your shirt?"

Xavier tugged his jacket around himself. "I did no such thing." Catherine laughed. "I had to play God and demonstrate to two people how quickly I heal. I ripped my shirt off to show them."

Harriet appeared in the doorway, her brow wrinkled. "Is he still going on about the plot with Denmark? I warned them it will never work. They'll all die." Xavier nodded, afraid Harriet may erupt at him. Instead, she came in and sat on the arm of his chair. "Well, better to get on with it then. It's a good warning for me to stay away from Malcolm. They're all as good as dead."

"What if they succeed?" asked Xavier.

"I'll be the first dancing in the streets and on the graves of the white man. Present company excluded." Harriet took a strand of Catherine's hair and played with it.

"So you lost your shirt." Catherine reached in and pinched his nipple, so he slapped her hand away. "What else did you learn?"

"That's just it. Malcolm showed me a vision of where they're keeping Duncan. He's right in Charleston. Thinking I found him and could free him, I rushed to the house and stood outside, planning how to invade, but then I got sick."

Harriet and Catherine both jerked their heads toward him at the same time and spoke. "Sick?"

"Yes." Xavier nodded. "Sick. If I were human, I would've rushed into private to throw up. I knew it was impossible, but I almost became ill, and then I was disoriented. I stumbled away and did not regain my senses until I'd walked a few blocks. So I came back here."

"Magic." Harriet looked from Xavier to Catherine with a serious expression. "This isn't something random we're dealing with."

"Can you help us?" Catherine reached up and grabbed Harriet's arm.

Harriet shook her head to one side. "I told you, love. I won't get involved. I'm needed, alive, not in a Vampire Council's prison."

"Of course," Catherine said. "At least tell us what to do."

Harriet stood and paced the room. She turned back to them and leaned against the fireplace. "You were under a spell, cast by the woman in the window. She knew you were coming. You won't be able to crash in there for no reason and without her knowing in advance. Here." She reached in her dress pocket and then walked across the room and put something in Xavier's hand. "It's a talisman, to protect you from evil. You'll need help to figure this out. Be careful."

Catherine stood and pulled Harriet toward her. "We'll be in touch." Harriet nodded, and the silent communication between the two sent Harriet away after a kiss on the cheek from Catherine.

Xavier also kissed his sister goodnight and retired to the coffins Harriet had hidden in the cellar, where he slept but tossed and turned the whole day. He saw visions of Thomas, angry and casting him out of his life forever, followed by dreams of Denmark, Gullah Jack, and Malcolm being beheaded for their deeds. Next his head swam with sickness, as it had the previous night under the curse. Throughout, Xavier dismayed at his quest, worrying he made too many mistakes and endangered too many people. He wanted Thomas back. He wanted to hide in the safety of France, away from slavery, away from his moral qualms, in the comforting arms of his lover.

As he cried out in his sleep, St. Michel visited him again, his sword held high above his head. Xavier flinched, waiting for the fire or pain to again tell him about the error of his ways. The archangel looked down upon him, his face stern but his words soothing. "You despair too much. You're too delicate. Trust your instincts. Trust your *soul*." St. Michel's sword pointed in another direction, and Xavier found himself floating through the air.

He stopped in a room of white, his regal brother once again standing before him. "Michel." Xavier leaned forward and pulled his brother into a hug as he wept. "I've done terrible things. I've endangered Catherine too. I want to help, but it's hard."

Michel's hand caressed the back of Xavier's head. "I thought we cleared this up with you, long ago. I thought Anne and Catherine purged this guilt of yours." Michel grabbed Xavier by the chin and forced eye contact. "You're still such a sensitive soul. So worried. So convinced you always do wrong. St. Michel sent you on this mission for Anne. Yours isn't to ask why. I'm here to build your confidence. Trust yourself. You're a good person. Here, take this." Michel took one of the medals from his chest and pressed it into Xavier's hand. "Whenever you doubt, whenever this becomes overwhelming, take this and know heaven watches over you."

Xavier woke screaming, with Catherine pounding on the lid of his coffin. She ripped it open and stared down in alarm.

"What? What is it?" she screamed.

Xavier started to tell her they had to abandon their mission—it had become too much for him, when he felt the ribbon and medal in his hand. He clutched it. "Nothing. A bad dream. Let's get to work."

Xavier leaped out of his casket and brushed himself off.

"Work? What are you talking about?"

"We have Duncan in our grasp. We have this." Xavier held up the talisman from Harriet. "And now this." He held up Michel's medal.

Catherine crossed over and touched it, then stared at Xavier. "Where did you get this?"

"You know." Xavier watched Catherine touch it and move away. He scurried around, looking in his bag to find a shirt so he could dress.

When they gathered everything, Xavier hurried them to Charleston and checked into a fine establishment, hoping to appease Catherine with their quarters because she became irritable. She mumbled about his chasing Harriet away, the medal and whatever it meant, and his keeping too many secrets. She started again with abandoning the mission and writing to Thomas. Inside their new rooms, she flopped on the bed and cooed about sleeping in refined lodging once again.

"Do you blame me for Harriet's leaving?"

"Of course not. She and I discussed it. We knew it was a possibility. She wanted to help. You have to believe. But she couldn't risk it." Catherine pulled Xavier down to lay beside her. "Thank you for these rooms. They're lovely, and just what I needed." She stood and pulled Xavier to his feet. "So, what should we do tonight?"

"Free Duncan."

Catherine and he walked through Charleston and once again stood outside the home where Xavier fled the night before. He peered at it, waiting for the nausea to hit but felt nothing. He glanced to Catherine, who wiggled her eyebrows but otherwise looked unfazed.

Convinced they were safe, Xavier launched into action before his courage failed him. He stormed up the front steps and kicked in the door. A muffled scream led them to a side parlor, where a lone man sat tied to a chair, shaking in fear. As Xavier untied him, he recognized the face of Duncan's white master.

"Save me," the man pleaded when Xavier freed the cloth from his mouth. "Please. You have to help."

Xavier jumped when Catherine appeared beside him and smacked the man across the face. "Where is Duncan? And your wife?"

"I've no idea." Catherine slapped him again, harder. He wailed in grief.

Catherine leaned over and pulled out a chunk of his hair as he cried. "Talk," Catherine said.

"I've no idea. They tied me up here and left. We were in this together. We always were. The vampire. The magic. We did it together. But she wanted him as her exclusive sex slave, and I put my foot down. So she and her servant did this to me. They've got Duncan under a spell and run away."

"Who are you talking about? And is that all you know?" Catherine asked.

"My wife. That's all I know. She abandoned me."

Catherine stood up, grabbed him by both sides of his head, and twisted until his neck snapped.

"Shit! Catherine? What are you doing?"

"Killing him. He gave us everything he knew."

"Did you have to?" Xavier hated the sight of his head hanging in the opposite direction and turned away.

"No. But he deserved it. What now?"

Maybe she was even worse than Thomas! Xavier led them outside away from the house. He gathered himself and then looked at his sister, which sent him into hysterical laughter.

"Something funny?" she asked.

"No. Not at all." But he still giggled, which caused her to join him. "I thought I'd left Thomas behind. I didn't think anyone could ever make him look like an angel."

"Well, someone needs to seize control. I suppose we could've fed on him to save the trouble of hunting later. But I thought it best we get out of the house. You know he deserved it, don't you?"

"I do."

"Good. Then instead of brooding, why don't you tell me what's next. She must have been putting a spell on you, and it's gone with her. How are we going to find her?"

"We may only have one option," Xavier said and hurried down the street with Catherine in tow.

Twenty-Nine: A Mistress and Her Possession

15 MAY 1822
Charleston, South Carolina

Xavier paused outside Malcolm's house and felt in his jacket pocket for the talisman Harriet gave him, then took a deep breath. "This is the witchdoctor Harriet sent me to," he said to Catherine and jerked his head toward the house. "He found Duncan once. Let's see if he can do it again."

"I'd better stay here," Catherine said, which surprised Xavier.

"Why?"

"Harriet suggested we avoid too much entanglement with Malcolm and his plans. She thinks his magic is impeccable but his other schemes dangerous. We should keep this simple."

Xavier nodded and strode across the street to knock on Malcolm's door. The old man himself answered, ushering Xavier inside without a word.

"He disappeared again." Malcolm shuffled over to his bench and pulled the table out, where the crystal ball sat.

"How did you know?" asked Xavier.

"I kept track of you, after you left. I wanted to see if you succeeded. I saw the woman put the spell on you, so I thought I'd better monitor things for a while."

Xavier sat opposite him, unsure how to feel. He hated being spied upon but needed Malcolm's help. And it appeared Malcolm sympathized with Xavier's mission, or had nothing better to do at the moment. Malcolm leaned over the crystal, beginning a chant, but nothing appeared above it. He hunched closer, peering into the crystal at an image unseen by Xavier. When he finished, he pulled the table aside and leaned on his cane toward Xavier. "Of course, our agreement ended, as you know. You visited Denmark, and I gave you Duncan's location. I'll tell you upfront I don't have access to the same kind of information this time because she blocked it. I can help, though, if you'll help me."

Xavier hesitated. He'd worried he sent those two men toward their ultimate doom on a fool's errand. Desperate for information, he once again pushed aside his qualms and nodded for Malcolm to continue.

"You told Denmark to do it on Bastille Day. He liked that. Likes the French, from what he learned in Haiti. If you promise to come back again in a month or so, to give him a bit more courage to continue, then we're set. I'll help you, with the promise of a future return payment."

"He won't succeed." Xavier ran his hands through his hair then reached for his cross, which had fallen out of his shirt. He rubbed it. "I understand what you want. I want the same thing. I wish I felt differently, that such a plot could overthrow this entire institution. I don't agree. I think it's dangerous. There must be something else you can come up with."

Malcolm's posture went rigid. "You may sympathize with my people, and we appreciate it. You can worry about us all you want." Malcolm pointed his finger at Xavier. "You can't know what it's like. You preach caution, but look where that's gotten us. Some of us won't sit quietly anymore. Denmark is a powerful leader, charismatic as anyone I ever met. And Gullah Jack gives us much more of a chance. Yours isn't to sit in judgment over us and what we plan. You can go along, or you can go to a different place. It's up to you."

"What if I take the information I need and decide not to return?"

Malcolm smirked. "It's not in you. What will it be? I've got other things to consider this afternoon."

Xavier's voice quavered as he assented to Malcolm's wishes. "I'll return."

"This is what I know." Malcolm tapped his cane on the floor. "It was the mistress in league with the vampire you killed. The master went along with it. Profited from it, and kept his wife happy. She wanted sex slaves. That's what she's after, and that's why she's got Duncan. She's learned magic, from the vampire no doubt. But she's not very good at it."

"She knew enough the other night to disorient me."

Malcolm smiled. "That's just it. It took all her energy to do it. What I can see in the crystal came from her husband, after you killed him. He's an angry spirit. I reached out to it because when I looked for Duncan nothing came up but the master's ghost, livid and sticking around here. The mistress panicked when she saw your approach in her vision, recognizing you for a vampire. So she scrambled around for her books and started throwing out a chant. It worked by mistake more than anything. She passed out right after, hit her head hard on the window sill. When her servant found her, she ordered her to pack while she ran around gathering things, preparing to leave. She figured out a clouding spell to keep me from seeing things and then tied up her husband, after they got into an argument about Duncan. She got real angry when he tried to talk her into giving him up."

"So Duncan's still with her?"

Malcolm nodded. "Under a trance I've never seen before. He's not himself at all. That's all I know."

Xavier stood and looked out the window. He fidgeted with his cross and then dropped it down his shirt, back against his chest. "So how can I find them?"

Malcolm pushed himself up and left the room. After a couple minutes, he returned and handed Xavier a small sheet of paper, no bigger than four inches square. Xavier flipped it over and saw neither side had anything on it. He looked up with a scrunched brow.

"Magic, son. Magic. It'll show you what it can, when it knows information. Don't ask for miracles. It's all I've got."

When Xavier looked back at the paper, it had words on it.

"Stay in Charleston."

Xavier tucked it in his pocket and shook Malcolm's hand. "Thank you." He went to the front door but paused before exiting. "I hope you succeed. Regardless of what I think or said earlier, I'll fulfill my end of our agreement."

"I know you will." Malcolm came over and patted Xavier on the back. He stepped out and went around the corner to find Catherine.

"Well?" she asked.

"I'm afraid we lost them again. But he gave us this." Xavier showed her the small note, which again had nothing on it.

"That's it?" she asked.

As an answer, Xavier held it up to her again. Catherine gasped and looked back at Xavier with her mouth open.

"Believe"

Part Seven

Friendship Betrayed

Thirty: Southern Aristocracy

1 JUNE 1822
South Carolina

Thomas brooded in the carriage next to Anthony as they rode toward Charleston. He wanted to go there afoot, at vampiric speed, to get a head start on his search for Xavier. But Anthony slowed him down, insisting the next step would require the assistance of more humans and thus called for appearances. Since when did vampires worry about such things?

Instead of rushing to Charleston when the latest report again indicated the rogue vampires operated near there, they had sent word ahead to one of the finest hotels, paid a mock staff consisting of a few teenagers to join their charade, and prepared to parade into town as European royalty. Such a game bored Thomas. And he suspected more and more Anthony aimed the charade at him, not the outside world.

"Explain all of this nonsense to me again." Thomas rolled his eyes.

Anthony whipped his head around to look at Thomas as the carriage hit a huge bump. "I've explained it a thousand times. What's the use, when you don't listen to me anymore, anyway?"

"I'm all ears. I'm riveted. Explain. One minute we dash away from Atlanta, hurrying to capture these evil beasts as soon as possible. Next, we do nothing for a week while pretending to be something we're not so we can make a grand entrance. It makes no sense."

Anthony took a deep breath. "These two are messing with more than the vampire ethic. We may have to cover more tracks than a few escaped slaves here and there. We have to hook up with the power establishment and thus become Southern aristocracy for the time being."

"Should be easy." Thomas sat up from his slumped position. "There are a lot of half Indians running around with rich white men in the South, I'm sure. And all sorts of men who come out at night. Plus, your British accent sounds so Southern. Doesn't this violate the ethic? We could arrest ourselves while we're at it."

Thomas started when Anthony pounded his fist against the carriage side, denting the wood frame. "Shut up. I brought you along as a favor. The last thing I need is your snide attitude making an impossible and unpleasant task all the more difficult."

Thomas fell back into his seat, a million nasty comments floating through his mind to shoot back at Anthony. He bit his tongue instead.

Outside the hotel in Charleston, Thomas flung the carriage door open before the bellman could do it and stormed into the night. He strode down the street without looking back and went to the wharf, where he found a quiet corner in which to collect himself. He sat with his feet dangling over the edge above the water. Despite his questioning, Thomas knew what Anthony plotted. He wanted contacts within the white Southern power structure so he could alert them to the possibility of the slaves escaping, thereby hoping human interference would slow these vampires down as they continued to hunt for them.

And much as he understood Anthony's motivation, it repulsed him that his good friend would in any way facilitate the awful institution. Not that Thomas had the same conviction against slavery as Xavier, because nothing in human society moved Thomas to such a degree. Still, certain of their practices bothered him more than others, since his own people faced enslavement and fought wars to protect themselves from the white men. Anthony preached goodness and doing the right thing, always insisting vampires could help make the world a better place. Yet here he aligned himself with the evil.

Perhaps it sickened Thomas because he knew with certainty they hunted for Xavier and Catherine. He peered across the water, toward Europe, and saw Xavier standing before him on the last night before he fled. He'd sensed something different in Xavier's demeanor when he exited Notre Dame. Rather than relief or determination at having a better direction, Xavier acted aloof and distant. Thomas convinced himself it was the stress of the visions that had Xavier acting out, but he knew Xavier acted to hide his plans from Thomas.

A blood tear trickled down Thomas's cheek. He let it land on his white shirt, not caring about the permanent stain.

Where had he gone wrong? He loved Xavier with all his heart. He lived to protect him, and they reveled in every night they spent together. So why had Xavier done it? More tears streamed down his face as Thomas guessed the answer. Xavier determined he had to act, and Thomas would have done anything and everything in his power to stop him, fearing it would lead to their current predicament—with the Vampire Council hunting for his love, to execute him.

Didn't Xavier know, however, in the end Thomas would have allowed them to go? Did he fear Thomas because of the fateful hit during the revolution? How could Xavier not know Thomas would follow him anywhere, on any mission?

Thomas slammed his fist into the pier, splitting a pole down the middle, sending splinters flying through the air.

"Are you going to join me? Or are you content beating inanimate objects?" On most nights, Anthony's sarcasm would have made Thomas laugh, but not tonight.

"Where are you going?" he asked without looking up.

"To our rooms."

"Oh, I can't wait." Thomas sat motionless.

From behind him, without warning, Anthony reached down and yanked Thomas to his feet. "I'm tiring of you."

"At least the feeling is mutual." Thomas, nonetheless, followed Anthony around the corner and back to the hotel. The doorman bowed as the men entered and started up the stairs toward their quarters. Anthony arranged for them to stay in the most opulent of rooms, though he stowed their trunks, in which they would sleep, a few rooms away to avoid prying eyes.

Inside, Thomas fell into a lounge chair and looked up at Anthony, who hovered above him. "What's so urgent? I was so enjoying the pier."

"This is serious, and no pouting or inappropriate outburst of anger is going to help you this time. You're at risk, too, so you'd better come out with the full story. I'll murder you with them if I have to. Thomas, I love you. But I have a duty."

Thirty-One: Suspicion Revealed

1 JUNE 1822
Charleston, South Carolina

Thomas pressed his lips together, once again biting back a million snide comments he wanted to unleash upon Anthony. Duty, indeed. Why did Anthony always hide behind his obligation to the Vampire Council whenever he disagreed with Thomas? Why did duty trump anything Thomas had to say? Thomas always put up with it, knowing his friend's strong feelings about sitting on the Council in service.

But it was personal. Anthony threatened Thomas with the demand Thomas tell him the whole story because he was at risk too. What had Thomas done to deserve such a slap in the face?

Worse, it meant Anthony had already convicted Catherine and Xavier. There would be no pleading or reasoning with Anthony or the Council. Anthony sounded as if he determined the crime and a preordained punishment. If he had, then why sit there, thinking Thomas would unleash a tale to further implicate Xavier? Was Anthony so dense?

Thomas had vowed to die in defense of Xavier. It felt more and more like he would have to do it, even if it meant attacking his very best friend. Seeing that Anthony sat opposite him, his face bright red, Thomas waited a few more moments to say anything. "I don't know what you want me to say." He tossed his hands in the air. "What do you expect?"

"The truth. All of it. No more concealing what you know. No more games." Anthony leaned forward and pointed an accusing finger at Thomas. "You know more than you're telling me. You've kept information from me from the start. I've no idea what you thought you could accomplish, but you were mistaken. If anything, you've made the situation worse. Tell me everything, and we can discuss your future and what we need to do. Continue this charade, and you may doom yourself."

Thomas jumped out of his chair and stormed across the room. He grabbed a decorative vase from a shelf, walked with it over to Anthony, and smashed it on the ground in front of his friend. "Explain this to the hotel staff. And keep playing coy with me, and we'll see how far I can go in making your life more miserable."

Anthony leaped to his feet, pushing Thomas back into a couch and leering above him. Thomas struggled to get up, but Anthony pushed him back down. "You think this is another one of your fucking games? You think you can toy with the Council again? This is serious."

Thomas nodded. Anthony relaxed his shoulders and sat next to Thomas, inches from him but without the snarl on his face. Thomas rubbed his neck, surprised at his friend's lashing out. Anthony had scolded him a million times before, but the current issue took the rebuke to a different level.

"We both have secrets from one another." Thomas started with the obvious. Part of him wanted to reconcile with Anthony, to search for a way to heal their relationship. Perhaps if they put everything in the open, they would better understand one another and come to a solution for both of them. Yet, at the same time, Thomas's fierce protectiveness of Xavier told him to proceed with caution. As much as he wanted to find peace with his best friend, Xavier came first. "Though I'm not sure how secret anything is at this point. It might be better to say we both know the same thing but refuse to talk about it. For the sake of our friendship, silence might be best."

"Or it may doom us." Anthony leaned back on the couch. "I've tried to remain patient with you because I understand your motivation. I played along, hoping to show you reason. Your avoidance and vagueness made things worse. I don't know how else to communicate the seriousness of this situation. This is more dire than anything we've ever faced together. I got you out of trouble before, but this problem goes beyond that."

"I'm not dense." Thomas rubbed his hands together. "I heard you every time you lashed out at the rogue vampires. I listened every time you covered the litany of vampire laws they've violated. I get it."

"But you feigned ignorance the whole time."

"What did you want me to do?" Thomas clapped his hands together. "Shout my approval they deserved death? Volunteer to execute them myself? I wanted to find a middle way to make this easier for all of us."

"No such path exists." Thomas was more annoyed than usual over how Anthony sat so stoically during an argument as he pronounced they could not compromise. Thomas wondered how Anthony could remain so calm as they discussed what might happen to Xavier, whom he claimed was a friend.

"I know now." Thomas squinted his eyes shut in anger for a moment. "Which brings us to the essential problem, doesn't it? Choosing sides." He opened his eyes and stared at Anthony. "You've tried to pull me to your side, but you must have known all along I would never go for it. I'll protect him with my life. He means everything to me. *Everything*. And you and the abomination of a Council with your black-and-white rules need a lesson in the gray areas of life." Thomas narrowed his eyes. "You're my dearest friend and for so long, the only one. The tension between us is killing me. I'd do almost anything to preserve our bond—except betray him. If I have to fight you, so be it. I've done nothing wrong, but I will if I have to."

Anthony stood, having listened to Thomas's lecture without reacting. He walked over to a case and opened it, searching through papers before pulling out three envelopes. At first, Thomas had no idea how it related to their conversation, but then he recognized the purple stationary. Anthony held them in the air. "You're not innocent in all of this. You concealed information from the Council and me. You may not have done the acts they committed, but you've decided to abate them. You could be punished too."

"You spied on me?" Thomas was livid. His pulse quickened, and he fought with every ounce of his willpower not to smash his fist into Anthony's face. Instead, he grabbed a porcelain statue and threw it against the wall. "You stole those from me."

"Just to prove my point to you. I already knew their content." Anthony flung the letters at Thomas and paced in front of him. "Shall we review? Renegade vampires are rampaging through the South, killing other vampires and freeing slaves, all against the vampire ethic. At the same time, Xavier disappears, from you of all people." Anthony jabbed his finger in Thomas's direction. "And, what? Catherine is missing too. Up and left, with no word as to her destination or expected return. A female and male vampire, so angry about slavery they think they alone can eliminate the entire institution. Using vampire powers in full view of the other slaves. And who have I heard rail against slavery, time and again? Who has questioned me about why vampires can't do more to stop it? I'm no denser than you, Thomas. Your lover and his sister have violated the vampire ethic. At best, I may be able to convince the Council to sentence them to a very long prison term. Perhaps centuries. That's *at best*. So get mad. Have one of your fits. Smash this place into oblivion. Threaten me. It won't change anything. It won't help a thing. And then I'll have more reason to imprison you too."

Thomas stared at Catherine's letters. Each time he got one he hoped she would reveal their location and at last lead him to Xavier. She pled with him to come to the South to force Xavier to stop, and in the second letter indicated their exact whereabouts. Thomas stole away from Anthony one night, thinking he would find Xavier and Catherine at last but instead found they already moved, with Catherine leaving behind another note for Thomas. It explained Xavier's trips to Charleston and how he almost found Duncan, and that they settled for a while in Charleston, once again with Catherine urging Thomas to find them. Thomas had no idea if they remained here, or if they once again headed to a new locale. Instinct told him he was closer to finding them than ever before, but he did not want to get his hopes up to have them crushed.

"They're old." Thomas shrugged and pointed to the letters. "We don't know for sure they're here."

Anthony smirked. "He's looking for this Duncan, whom the letters say they found in Charleston. All the other reports and evidence point to them being here, including the human indications about the freeing of slaves by unknown outsiders. You may think me a fool, hoping to protect him. But it won't work."

Thomas nodded but twirled his finger in the air at the same time. "Impressive. You're quite the detective to figure out all on your own so much. It doesn't resolve our problem, does it?"

"There's nothing to resolve." Anthony stooped over and gathered up the letters. "Xavier has violated the ethic, without remorse and knowing he did it. He started on this quest to find and free Duncan, in and of itself a major violation that would warrant severe punishment. But along the way he transformed Catherine, knowing it violated the ethic. He disregarded the ethic for his own gain. Then, to make matters worse, he parades around the South interfering in human affairs, freeing slaves and showcasing his vampiric powers to anyone in his vicinity. Resolve what, Thomas?"

Thomas drew in a deep breath, searching for a way to continue the conversation. He knew it was futile, but he had to try. "I know how it sounds. Everything you said is true."

"Exactly."

"Let me finish." Thomas tried to avoid a nasty tone but failed. "He felt called by a divine authority to find this Duncan. No doubt he transformed her because he needed help and was afraid to go alone. He's under tremendous stress, feeling an awful obligation to his friend, Anne, that he can't fulfill. Then he sees slavery all around him, and we know how much he hates it. The stress is acting out, not Xavier. He's not of his right mind. The Council has to take into account his frame of mind."

Anthony raised his eyebrows. "Not in his right mind? He calculated enough to remove you from his presence. Why?"

Thomas winced at the reminder. "Because I would have stopped him. To protect him."

"Which proves he did all of this of sound mind and disobeyed all vampire rules with intention. This is willful negligence. This is an utter disregard for the ethic and the reason it exists. I'm sorry. There's no other way but to punish him. If he had stopped earlier, or confined it to the Duncan matter, it might be different. But he kept going, deeper and deeper. Let's hope the Council will settle for a long prison term."

Thomas shook his head. "I won't allow it."

"Won't allow what? Like you have any say in the matter."

"You won't put Xavier in one of those boxes over the fire in your mountain cavern unless it's over my corpse. He went on this mission for all the right reasons. He meant no harm. He respects the ethic, more than I ever have. You know that. He was protecting the innocent and still is. The Vampire Council can condemn him all they want but they have to see reason. They have to take his motivation into account."

Anthony paced the room as Thomas seethed inside. If the Council could not see the rationale behind what Thomas explained, then he wanted nothing to do with it anymore. He would raise an army of vampires against it to defeat such an uncaring lot who valued their rules more than the vampires they pledged to protect.

"Come. We won't solve anything this way." Anthony motioned for Thomas to follow. "Come on. We need to go meet someone." Thomas followed. Anthony was right. No further talk would abate their situation, but where was he taking them? Thomas wondered if he should remain with Anthony or if he should sneak away and work on his own to find Xavier and Catherine before his friend could.

Thirty-Two: Parting Ways

1 JUNE 1822
Charleston, South Carolina

Thomas sulked behind Anthony, as he sauntered through the hotel, watching his "friend" act nonchalant, pretending to be human, as if without a care in the world. Thomas thought he drew out the procession in order to torture Thomas, though it did give Thomas time to ponder his next move. He would go with Anthony, curious about his announced meeting with a mystery guest. Thomas doubted, however, it would do anything to solve their feud and so determined to strike out on his own afterward with the hope of finding Xavier and Catherine first. He would do whatever it took to force Xavier out of here away from the South, back to Europe or perhaps to another exotic locale where they could hide from the Council. But Thomas doubted more and more such a plot could succeed, that anyone could hide from the Council.

Anthony stopped his charade and motioned for Thomas to follow outside, where they started walking down the street. "I thought you understood we have to blend into their society this time. You're not helping things with your morose attitude and by hanging in the background."

"I never signed onto your idiotic farce. I think it's stupid. Doesn't this all violate the ethic, or did God ordain you as Vampire Master?"

"It's part of trying to fix the problem so the ethic remains in force. If you're going to stay with me, we have to do this together or it won't work."

Thomas almost shot back he'd be leaving soon enough but thought better of it. Instead, he rolled his eyes and kept walking.

Anthony kept them at a human pace as they neared the outskirts of town and headed away from the city. "I don't mean to be so cold."

"Then stop it." Thomas almost regretted not sympathizing with Anthony, but something kept him from believing his latest admission would change anything. He was in no mood to humor his friend for the sake of small talk.

"I suppose I deserve your scolding. Listen, I understand how you feel about Xavier. I'm trying to explain I'll do anything in my power to protect him too. He means a lot to me. And you're right. I know he'd never do anything unless he felt a strong calling for it. I know he wants to help people and has the very best of intentions. He cares so much about those around him. And I realize, more than anything, the lengths to which you'll go to protect him. I promise to you and to Xavier, as a friend, I'll try to minimize the punishment. If the Council has ever listened to me, and I think they will, I'll save his life."

"I suppose you expect a thank you." Thomas glanced over to gauge Anthony's reaction and saw an understanding face. So Thomas pushed it further. "Or my eternal gratitude."

"I just wanted you to know. You're my friend, and my obligation to the Council has gotten in the way of our friendship. I can't do anything about my duty, but I can use my influence to help you...and him. I didn't tell you this to patch things up between us."

"Good." Thomas suspected Anthony knew far more than he said; he had more influence than he admitted, and somehow none of it would prevent the horrific from happening to Xavier. He pressed for more information. "Will you use magic on him?"

"I don't know. We use magic to subdue a recalcitrant vampire. Xavier never struck me as the type. You know him better than I, but I can't imagine him putting up much resistance."

Thomas nodded. Thomas had already feared Xavier would be compliant and follow Anthony like a scolded puppy.

"What about against me?"

"Why would I need to do anything against you?" Anthony picked up their pace.

"I violated the ethic by not telling you everything I knew. How many times tonight did you threaten me? So I may need punishment. I don't suppose you expect the same docile response from me you think you'll get from Xavier?"

Anthony smiled when he saw Thomas smirking. "Touché. Docile never described anything about you. Or Catherine, for that matter."

"So you *would* use the magic against me?"

Anthony halted and turned to Thomas. He put both of his hands on Thomas's shoulders. "I'd do whatever I thought necessary to maintain the vampire ethic, to enforce the Council's rules, and to do my duty to all vampires and humans to keep us safe. But I'd also do everything in my power to protect you, Xavier, and Catherine. You most of all. Even if it meant protecting you from yourself. Much as I may want to, I can't make exceptions. The Council can't make exceptions. Making exceptions and letting one Council member handle a close relationship on their own led to the battle that destroyed so many vampires. The woman on the Council tried to stop the one who wanted to destroy us, once she learned of his deceit and plans, but it was too late. Years of overlooking his transgressions allowed him to assemble allies and mount an enormous attack against all other vampires."

"And that's why you said there are only about one hundred vampires left?"

"Yes. And the fact we restrict the number of new vampires. He was suspicious. We all knew it, but we trusted his maker to control him. He destroyed her and then started the vampire war. A few survived. I lost a lover. We can't allow the possibility of that happening again. The ethic exists to protect *all* of us."

Anthony linked their arms together and pulled Thomas forward. He'd never answered the question about magic, but his evasiveness told Thomas everything. Missing Xavier and contemplating all of the awful possibilities brought Thomas's rage to the boiling point once again.

They traveled a short distance into the countryside and headed into a dense forest of trees, where Anthony lit a couple of candles and leaned against a tree.

"Are we having a séance?" Thomas kicked a stone across the ground.

"Shh. Don't make such a ruckus."

"Fuck off." The scolding irritated Thomas, though he regretted losing the moment of affection they had shared. "A lit candle won't bring attention, but one little rock will? I already had one father in life. I don't need another."

"If you don't—" Anthony halted and put his finger to his mouth. Seconds later, the woman whom they had met before, the former slave who went around protecting slaves from evil masters, appeared through the trees. She smiled again at Anthony, though she pulled back from their hug. Then she surprised Thomas by turning to him and embracing him. She remembered his name and patted him on the hand in a familiar way. Thomas remembered her name, Harriet.

"You summoned me?" she asked Anthony. "Have I become your dog?" Thomas thought she sounded defiant but noticed she smiled, as if teasing Anthony. Yet she emanated a tension Thomas had not sensed the first time they met her.

Anthony chuckled. "I would never treat you like a dog. But this investigation gets more and more complicated. I may need your help." He narrowed his eyes at her.

"I always do what I can for you. But I haven't seen them or any sign of them since last we met."

Anthony picked up a candle and stared into it. "There's strong evidence they're in this area."

"Charleston? Interesting." Harriet kept her distance.

"Will you keep your eyes and ears open and tell me if you hear of anything?" Anthony gave Harriet their hotel information, and she agreed to get any information to him as soon as possible. She also promised to stay in the region in case she came upon anything.

She hugged Anthony again before she left, the affection of their first visit seeming to have returned. Then she came over to Thomas, who stood a short distance from the two during their conversation. She watched Anthony as he went over to extinguish one of the candles and then whispered to Thomas as she hugged him. "Tomorrow. Here, same time. Alone."

She turned back to Anthony and touched him on the arm. "You'll keep me posted too? Lest you find them and leave me wandering around here for no reason?"

"Of course." Anthony hugged her again.

Harriet walked into the night, leaving as mysteriously as she appeared but with Thomas more intrigued than before.

The second Harriet disappeared, the tension between Thomas and Anthony reignited. They'd had arguments before, as Anthony attempted to get Thomas's anger under control in their early years, when he courted Xavier during the French Revolution. They survived each time, with a stronger friendship. But this time felt different to Thomas because in the past a part of him knew he was wrong. He had always understood that truth on some level, and so their disagreements healed as Thomas came to accept himself and control his extreme ire. No such personal flaw inhibited their relationship. Thomas would argue his case to the ends of the earth and saw no reason to trust Anthony, because it necessitated he also have faith in the damnable Council.

The end game had arrived, so Thomas determined to make it happen once and for all. He would give Anthony one last chance before striking out on his own. "So, what's next?" Thomas looked to Anthony, who stood motionless nearby with a blank look on his face.

"We hunt for them. Can you?"

"Probably not." Thomas started to explain but thought better of it. "Not in the way you mean, anyway. I want you to hear me out, though. Let me explain to you before this thing gets any worse. Will you do that for me? Listen, without judgment or interruption?"

"I don't see how it will do any good." Anthony crossed his arms.

Thomas resisted the impulse to storm away as the rage built within him. "We've come too far not to give it one more chance, haven't we?" Thomas cringed at the finality of what he had said. "Let me plead before the Council." Before Thomas could say another word, Anthony tossed his arms in the air and rolled his eyes. He started to speak, but Thomas interrupted. "I asked you to listen to me first. Please." Thomas felt his heart pounding as he again resisted the urge to yell back, to lash out at Anthony's behavior. He took a deep breath, when Anthony nodded and stood still, rigid but at least listening.

"You scold me whenever I claim the Council issues arbitrary rules or penalties. You get *so* angry whenever I accuse them of hiding too much and not explaining what it is they want or need. But how else should any vampire feel? No one I've ever met knows anyone on the Council, except you. Yes, they publish the laws and pass them down from maker to new vampire. But what about the gray areas any legal system contains? How does the Council deal with them? Not everything is black and white."

"And I suppose you think these violations by Xavier and Catherine fall into a gray area?"

Thomas nodded. "I do. Not that they didn't violate the ethic. The *reason* for the violation has to be taken into account. Motive plays a part. It's unfair to lump Xavier with other rogues who murder for murder's sake or attack one of our own kind without provocation. Yes, he was wrong. Yes, he violated the ethic and has continued to do so over and over again throughout the last few months. But he can be taught. He can understand why it was wrong if given a chance.

"And, think about his motivation. He wanted to save a poor soul who was stolen into this abomination of an institution. Don't tell me the Council can't factor slavery into their judgment, because in other things they consider human factors and realities all the time. We aren't allowed to kill or hunt the innocent. What is that, if not a protection of humanity? Extenuating circumstances should force this Council to rethink its penal code. For Xavier's sake, you have to let me talk to them. If you give me a chance, I think I can make them see reason and give Xavier a light sentence. I'm not sure Catherine deserves any punishment at all because no one taught her, except Xavier, who was in the midst of his quest."

Thomas knew he'd lost the argument by looking at his friend. Anthony stood like a statue, his jaw once again clenched together. "The Council doesn't work that way. Your proposal can never happen."

"Why not? Did you hear a word I said?"

"I heard every word." Anthony started pacing. "*Every* word of it. But you never hear anything I have to say. How many times do I have to explain the Council's secrecy? How many times do I have to tell you how these laws and procedures were developed after the catastrophic event? Secrecy is essential. Even from you, though you know I love and trust you. Your suggestion won't work."

Thomas's blood began to boil. Not a conversation. Not a nod toward Thomas acknowledging he made good points. Nothing. God Himself must exist and sit atop the Council issuing decrees and orders. "Who do you think you are? Jesus? Yes, that must be it. Christ walks in my very midst. Should I bow before your feet? Or are you the pope, pretending to do God's will while satisfying yourself?"

"What are you talking about? I thought we got your temper under control. Now we can't have a reasonable conversation?"

"Reasonable conversation? You didn't hear anything I said. You won't explain why you disagree with me, only claiming I have incorrect thinking. What kind of conversation is that?" Thomas snapped a large branch off a nearby tree. "No, God Himself sits atop this Council, and that's why you can't tell any of us what's going on. That's why the rules are so final. Because God doesn't allow any questioning. Which means all these years you hid your divine nature from me. I'm so sorry not to have recognized your divinity sooner."

Anthony backed away as Thomas ranted, then postured himself as if Thomas might attack him. Thomas had no such intention. Instead, he walked closer and lowered his voice to a whisper. "A true friend would never betray those he claims to love."

Thomas whipped around and ran through the night as fast as a vampire could run. He hurried to their quarters, ignoring the charade he was supposed to act as an aristocratic European as he brushed by the people in the street and in the lobby. He gathered the few personal items and clothes he brought along and stormed out again, but not before breaking a few more decorative statues and a glass, stealing back his letters from Catherine, and ripping up all of Anthony's clothes as a message. He needed Anthony to comprehend the finality of the moment.

Thirty-Three: Clandestine Meetings

2 JUNE 1822
Charleston, South Carolina

Thomas woke the next night determined to defeat Anthony. He had no idea how to find Xavier and Catherine, how to conceal them if he did, nor what he would do if faced with Anthony and his magic. Yet he would succeed. He had to.

Last night, Thomas found a large crypt in a serene cemetery. As he settled in, he missed Xavier more than ever. His love. His everything. Without Xavier, Thomas hardly believed the sun set every night. Without Xavier, he would still be walking around in a complete rage.

And that was the crux of the matter. If he could save Xavier, not just preserve his life but also avert a long prison sentence, then perhaps he could repay Xavier for having so saved his life. He had to do something in return, and saving him could be it.

He could already hear Xavier scolding him that they owed each other nothing but their love. Which was true. But it would make Thomas feel so much better. He could show Xavier the lengths to which he would go to protect him from *anything*.

To be sure, Thomas was miserable. He ached at the loss of Anthony. He worried Anthony would find Xavier first. And he so missed Xavier his heart hurt.

Thomas hurried out of the crypt with renewed energy and walked toward the woods where Harriet asked him to meet her. Strange that she requested a secret meeting. Perhaps it presented the way to get ahead of Anthony.

He sensed Harriet's approach several seconds before she appeared but kept his guard up in case Anthony concocted the whole rendezvous as a test.

Harriet strolled into the small clearing and smiled at Thomas. "You came."

"You piqued my interest." Thomas felt at ease with her. "Anthony's instructions to you last night didn't seem to resonate with you in the same way as when first we met."

"Circumstances change, don't they?" She linked her arm through Thomas's. "Come, let's walk and talk. I love the power of owning the forest at night."

They went deeper into the woods. Thomas grabbed Harriet's hand. "The first time Anthony introduced us, I thought you were an obedient vampire. Obeying the ethic. Informing on the rogue vampires. Listening to Anthony's every whim. I detect I was wrong."

Harriet whistled for a moment before speaking. "Life is complicated, isn't it?"

"Indeed. Which led to your summoning me. Perhaps Anthony told you about my rebellious nature. Or you sensed it?"

Harriet pulled away and picked a flower. She sniffed it, handed it to Thomas, and then picked another one for herself. "Violets. My favorite." When Harriet sat on a fallen tree, she patted the space next to her for Thomas to join her. He did, twirling the flower in his fingers.

"At first, I thought these vampires had wandered into the South to kill a bunch of other vampires. I feared a vampire war was upon us. It was strange the Council hadn't acted yet. And those two had killed one of our own, after all. It wasn't until afterward I heard the stories of two angels roaming the South, freeing slaves and killing the masters and overseers." Harriet paused. "Make no mistake about me. I don't obey the Council because I agree with them. I obey because I don't want to die, and most of all because alive I can at least do a little to alleviate the worst of the suffering. If I was braver and less concerned about leaving my people with nothing, I'd do what Xavier is doing too."

"You know his name?" Thomas perked up at the mention.

"I met him. And Catherine. If I found them again, I'd never report to Anthony. I can't join them, though I wish I could. Instead, I offer you this: I can protect you from any spell Anthony tries to inflict upon you, so you can defend Xavier and Catherine. Anthony confided he's worried about what you'll try to do, and he's preparing to cast a powerful spell against you. I know someone who can counter it. I'll help you, if you'll help me."

Could it be true? Was there a way to counteract Anthony's spell, to give Thomas a chance against Anthony? "What's the condition?"

"First, leave me out of it. Protect me so I can continue with my work. My people need me."

"I would have done as much without your asking."

"Thank you. Second, whatever you do for Xavier, however you free him or help him escape, you have to promise to do the same for Catherine."

"I won't have a choice in the matter either. I can tell you already Xavier would never leave her behind, regardless of how much I pleaded for it, or even if Catherine ordered him to do it to protect himself."

"Is that a promise then?"

"Yes, it is. I was trying to explain both of your requests would have been met without your asking."

Harriet stood, leaving her violet sitting on the tree. "If you succeed, I want you to come to me, to tell me. I want to know what happens. Come here, to Charleston."

"You have my word."

Without responding, Harriet waved for Thomas to follow and sped away, back toward the city. Thomas remained alert for Anthony, especially when they got to Charleston, but never sensed another vampire or presence anywhere. Harriet knocked on the door of a small but well-kept house in the free black community, where an old woman answered the door and kissed Harriet on the cheek as she ushered them inside.

The woman then left the room, promising to send Malcolm at once. The room looked innocent enough, like almost any sitting room one expected to find in a typical house. But tucked into the corners and on a few shelves, Thomas spotted the accouterments of a sorcerer. A crystal ball, a crow's claw, a rack of spices. He stood gazing at a tiny skull on a shelf when a person shuffled into the room. He turned to see an elderly black man, leaning on his cane.

"Well, if it isn't more vampires. I never thought I'd see so many vampires in my life. Never wanted to. Harriet? What this time?"

Harriet walked over to him and took him by the arm, assisting him to his chair. "I've never asked for repayment. I bought and freed your children because it was the right thing to do."

"But nothing's ever free in life, is it?" Malcolm tapped his cane on the floor. "And you've come to collect."

"It's a small matter. This is Thomas." When Harriet pointed to him, he bowed to Malcolm. "Thomas, this is Malcolm. An old friend."

Malcolm chuckled. "More of a business associate, I'd say."

"I'm pleased to meet you."

Malcolm nodded but turned back to Harriet. "This isn't your run-of-the-mill request. Call it what you will, but this 'small matter' carries the weight of life and death."

Harriet smiled. "I'm testing your skills to see if you've lost anything in your old age."

Malcolm straightened in his chair. "If anything, I'm stronger than ever."

"That's the spirit!" Harriet laughed, and a smile spread across Malcolm's face.

"She likes to antagonize me," he said to Thomas. "What do you need?"

"A protective spell." Harriet sat in a chair opposite Malcolm.

"For you?"

"No, for him. Sit down." Harriet pointed to a chair opposite Malcolm, so Thomas obeyed.

"Easy enough. You didn't need me. Any voodoo priestess in the area could accomplish your need."

"I'm afraid it's not so easy. It's an old and powerful magic. Almost omnipotent." Harriet leaned forward in her chair. "Against vampire magic. I don't know much about it, except it's more potent than anything I've ever seen before."

Malcolm peered straight ahead for several minutes before he spoke. "I see. You need a powerful spell, then. Protective, of a force you can't describe. This return payment won't be easy." Malcolm strained to get out of his chair and shuffled over to a cabinet. He unlocked it and pulled several vials out. Despite his age and crippled body, he arranged them on a table in front of himself and called Thomas over to sit opposite him.

"Harriet, you'd best leave."

"I'll wait for you outside."

When she had gone, Malcolm peered at Thomas through glassy eyes. "Of course, no magic or spell comes with a guarantee. You must be preparing to face a very strong witch to need this. I'll do my best, but you better think long and hard about whether or not you need to confront this demon."

"It's no demon, but a friend. And I assure you I have no choice."

"Then I need you to close your eyes and wait. You'll feel funny, almost drunk and very lightweight. Keep your eyes shut and don't move until I give the word. I'm sure Xavier is worth it."

Thomas wanted to question how he knew Xavier's name, but the light-headedness had already begun. The room felt like it swayed under Thomas and a rainbow of lights flashed before his eyelids. He wondered if his body lifted out of its seat, and at the very thought, he felt the cushioned chair beneath him again. A wave of heat hit Thomas in the face, and then everything became still. Thomas entered a different realm. Away from Charleston. Away from earth. He floated in total darkness, yet unafraid and wrapped in a cocoon of protection.

"Open your eyes."

Thomas looked around and took a moment to regain his senses. The drifting sensations of moments ago had passed. He felt like himself, with nothing wrong or different.

Malcolm got out of his chair and told Thomas he could go.

"I don't feel any change. How do I enact the charm? Are you sure it worked? This is important."

"The charm worked. You shouldn't feel different, or it would signal to the witch you were protected. When you need protection, *it* will know. Harriet's waiting."

Thomas walked to the door but paused before going out. "How did you know?"

"I met him. You wear him on your sleeve, the same aura."

Thomas closed the door behind him and greeted Harriet. "I'll be going now."

"Don't hurt Anthony if you can help it. He's a good vampire. A gentle, caring soul. A good man. He wouldn't be doing all of this if he didn't think he had to."

Thomas kissed Harriet on the cheek and walked away. He did know about Anthony but was grateful for the reminder. They were all trapped in a game, not just Xavier and Thomas.

The old man had sensed Xavier's very essence on Thomas. How was such a thing possible? For the first time in months, Thomas smiled.

Part Eight

Discovery

Thirty-Four: Slave Rebellion

8 JUNE 1822
Charleston, South Carolina

Xavier clutched Michel's medal in his hand as he walked at a brisk pace through the free black community in Charleston on his way to see Denmark Vesey. Leaving Catherine behind tonight pained him because they had once again parted with an argument. She wanted to hunt, feeling drained and in need of blood. When Xavier suggested they do so after he finished his business, she'd balked.

"We've done 'business' every night for several weeks. We have to feed, or we'll get too weak. We have to enjoy ourselves, too, or this becomes too much."

"I'm sure the slaves feel it's too much every day too," Xavier snapped. "No doubt Duncan thinks the same thing but can't get away from his captor."

Catherine stomped her foot. "This has got to stop. It's making you crazy again. You've replaced an addiction to wine with an addiction to this cause. We need to reconsider. Let's get Thomas's help."

"This argument again? I'll tell you what. You take a night off. You go do what you need to do, and I'll do what I *have* to do. But I don't want to rehash everything. Going to Thomas at this point is out of the question." Xavier slammed the door behind him, and Catherine didn't follow.

Of late, she pushed more and more for them to get Thomas involved, and more than once, Catherine pleaded with Xavier to go back to Europe and forget the whole crusade to find Duncan. She had broken down in tears a few nights ago, afraid the Council would kill Xavier, afraid she was powerless to stop it.

As much as he might wish to put an end to it all and flee to Thomas, Xavier had to finish what he'd started. What further proof did he need of his divine calling than the bald spot on his head where St. Michel seared a brand onto him or the hard medal in his hands, off Michel's chest straight from heaven?

Perhaps he *had* become addicted to his quest. But Anne once saved him from himself, from drinking, and a life of utter misery. If it took another addiction to repay her, so be it. At least he saved enslaved souls in the process. At least in trying to free Duncan he could exact justice for the innocent.

He stood outside Denmark Vesey's, having returned to fulfill his latest and last promise to Malcolm. Xavier loathed the idea of the slave insurrection and thought it doomed to failure, more than ever before. Yet a pact was a pact, and Malcolm insisted upon Xavier doing the visit.

Xavier glanced around and went to the back of the house. Seeing no one, he leaped to the roof and stomped across it like on his first visit. When he crashed through the bedroom window, he found Denmark and Gullah Jack waiting for him.

"We sensed your approach," Gullah Jack said. "The angel returning with his message."

Xavier winced at the sacrilege. "No angel, I assure you. Just coming upon my business. Are you preparing?"

"Yes." Denmark nodded. "I have a whole army of folks following me. We've been stockpiling arms in secret. We're gathering help. We'll be ready to get this done, in honor of the Bastille! In honor of all people enslaved all over the world. Tell God. We'll be ready."

Xavier walked over to where Denmark and Gullah Jack knelt before him. He helped each to their feet and then stared back and forth into each of their eyes. "No one deserves slavery. Your hearts are in the right place. If, however, at any time you think you may fail, if you ever fear getting too many innocent people slaughtered in the process, you can reverse course."

Denmark tilted his head and furrowed his brow. "I thought you urged us on? I thought God sanctioned this?"

Xavier struggled to respond. He went too far in his last statement, knowing it violated his agreement with Malcolm. He had to make things right, to appease his own conscience but without betraying his promise to Malcolm. "I want you to succeed. God doesn't want slavery to continue. We know, in our hearts if nothing else. God wants to protect all people from harm."

Xavier patted each man on the shoulder. "Here." He handed them a small slip of paper with an address on it. "Go there. Here's the key. You'll find more arms for your mission." Xavier spun around and launched himself out the window and ran down the street, disappearing from their view in mere seconds. If they insisted upon their fool's errand, he wanted them to at least have as many weapons as possible. The small stockpile he'd squirreled away for them might help.

Xavier wanted to do more, but Malcolm's small slip of magical paper warned against it. He dug it out of his pocket one more time to check.

"Patience. Tomorrow."

Without any other options, Xavier decided Catherine was right; he needed to feed. He meandered toward the center of town where loud revelers drank and sang in bars. Around a corner, barely concealed from the main street, if at all, he found a young white man lifting the skirt of a black woman.

"Please don't, master. What would your father say?"

"He'd say it was time I took my pleasure with the whore."

"I raised you. Please." Though she beseeched him to stop, she made no attempt to resist as he pulled his pants down, and Xavier saw his white ass in the moonlight.

Xavier grabbed the youth from behind and spun him around. Snatching him by the hair with one hand and grabbing an arm with his other hand, Xavier yanked his head back and sank his fangs into the soft skin of his neck. The blood flowed down Xavier's throat, intoxicating him with the man's story of tormenting slaves and raping women. Lost in his hunger, Xavier almost failed to hear the running footsteps or the screaming woman he saved.

He looked up to see her pounding on him to stop as she yelled at the top of her lungs. A gang of men stormed toward him, so Xavier flung the body aside and ran the other way. He wanted to use his vampiric speed but thought better of it, knowing it would give away his true nature. Of course, hadn't he already done that right in front of her by drinking the man's blood? But a larger audience came at him. He ran a few blocks with them trailing behind until he turned a corner and raced away down an abandoned street. By the time the mob got there, he was out of sight.

Back in their quarters, Xavier fell into a chair. Why had he become so careless? The sight of the man, no more than in his late teens, raping the poor helpless woman got to

Xavier. Catherine warned him the other night he started to act the part of God. Her accusation offended him, but perhaps she was right? Perhaps he had become too careless. He had to get ahold of himself and maybe protect Catherine in the process.

He hoped that the note in his pocket was correct. If so, they could end it all tomorrow and go back to Europe and away from slavery because Xavier found it almost impossible to control himself anymore. Grabbing the small sheet from his pocket again, Xavier asked it for assurance.

"Tomorrow. Freedom."

Thirty-Five: Liberating Duncan

9 JUNE 1822
Charleston, SC

Xavier woke confused and worried about his increasing rift with Catherine. She pouted around their rooms after returning the night before and going to her crate without saying a word to him. He had enough to cope with, being away from Thomas, searching for Duncan, and the trouble he got them into because of freeing the slaves. He could not deal with Catherine being angry with him too. As he dressed for the evening, he determined to reconcile with her.

Putting Michel's medal in his pocket, he glanced at Malcolm's sheet of paper with wide eyes. It had a Charleston address on it and nothing else. Based on its messages from yesterday, it had to be the location where they would find Duncan. Perhaps he and Catherine neared the end of their task, and he could appease her sooner than anticipated.

Xavier hurried into the front room and found Catherine writing letters. She looked up and smiled at him, sending a wave of relief through his body. "Look at this," he said as he placed the paper in front of her. She looked at it and then at his face, as if trying to read him. "It has to be where they have Duncan."

"Do we know for sure?" Catherine dropped her quill and stood up. "What does this mean?"

"Well, it doesn't say much. But whatever puts the messages on this paper, whatever magic Malcolm used, he attuned it to our quest for Duncan. It's given solid advice and guidance since we got it. Whatever the paper means this time, it wants us to go to this address."

"Then let's go." Catherine hurried about the room, gathering a few items and adjusting her appearance to a proper Southern woman. She spun around in her hoop skirt and laughed. "These are hideous, aren't they?"

"You could hide a lot of stuff under there."

"Maybe I should put Duncan in there. No one would dare spy under a lady's dress for a missing black man."

When she finished sashaying around the room, Xavier went over and hugged her. "I need you, now, more than ever. Please don't be angry with me. Please."

Catherine nodded. "I can never stay angry with you, anyway. I just worry. You know that. Besides, it may end tonight. Promise if we free Duncan, you'll leave with me tonight. We'll find Thomas."

"I promise. Do you need to feed before we go? You can't be weak tonight."

"I should. Will you join me?"

"No. I'm too nervous. I'll wait here."

Catherine kissed him on the cheek and headed out. Xavier examined a shelf of books when a knock came on the door. He was surprised to see Harriet on the other side. They greeted warmly, but her serious expression alarmed Xavier. "What is it?" he asked.

"I got here last night and have been waiting to see you alone. I need to tell you something."

Xavier ushered her into the room and sat next to her on the couch. When she finished her story, Xavier nodded. Then they hurried Harriet out the door, before Catherine returned.

"Better?" Xavier asked.

"Yes. Much." Catherine grabbed Xavier's face in both hands. "What's wrong? You look pale."

"I'm dead. It does awful things to one's complexion."

"Stop it." Catherine squeezed his cheeks harder. "You know what I mean. Are you ill?" She tugged his face from one side to the other, examining him like a prized horse, until he reached up and stopped her.

"I'm fine. I already told you I'm nervous. And anxious to get to this address."

Charleston already sweltered with heat and humidity despite it being June. Though not affected by the weather himself, Xavier saw it in the scowling and sweating faces of the men they passed as he and Catherine walked through town toward their destination. They arrived outside a large home in the center of town, surrounded by a gate but with no sign of life in it.

"This is it," he said and walked back and forth, wondering what to do. It stood two stories tall, with a balcony wrapped around the entire second floor. The windows were all shuttered.

Catherine stared at the house through squinted eyes. "It's rather abandoned for this time of night. Odd. Not even a servant in sight."

"They have it shuttered. They could be hiding in there. If the magic on the paper brought us here, perhaps the magic she knows warned them in advance of our approach. We have to be very careful."

"She could be watching us right now." Catherine reached into her pocket and held up the charm Harriet had given her. "Do you have your talisman? Harriet said it would protect us against her spells."

Xavier remembered the last time the woman saw him, after Malcolm led him to another home where she had Duncan and later abandoned her husband. He recalled how he walked about feeling human again and very ill after seeing a woman's figure in the window. He had lost his bearings. She would be more desperate, and more on guard. He held his talisman up to Catherine and then tucked it back into his pocket.

"We'll need to surprise them."

Catherine laughed. "Anything else obvious to report? Perhaps you should remind me it's night out? Your observation doesn't give me much direction."

"Don't tease me. You'll make it worse." Xavier had nothing else to say. No plan of action. No theory on what to do next. "When I saw the address, I wanted to get over here fast. I didn't get any further with my thinking. Thomas would kill me right now."

"Let's try this." When Catherine finished explaining her idea to Xavier, he nodded and sprang into action by speeding around to the back of the house. He spied on the slave quarters but found all of them inside, eating together and locked in their rooms from the outside. He returned to the Big House and counted out a few more seconds until he knew Catherine would have begun her part too. He climbed onto the second floor balcony and entered the house.

Nothing made a sound. He inched his way through the darkness into the hallway, where he found Catherine coming out of another room. She shook her head, so they searched the other three second-floor rooms but found them all unoccupied.

Stepping down the stairs, Xavier listened for any sign of habitation but heard nothing. Finding the first floor empty, they headed for a cellar door, open inside a serving area at the back of the house. Below, the faint light of a candle glowed and beckoned for them. Xavier led the way down, with Catherine following him with her hand on his back.

Xavier realized they'd lost any element of surprise because the mistress waited for them in a dungeon-like room full of implements used in torture and other items that looked like elaborate sex toys. With his wrists tied to an overhead beam, Duncan stood naked in the middle of the room.

"I'm pleased to meet you at long last." The woman bowed in mock deference as Xavier and Catherine walked into the cellar. Before either could react, she raised a knife in her hand and held it in front of Duncan's throat. "Don't try anything, or he dies." With her free hand, she felt down the side of his body and reached around to grab his erect penis. Duncan's glassy eyes revealed the trance under which she controlled him. "I'm Matilda. And who are you?"

"I don't think pleasantries are necessary"—Catherine stepped in front of Xavier but kept her distance from Matilda—"or desired."

Matilda laughed, sounding like a crazed asylum inmate. Nothing about her demeanor, words, or appearance seemed sane to Xavier. He was thankful Catherine took over. Reaching into his pockets, he clutched Michel's medal in one hand and the talisman from Harriet in the other. His slip of paper fell out of his pocket as he pulled the items out. The paper glowed a golden yellow with no wording on the floor beneath him.

"You killed my dear friend, and we had such a nice arrangement. Do you know how difficult it was to find a vampire to cooperate with me? Perhaps the two of you would like to take his place? Imagine the power the three of us could have. My magic." Matilda placed a hand over her heart. "Your abilities." She gestured toward the two of them. "Instead of one vampire, two. Why, we could rule the South. You both seem so much smarter than he was. Because he was black, don't you think? I imagine it's the same among vampires. The white vampires are far superior to the black ones? Maybe not in sex, but in intelligence."

As she spoke, Xavier spotted three other white women cowering in a far corner in fear. Were they slaves to Matilda too? Accomplices? They gave no threatening aura, but Xavier kept his eyes on them.

It was Catherine's turn to laugh. "What a charming proposition. Join forces with a madwoman and exploit people for sex. Care nothing about anything other than yourself. But that's not in our plans."

Matilda sneered. "You wouldn't want to take a ride on this?" She flicked Duncan's penis. Xavier grimaced when she leaned over and licked it, moving the knife to threaten his scrotum. "Why, he's almost white." She stood and put the knife back at his throat. Duncan hung there, as if he had taken leave of his senses.

"Give him up and we'll leave." Catherine spread her arms before her and clapped her hands together. "We'll be gone and out of your way in seconds."

Matilda disliked the idea, for she reached into her pocket and chanted a spell as she flung white powder about the room. The talismans from Harriet did their job, for nothing affected either Catherine or Xavier, both of whom sprang into action.

Matilda dropped her knife, perhaps self-assured her spells would work. Catherine launched across the room and grabbed Matilda around the waist, dropping her to the floor. Matilda may have counteracted Catherine's power with her next move if Xavier hadn't seen it. She clutched a small hat pin in her hand with blood dripping from the tip. Before Matilda could jab it into Catherine, Xavier stepped on her arm and held it there. Matilda shrieked in terror and tried to thrash about, to no avail.

As Catherine sank her fangs into Matilda's neck and drained her blood, Xavier kept watch over the three women still hiding in the corner, but they made no move whatsoever.

Xavier knew Matilda died before Catherine even finished drinking her blood when Duncan cried out and yanked at the leather straps attached to the ceiling. After getting him to stop wriggling around, Xavier unhooked him, then wrapped Duncan in his coat. The poor young man shook and glanced around, afraid.

"You're safe. We'll protect you." Duncan pulled away from Xavier, his eyes wide with terror. "Your grandmother sent me. Anne Hébert. Duncan, listen to me. You're safe."

"You knew my grandmother?" Duncan's deep baritone sounded confused.

Xavier held Duncan by both shoulders in front of him. The glazed and fearful look gave way to comprehension over the next few minutes.

"Yes. In France. She was a dear friend. She knew what happened to you and sent us to help. We're here to free you."

Duncan slumped to the ground and wept. Hearing his cries of relief and despair, Xavier cried too. He wiped at the blood tears to try to conceal them, afraid any more trauma would send Duncan into a fit of insanity. When he got his own emotions under control, Xavier sat and wrapped Duncan in his arms.

After everything, after all he had done in freeing other slaves, running away from Thomas, violating the ethic, and risking Catherine's and his lives, it all came to an abrupt end.

He wondered if he would feel better had Matilda put up a better fight. Or if she had done something more innovative than capture innocent people to become her sex slaves. It all seemed too dull, too mundane for what Xavier risked.

Catherine went over and pulled the three cowering women out of hiding. They confessed they assisted Matilda because she promised them a fortune. If they disobeyed, she would turn them into the authorities or have them killed. Two of their friends met such a fate already.

When Duncan stopped sobbing, Catherine and Xavier moved the three women and Duncan upstairs to a grand banquet hall.

Xavier whispered reassurances to Duncan the entire way. Before they did anything else, he sat in a quiet corner with Duncan, trying to gauge whether or not Duncan could proceed or if he remained too emotional. All of those years of counseling his parishioners in Paris came back to help Xavier. When Duncan asked more questions about his grandmother, he seemed to be on the mend or at least stabilized.

"Can you continue?" Xavier asked him.

"I don't want to speak of it. I know I'm not well yet. I may never be. I have to move on. I have to keep going." Duncan sat up straight in the chair, glaring straight ahead.

Xavier hugged him again, then rushed upstairs and found Duncan appropriate clothing. After giving them to the young man, Xavier headed outside to the back of the house. There, he unlocked the door to the slave quarters and undid the shackles of a few who were chained to the wall. He freed all the slaves owned by Matilda and instructed them to wait for him right there, to avoid detection. He promised to take each of them to New York City.

Back inside, Xavier asked Catherine to organize the household and all of the people, while he arranged for transportation. After asking around among the slaves and free black people milling around the port for a safe shipper to engage, Xavier paid a Northern captain three times the cost of a full load to smuggle a group of free blacks to New York. The man balked, afraid capture would lead to his death. "Those aren't free blacks you want me to transport, are they?"

"Do you believe in vampires?"

The old man laughed hard at Xavier and spit on the ground. "Get the hell outta here, you crazy idiot."

Xavier opened his mouth and descended his fangs. With one motion, he moved next to the captain and grabbed his wrists. The man struggled to get away, to no avail. Xavier released him. "Still don't believe?"

"So what do you want? Go ahead, kill me."

Xavier shook his head. "I told you already. Passage for my friends. Their master died this evening, freeing each of them. A free black man and my sister will be accompanying them on your ship. She's like me, and will protect you from any threat. I'll see you get safely out of Charleston with her, and then she and Duncan will take you the rest of the way."

"I suppose I don't got any other choice. You going to give me the money anyway?"

"I'm a man of my word. Here's half now." Xavier handed him half the money and then told him to ready the ship. Back at Matilda's, he found the group assembled. Catherine had told them of their plans to get a ship to take them to New York. All but the three women wanted to go. Southern by birth, they didn't want to leave, so Catherine tasted their blood to confirm the truth of their words and set them up to inherit Matilda's wealth, except the slaves, of course.

"Catherine, a word before we go?" Xavier motioned with his head for her to follow him upstairs.

"The boat and captain are ready." Xavier sat on a bed and had Catherine sit beside him. "I showed him I'm a vampire to convince him to do this. He knows you are, too, and you'll protect him."

"What if he decides to kill us through the day? Was that wise?"

"He won't, because I'm not going with you."

Catherine stood up. "We can't separate."

"Hear me out." Xavier reached for her hand. "I have to contact Thomas. It's time now. I'll write to him from here and tell him to meet us. In fact, Malcolm is going to use magic to get the letter there faster than by traditional means. He said he could dispatch it for me in less than a week. I need you to get Duncan to New York with the other slaves. The captain won't do anything to you, knowing I'm out there, waiting for revenge if he tries anything. I promise I'll be right here when you get back, waiting. Maybe Thomas will have arrived by then."

Catherine at least relaxed her posture but still stood in front of Xavier. She clutched his hand. "You'll write to him right away? And have him come here soon?"

"You have my word." Xavier held both of Catherine's hands.

"What else? What are you planning?"

Xavier shook his head. "No. I'll wait here, for you and Thomas." He hated yet another deception of those he loved, but once again, his quest demanded it.

Catherine agreed, so they headed back downstairs and arranged for the slaves to get to the wharf and waiting ship. They had to go separately, lest a band of twenty black people marching through Charleston attract too much attention.

Duncan and five others went one at a time, with fake papers from Matilda sending them on an errand in case anyone stopped them along the way. Catherine took another six and Xavier the rest. Despite the tension, everybody arrived at the ship.

Xavier paid the captain the rest of the promised money. "There's more when you get to New York, if everyone arrives safely. If not, you'll die." The captain shot Xavier an alarmed look. Xavier nodded. "You heard me. If anything happens to anyone on this ship before they get to New York, I'll hunt you down and torture you for years before killing you. Understand?"

The captain nodded and Xavier left the ship. He hated threatening people but learned from Thomas you had to do things threatening to get what you wanted. No doubt the man and his crew would do everything in their power to get the ship and its cargo to New York City. Even without the threats, they stood to gain a large sum of money if successful.

On the dock, Xavier said goodbye to Duncan and vowed to send him money for his new organization. Duncan determined to create a new black abolitionist group, and Xavier and Catherine promised to fund it and a full salary for Duncan.

Once alone, he hugged Catherine. "Take care of them."

"I will." Catherine patted Xavier on the shoulder. "You'll be here?"

Xavier nodded and watched Catherine head up the gangplank. Once she was on board, the captain shouted orders and the ship began to move away. Xavier waved to Catherine as the ship sailed into the darkened sea. The abandoned port had an eerie feel about it late at night after everyone left.

Watching it glide away, Xavier grimaced at once again having sent a loved one away with a lie. Yes, he would write to Thomas and Catherine. Yes, he wanted to wait here for her to return so they could be reunited with Thomas. He doubted, however, it would happen.

He did not flinch when Harriet strolled up beside him. "She's safe this way," she said.

Xavier nodded. "Thank you. For letting me protect her. I know it wasn't easy for you either, to let her go. And to not talk to her. She has no idea."

"You're a good man, abbé."

No one had called him by his official designation in a long time. "Abbé?"

"That's what Catherine said they used to call you, isn't it? Their abbé? For doing all those things for the people of France. Looks like the abbé came to America to help. And protected his sister in the process. I think we can get the Council to leave her alone. If you confess everything to Anthony."

"You told me he was here? Where?"

"Tomorrow night. I'll take you to him."

Xavier considered for a moment. "You were supposed to inform on me. I know why you don't want to. But we could protect you too. We could arrange for you to discover me tomorrow night. Then you take me to Anthony and you'll be free too. Free to leave. Free to continue doing *your* work among the slaves."

"You'd do that for me?" A blood tear appeared at the corner of Harriet's eye.

"Of course. Tomorrow you'll turn me in. And I'll accept my punishment, so long as Anthony can get the Council to promise not to punish Thomas or Catherine."

Thirty-Six: Double Cross

10 JUNE 1822
Charleston, South Carolina

The following night, after cleaning their quarters and preparing to leave, a strange calm overcame Xavier. He thought being caught would make him panic or be fearful, but after all these months of running and hiding, he needed to face his fate. He was ready, relieved to know he would meet Anthony tonight.

With his time before Harriet arrived, Xavier went back to Matilda's house. Last night's events felt so anticlimactic he wanted to see the place again, especially the chains that tortured so many victims. Back in the basement cellar, Xavier saw the blood on the walls and floor. He sensed the vile acts perpetrated against innocent people and almost vomited when exploring the attic and discovering a dozen decaying bodies. No, he had done the right thing. He didn't need a grand finale to know.

Checking in the cellar one last time he spotted his talisman on the floor, next to the slip of paper from Malcolm. Reaching down to pick them up, he jumped back when both items burst into flames. He smiled as he climbed back to the first floor and returned to his quarters to wait for Harriet. Even the artifacts knew Xavier had finished his quest. Perhaps their combustion provided the divine signal Xavier longed for, which ended his mission.

Next, Xavier sat at the desk with a heavy heart and took paper and quill in hand. Whatever he managed to write would be inadequate, but he saw no other way to communicate with Thomas and Catherine.

My dearest Thomas and Catherine,

When I undertook this quest, I had no idea it would one day force me to pen this letter. I suppose I should have seen it coming, for it seems obvious now. St. Michel visited me. I'm sure. I can feel the bald spot on my head still, and Michel's medal sits on the desk next to me as I write. How could one deny a task given by God? Whether delusion or real, one must follow one's conscience. Though its leading me away from both of you pains me more than any words could ever convey.

I must face Anthony tonight. In doing so, I hope to protect both of you, who were innocent in this entire escapade. Neither of you deserve punishment for my deeds. If I am handed a prison sentence, then I will see you before long. A century or two for a vampire is nothing, right? I deserve whatever punishment the Council sees fit because I knowingly violated the ethic. Not for personal gain or glory, not out of defiance or disrespect for the Council and its rules. But I disobeyed, nonetheless. I deserve the same punishment anyone else would receive. If it means death, so be it. I accept such an outcome. And if that is my fate, know this:

Catherine, you are everything anyone could ever have wanted in a sister. I love you. Giving you the gift of vampirism at least repays a small part of what you've meant to me all these years. At least, take it as a token of my love and devotion. You are a wonderful person. Thank you. I love you.

Thomas, I don't know how to write everything you mean to me. My life. My love. My inspiration. My savior. God willing, I will be waiting in heaven should something ever strike you down. Know either way, my heart belongs to you and always has. No lover could offer his devotion more than you. At least my final years before this quest were spent in the utter bliss of your companionship and love.

With all my heart, Xavier.

Xavier anticipated tears but none came, though a sense of calm enveloped him. He said a prayer and then left the letter sealed on the desk, addressed to both Catherine and Thomas for whomever found it first. Then he penned a brief note to Thomas, asking him to come to Charleston. He hurried out the door and got the letter to Malcolm, who required no payment for the favor. He assured Xavier the letter would reach Pierre in Paris in a few days.

Xavier returned to his rooms to find Harriet sitting in a chair, looking out the window.

"He's waiting," she said and cast her eyes to the ground. "In the next room." She walked over to Xavier and hugged him. "Thank you."

Xavier kissed her on the cheek and watched her walk away. When she had gone, he straightened his coat and went next door, knocking. Anthony's authoritative voice answered from the other side and Xavier entered.

Xavier had no idea what to expect but found Anthony his usual, welcoming self. He wrapped his arms around Xavier and kissed him on the forehead. They sat and chatted for several minutes, as two friends catching up after a long but expected absence. When an uncomfortable silence fell between them, Xavier fumbled under his shirt to clutch his cross.

Anthony leaned forward and patted Xavier on the knee. "It means a lot you came of your own will. Without resistance. That will mean a lot to the Council too."

Xavier nodded without speaking.

"I hope you understand I love you. I cherish you as a dear friend. Anything I say or do while we go through this process comes from my duty as a member of the Vampire Council. I trusted you the minute Thomas brought you into my life, often more than I trust him. This hurts me. I hate it."

It was Xavier's turn to find words of comfort. "Of course I know. Or I wouldn't have come so easily. Peacefully, always. Easily, maybe not." Anthony laughed, making Xavier feel better. "There are two things we need to discuss before you determine my fate."

Anthony nodded. "What?"

"Catherine and Thomas. You have to let them go free. You have to convince the Council of their innocence. That's my one condition for surrendering to you."

"I'm not sure how much negotiating can be done." Anthony leaned forward and then rubbed his face in his hands. "Even if those two acted at your behest or to protect you, they engaged in the behavior of their own will. You didn't coerce them into cooperating."

"But I did." Xavier jumped out of his chair and walked back and forth in front of Anthony. "Thomas had no choice, believe me. I deceived him and disappeared, leaving him the impossible options of either betraying the Council or me. I suppose it's easy for others to insist the law ranks above a lover, but I don't think it's so easy. Catherine had a choice not to become a vampire, true. But she was human and not governed by the Vampire Council. What human would deny eternal life? Except she had, until I insisted I planned to violate the ethic with or without her. With her would be easier, and perhaps save my life. So then she allowed the transformation because of me. No, I left them little choice and manipulated them into the entire thing." Xavier positioned himself near the window, intending to launch out of it and attempt to flee if Anthony could not guarantee their safety.

Anthony remained seated. "If the Council allows this then others will attempt the same thing. The law must be solid, without question, or it endangers us all."

"Thank you for your candor." Xavier inched closer to the window. "I won't sentence them for my crimes. If I have to flee, I will."

Anthony stood and held his hands out in a gesture of peace. "Please, don't. Stay and talk." Xavier returned one step into the room, and Anthony backed away. "Can we begin by discussing your crimes and then worry about the other two?"

"I assume you know all my transgressions. What's to discuss?"

Anthony nodded. "Clarification."

"Again, I don't see the point."

"It wouldn't be fair to you to sentence you or bring your case before the Council without your having complete knowledge about what will guide their decision. You transformed a human to vampire without permission.

Fraternization with a family member who knew you in life exacerbates the crime. With a new vampire, you came to America and interfered in human affairs, time and again. You've risked exposing us all with your freeing of the slaves. So many of them know you, vampires, exist. You pursued Duncan, when humans had determined his fate, and along the way you killed one of our kind without sanction for doing it. I've already learned last night you freed Duncan and all the slaves in the house, again against the ethic. You told them about yourself as a vampire. Then you left three white women go free who know about you and Catherine." Anthony started to list more crimes, but Xavier stopped him.

"I admit all of those crimes."

"Worst of all, your interference in human endeavors has gotten worse and worse, instead of better. This plot you want to orchestrate with Denmark Vesey is pure insanity."

"Wait." Xavier held up his hand to stop Anthony. "I didn't choose the path for them. They plotted it all alone, without me. I think it's foolhardy and dangerous. I tried to talk Malcolm out of it."

"Yet in order to get information from him, you agreed to reveal yourself to Denmark and urged him on this path. Regardless of your reason, it's another deliberate intercession in human matters with the use of your vampiric powers."

Xavier nodded. "Again, I admit to all of this. Punish me for each and every one of those things. I still don't understand why this has to implicate Thomas and Catherine."

"I'm trying to explain you don't have much leverage."

Anthony took another step toward Xavier, who backed toward the window. As he contemplated jumping out of it,

Anne Hébert's ghost drifted into the room. Xavier almost fainted, and Anthony stood transfixed. They both stared at her as she glided across the room.

"Good evening, gentlemen." Anne's ghost laughed her deep, guttural laugh Xavier so loved in life. "You look like you've seen a ghost." Again she chortled as she moved between them and turned to Xavier. "I wanted to thank you for freeing Duncan. I meant to help along the way. But I could only do so much as a ghost. I had hoped for more power, but alas death has its limitations. I could stay with Duncan and protect him as best as possible or help you. I chose him."

Xavier began to speak but no words came to mind. She laughed even harder and then turned to Anthony. "I don't want to be here. I don't want to be a ghost. I have better things to do." Anthony stood immobile, surprising Xavier because he had never seen Anthony without his total command of a situation. "But I had to see my grandson freed, and now I have to help the one who did it. You don't intend to negotiate in good faith with him." Anne lowered her head and peered at Anthony.

"Xavier"—Anne's ghost said without taking her eyes off Anthony—"listen. Things aren't all as they appear. There are layers here you don't see."

"Please," Anthony interrupted her. "Don't."

Anne nodded at Anthony, staring hard at him. "Good." Xavier's head spun, not knowing what these two were talking about. Anne turned and stepped back so she could see both of them. "Anthony and I have business to discuss," she said to Xavier. "You best enact your plan and head out the window. If all goes well, you and Anthony can continue this dialogue tomorrow. Go!"

Anthony moved toward Xavier but Anne stepped in his way. Without waiting to see what she did or if she could slow Anthony down, Xavier dove through the window, shattering glass all around and then running into the night as fast as possible. He wound around in circles and went all over the place, as Thomas taught him to do when pursued by another vampire. Not until the sun began to emerge did he stop and find an abandoned cellar in which to hide himself.

Thirty-Seven: Surrender

11 JUNE 1822
Charleston, South Carolina

Xavier woke to the comforting sound of Anne's ghost laughing next to him. "Not a very safe place for a vampire to hide. I found you easy enough."

"I didn't have much time. Besides, you have an unfair advantage. You're a ghost." She did have a point, however, that he slept in a cellar but out in the open.

"I came to tell you I'll be going now." Anne's ghost headed for the cellar door. "I don't think you and I need another emotional goodbye. I don't think my heart could take it." She laughed.

"Wait! Where are you going? And what happened last night?"

"Oh, that." Anne turned around. "Don't you mind where I'm going. I won't be here anymore. I am tired of earth. Duncan's free and on his way to New York, so my work here is done. Last night, another complicated question. I compromised with Anthony, which included promising not to tell you everything I know. So here's the pertinent information I can tell you. Go back to him. Tonight. He's agreed Thomas and Catherine will go unpunished if you turn yourself in. So it's done. Best of luck to you."

"What did you mean, there are layers I can't see? About the Council?"

Anne shook her head. "I can't say a word."

Xavier nodded. "One more thing." Xavier stood and brushed himself off. "Do you know if Anthony can persuade the Council to agree with any deal I make with him? How can I know for sure?"

Anne hovered in front of him for several seconds before she answered. "The Council, interesting question. Here's what I can say. The Vampire Council agreed not to punish Thomas or Catherine, just you. They've already determined your sentence, which is why you need to go see Anthony. You won't be seeing anyone but him. And I wouldn't be sending you there if it meant your death or a betrayal of the promise to keep Thomas and Catherine out of it."

As fast as she appeared the night before, Anne vanished. Xavier still wondered at everything she said and had no idea how she managed to negotiate with Anthony and get the Vampire Council to agree to everything already. Yet her news lifted an enormous burden from Xavier's shoulders. Thomas and Catherine, free! And Xavier avoided death. As much as he wanted to focus on having protected Catherine and Thomas, he felt the most relief at his own survival.

He would have died for the cause, knowing Michel and all his family and friends waited for him in heaven. But he wanted to live. He wanted to know he would see his sister again, even if it took centuries. Xavier wept, hoping in the distant future he would again feel Thomas's strong arms wrap around him and hold him.

Xavier gathered his wits about him and returned to his rooms. He ripped up the letter he had written to Thomas and Catherine, replacing it with an explanation of what he knew about the sentence and telling them to find Anthony for more details. He assured them the Council would not punish either of them, and told them about Anne's guarantee of it. He professed his love over and over again but did not have to say a permanent goodbye.

Dressed in the proper clothes of a gentleman, Xavier glanced in the mirror and smiled. Relief flooded through him once again. He was safe. He'd spared Thomas and Catherine.

Xavier wondered where to meet Anthony when someone knocked on his door. A beautiful young male with bright-green eyes, red hair, and a chiseled body smiled and handed him a note. Xavier knew who enlisted such a beautiful specimen in his care before he saw Anthony's handwriting on the envelope.

The brief note asked Xavier to come to Anthony's room. Once he arrived next door, Xavier knocked and was surprised when Anthony himself answered and pulled Xavier into a hug. "I told you I loved you yesterday, and I meant it. Come in."

"I don't understand everything Anne told me." Xavier sat without concern, despite the gaps in his knowledge, trusting her.

Anthony nodded. He opened a bottle of wine and handed a glass to Xavier. "I suppose it seems odd to fraternize with your imprisoner."

"It should. But I'm comfortable. Anne said you convinced the Council not to punish Thomas or Catherine. What changed your mind? And theirs?"

"Anne's a good negotiator. I'll be frank. I can't tell you everything, but you deserve to know this much. When you came last night, I didn't see any way for you to negotiate with the Council. While I understood your point about their innocence, the rules are the rules. Anne, however, threatened to reveal certain information she came across and to help you escape. In the interest of expediting this matter and keeping the secret safe, I agreed to her demands. Besides, I trust you. I know you're a good soul." Anthony came over and sat next to Xavier. "All along, I agreed with you about Thomas and Catherine. Yet it violated the ethic to let them go unpunished. Given the circumstances, I'm glad it worked out the way it did."

"Is the Council in Charleston? Did they assemble here because of me?" Xavier still didn't understand how it all happened in one night, in a matter of hours, after he left and before the sun rose.

"I can't tell you about the Council's methods or modes of operating. Let's leave it at this. Thomas and Catherine will receive stern reprimands and warnings, but no prison time. They'll be monitored for a time. But you succeeded, with the help of a ghost, in negotiating for their protection. I assume she gave you your sentence as well?"

Xavier had not thought about it, other than the fact he avoided a death sentence. "I don't have to die. She said nothing else." Xavier choked on the last word and cried. Perhaps the emotion caught up to him or the realization about how close he came to death hit home. Anthony pulled him into a tight hug and patted the top of his head.

"It's okay. You're safe." Anthony held him for several more minutes before Xavier pulled away. "You have a bald spot on your head. I never noticed before."

Xavier took his turn to keep mystery between them. "It's a long story." Xavier poured more wine for both of them. "Thank you for pleading my case before the Council. I took advantage of our friendship because you're on it. I can never repay you."

"Perhaps you should wait to hear the sentence before you decide."

Xavier nodded. He fumbled for the cross under his shirt and prayed his gratitude for having survived the ordeal. Then he asked for strength going forward.

"Regardless of what happened last night, I would have pled for the Council's mercy in your case. I would never watch them send a friend to death without arguing against it. Unless you had done something egregious, I would fight with all my power against it. Your motive meant a great deal in this matter. Therefore, the Council judged against death and for a rather light sentence, given the number and severity of the crimes."

Anthony fell silent, which unnerved Xavier.

"How long?" Xavier took a deep breath, waiting to hear.

"One hundred years."

Xavier fell silent for several minutes. "A century." Longer than he had even walked the earth. Would Thomas feel the same about him, after all those years? Yet they spared him, and he owed it to Anthony to accept the sentence. "What's next?"

"I have to take you there, tonight."

Xavier stood to leave. "I'm ready."

Anthony hugged Xavier again. "I wish it were that easy. This has to be done in secret. I'm going to do something to you, but I promise it won't hurt."

Before Xavier could respond, Anthony motioned at him and chanted. Xavier lost consciousness but had the sensation of being carried over miles and miles. He had no idea how long it took—hours? days? weeks?—but he regained consciousness inside an enormous cave.

"Where am I? How did we get here? What did you do to me?"

"I carried you here." Anthony put his hand on Xavier's back. "I'm sorry. I used vampire magic to subdue you to maintain the secrecy of this place. You're deep inside a mountain, inaccessible to humans. This is where we imprison vampires."

Xavier glanced around at the pit of fire, the enormous hole leading deep into the bowels of the earth, and the black iron boxes hovering about it. Torches high above illuminated everything. The chamber had an eerie quality. "Will I be put in one of those boxes?"

"I'm afraid so."

"Then let's get it done. So I can be free sooner." Xavier shook as Anthony moved one of the boxes from over the pit to right in front of him. The lid opened of its own accord. It looked like a gigantic, iron coffin. Anthony motioned for him to get in, and Xavier complied. "Will I be put into another trance?"

"No." Anthony shook his head. "It's part of the punishment."

The lid descended with a creak, but Xavier screamed for Anthony to wait. The lid lifted again, and Anthony peered inside. Xavier saw a blood tear trickle down his cheek.

"Will you do one more thing for me?"

Anthony wiped the tear from his cheek. "What?"

"Tell Thomas to wait for me. Tell him I want him to wait for me."

Anthony nodded and then stepped away. The lid clamped down, leaving Xavier in total darkness. He had the sensation of moving again, then felt the faint hint of heat below. In total darkness, he wondered what to do with his mind for the next hundred years. Could he maintain his sanity?

Part Nine

Revelation, Confrontation

Thirty-Eight: Finding Catherine

17 JUNE 1822
Charleston, South Carolina

Thomas trembled at the three letters in his hand. One he received two days before, dispatched from his New York office to his people in Charleston. Catherine had sent word to meet her in Charleston, giving an exact location. She'd reached out to him a number of times, each time sounding more and more desperate, but they never figured out a way to find each other. To try to end the game of cat and mouse, Thomas told her to use his American addresses because it eliminated the need for every letter to move back and forth across the ocean before he got it. Her latest note promised to wait there until Thomas arrived, and the other two letters he held gave him hope at last he would find Xavier and Catherine.

The first came from Paris, with Pierre apologizing for how he sent the correspondence to Thomas. Thomas had been sitting in a bar, asking questions of anyone and everyone in an attempt to find out if they had seen anyone like Xavier. His temper boiled each time he ran into another dead-end. His heart ached a little more with every passing night without Xavier. As he contemplated whom to feed off, if anything, to take out his aggression on a worthy victim, a small golden orb floated in front of him.

Without knowing why, Thomas followed it into the street and down a darkened alley, where the orb fluttered into his hands. The instant it touched his skin, it transformed into two letters.

My Dearest Master,

I am overstepping my bounds with this dispatch, but in my humble opinion with good reason. Allow me to explain myself. In copying the letters from America to you, I have sensed the urgency of finding Xavier, to no avail thus far. At last, getting the letter from him we awaited, I panicked at how long it would take to get word to you. I therefore enlisted a sorcerer, long known to my family, to send these letters by magic across the ocean in but a day. I pray forgiveness if this offends you. Heaven forbid the magic fails and this never gets to you. As a precaution, I am also copying it and sending it via traditional dispatch. I hope you can forgive my boldness. I would like to note, too, Xavier's letter arrived by means other than traditional dispatch. I suspect he, too, used sorcery to get it to me. More than anything, I hope you find Master Xavier soon.

In your service, Pierre

Thomas admired Pierre all the more for the daring step, because his instincts proved right once again. In the second letter, Xavier himself asked Thomas to come meet Catherine and him, giving the same address Catherine had in her letter. As he raced out of the alley to head to the location, once he got the two letters from Pierre, a courier hurried after him with the letter from Catherine, stating Thomas's hired man in Charleston paid him to track down Thomas. Three letters, two of which had the same address and message, all came to Thomas in the span of ten minutes. His heart beat with anticipation.

As he neared the address, the trembling in his hands started. He slowed as he walked toward the hotel, knowing his tan skin and black clothing caused people to look at him enough without his drawing more attention to himself by running around everywhere. He took a deep breath and walked into the establishment. Without as much as a glance at anyone, he strode up the stairs and walked down the hall, knocking on the room indicated in both letters.

Thomas's entire body shook with anticipation, fear, and worry. What would he say to Xavier? How would his lover react to seeing him after such a long time?

When Catherine answered the door, she pulled Thomas into a hug. They said nothing. Thomas felt the strength of her grasp around his waist, even stronger than a typical vampire, and marveled at how good she looked since last he saw her as an old, failing woman.

His awe at her vampirism dissipated when he scanned the room and found no sign of Xavier. "Where is he?"

Catherine pulled away and shook her head. Blood tears clouded the corner of her eyes.

Thomas's heart raced. "Tell me."

Catherine took a deep breath but the blood tears streamed down her face. Unable to talk, she walked over to a desk and handed Thomas a letter. He recognized Xavier's dignified script and nearly fainted as he read the words. Xavier sacrificed himself to protect Catherine and Thomas. He gave himself over to Anthony and the Vampire Council, all to accept a punishment he thought he deserved if the Council promised to leave Thomas and Catherine alone.

Thomas crumpled the letter in his hands as the anger pulsed through his body. "What happened? Speak to me. Do you know anything else?"

She shook her head. "He sent me away. Like a fool, I trusted him. We found Duncan and needed to help him and the others escape to New York. Xavier sent me on the boat with them in order to safeguard their passage. As soon as we got there, I raced back to Charleston but too late. He got rid of me so he could do this. That's all I know. He succeeded in his mission and then worked to protect us. I could kill him." Catherine laughed despite herself as she wiped at her tears.

Thomas walked over and pulled her into another hug.

"What will we do?" She sobbed into his chest, as if trying to release a huge burden for the first time in ages. Thomas felt the same emotion. He hid his angst and kept all his worry to himself for all these months, but having Catherine with him eased the burden of secrecy because she felt the same way. At least someone else understood and would work toward the same goal.

"We have to find him," Thomas said as he rubbed away a blood tear. "It's not the first time in our lives we've had to search the entire earth for him, without a clue as to his whereabouts."

"How could we ever find him? The Council issued their judgment. I'm sure Anthony took him away. Do you think he'll help?"

Catherine's words spurred Thomas. "No." He shook his head. "Anthony would just as soon sentence us for our crimes than help us free Xavier. He's too wedded to the Council. But I think I know where they took him. Come, we have to go."

Thomas allowed Catherine to gather herself, then insisted they both feed before leaving Charleston to embark on a long journey that would require as much strength as possible. Thomas hoped the spell Malcolm placed on him could hold out against Anthony's vampire magic as he told Catherine they were heading toward the Rocky Mountains, far into the American West.

Thirty-Nine: Xavier's Cell

18 JUNE 1822
Rocky Mountains

The sunrise approached by the time Thomas and Catherine got to the base of the Rocky Mountains, and Thomas retraced the steps he had taken with Anthony to where they went up into the mountains. Not knowing where Anthony had gone or what he intended to do, Thomas avoided the caves and locations they used together, instead finding an abandoned shack in the foothills and digging a deep hole into the ground, where he and Catherine slept through the day.

Even before the sun disappeared, Thomas woke and nudged Catherine. "We should get going."

She nodded, pulled herself out of the underground cave, and straightened her clothes as best as possible. "*Where* are we going? What are we *doing*?"

"We don't have time." Thomas started to walk away.

Catherine grabbed Thomas's arm and pulled him back to her. "Your impatience won't accomplish anything. You have to tell me what's going on. Look, you're turning bright red and clenching your fists like you want to punch me in the face. Will that help? Or is your rage so intense I have to wonder if you'll assault Xavier again in the process?"

Her words stung but worked. Thomas took a deep breath and nodded. He would never forget the night he'd slapped Xavier and almost lost him forever. "That will *never* happen again."

"So you've said. But your irrational anger isn't going to help us tonight, regardless of where you direct it."

"I'm not mad at him. Or you. It's the Council." Thomas touched Catherine on the arm and patted her hand. "Their arbitrary rules have always bugged me. And the secrecy drives me nuts. Why can't they be open about who they are? Why do they make all of their edicts and verdicts in secrecy? It seems disingenuous at best, deceitful at worst—a power play on their part."

"I agree. I've wondered throughout this ordeal why they couldn't at least hear Xavier out and take his motivation into account when they determined his fate. This cloak and dagger way of acting makes vampires resent their rules."

At last, Thomas thought, someone agreed with his point of view. Anthony, of course, always defended the Vampire Council. And Xavier seldom questioned them. He claimed it was because they were a reality and he and Thomas could do nothing about it, so why challenge the system and risk being put in prison? Thomas, however, suspected more lay behind Xavier's attitude. He thought Xavier replaced the Vatican with the Vampire Council in his life, to give him rules, structure, and principles to follow.

Thomas and Catherine walked toward an enormous pine tree. Thomas touched the bark, feeling the energy of the tree as it stood tall against the elements.

"And Anthony?" Catherine linked her arm through Thomas's and pulled him forward again. "You haven't said a word about him since you found me. I thought you two searched for Xavier together."

As briefly as possible, Thomas told Catherine the entire story of how he concealed the truth from Anthony until his friend admitted what he knew, about how they argued, about their parting company because they worked toward opposite ends. "So, yes. I'm mad at him for doing this to Xavier and for not doing more to try to convince the Council not to punish him. This could get ugly between us."

Catherine grinned. "Whatever happens, I'm on your side. Now, tell me. Where are we going?"

Thomas described the vampire prison as they quickened their pace up the mountain, watching as they journeyed for any signs of humanity, or worse—another vampire.

"And you're sure this is where they took him?" asked Catherine.

"No, I'm not. It's my best guess. I don't have anything else to go on. That's the whole plan: we go see if they took him here and find out if we can free him."

"But you have no idea how to do it? And we could face vampire magic?"

Thomas nodded, wondering if Catherine would stop them again and preach about the lunacy of their mission. Instead she trudged along.

Thomas moved fast but with deliberation after he described it all to Catherine. He went as fast as possible to see if they imprisoned Xavier but without complete vampiric speed for fear he would get them lost in the mountains. As they wound their way up the mountainside along the river bed, Catherine asked of Thomas the same questions he had of Anthony during his first journey here.

"Are we lost?"

"I recognize all of this," Thomas answered and grabbed her hand.

"Who would live in this desolate place?"

Thomas laughed. "No one. It's awful. Which makes it the perfect place for a vampire prison."

When they reached the clearing where Thomas once waited for Anthony, Thomas pulled them to a stop. There in the forest lay the mountain lion he had seen on his first visit. Catherine crouched, ready to take action, but with a wave of his hand Thomas calmed her.

Thomas stepped forward, staring into the eyes of the magnificent beast. She got up and took a few steps toward Thomas. Then, to Thomas's shock, she bowed before him by placing her front paws out in front of her and arching her hind quarters high into the air, with her regal head laying between her front paws on the ground. His mother's grandfather, the spiritual leader of his tribe, taught humans were connected to nature and the animals around them, and while Thomas always respected that point of view, he never before experienced it with such force. The wild cat imagined in her head she could tear any human from limb to limb but seemed to tell Thomas she welcomed him to her territory; the spirits sanctioned his mission.

When she turned and ran full speed in the other direction, Thomas laughed. With such spiritual ruminations, he almost sounded more like Xavier in his own mind than himself.

"What's so funny? That thing terrified me." Catherine returned to his side and pointed in the direction the mountain lion had just left.

"Nothing. I started to have delusions of grandeur because of her. I saw the animal last time when Anthony brought me here. She's magnificent, isn't she?"

"And deadly."

"You're a vampire now, remember? We could have leaped into a tree and out of her reach in less than a second. Even if she landed on us, we could choke the life out of her and heal in mere seconds. Come on. We're almost there."

Thomas led them the rest of the way, past the line where trees no longer grew, around a great bend, and deep into an area where the snow had yet to begin to melt. A slight depression in a drift told Thomas where to begin digging because the snow around it had been moved recently. Before he submerged them in the snow, he turned to Catherine. "Don't be scared. It's rather frightening at first, but there's nothing to worry about."

She nodded and helped him continue digging with her jaw clenched. They reached the enormous boulder soon enough and shoved it aside, gaining access to the tunnel leading down toward the prison. The hair on Thomas's arms stood straight up when they walked into it because the torches illuminating the way were already lit, and he could see the faint glow of light from the opening into the large cavern and fire pit. Someone was already there.

Catherine put the stone back in place and turned to speak to Thomas, but he quieted her, with a finger to his lips, before she said anything. He motioned for her to follow, so they crept down the passage, trying not to make noise, though Thomas suspected whomever guarded the iron boxes had magical abilities and already detected their arrival.

The closer he came to the chamber, the more his blood boiled at the thought of Anthony having forced Xavier into one of those boxes. He imagined Xavier's fear at hovering over the fire for an unthinkable amount of time, all because he tried to help a person.

When Thomas rounded the corner and saw Anthony standing there as if waiting for him, he wanted to run over and punch him in the face.

With a soft touch on his back, Catherine calmed Thomas. Her gesture reminded him of their goal, of what they needed to achieve, and signaled any rash move would reveal to Anthony too soon that Thomas had immunity from his vampire magic. Thomas took a deep breath and unclenched his fists, knowing he had to play the game to perfection for Xavier's sake.

Anthony stood across the way, neither smiling a welcome nor glaring a warning. In control. Calm. Assured of his rightness. The Anthony Thomas always admired, respected, and loved, until all of those characteristics came crashing down on Xavier's head.

Catherine stepped forward, as always, taking command of awkward situations. "Anthony," she bowed her head to him but kept her distance. "It's been too long."

"I see the afterlife serves you well." For the first time, the hint of a grin appeared at the corner of Anthony's lips.

"I do enjoy its many benefits. I think I was made to be a vampire."

Anthony laughed out loud, causing Catherine to smile. Thomas wished he could join their merry little reunion but could feel the presence of Xavier in one of those boxes, crying out to him for help. "I assume you know we didn't come here to exchange pleasantries?"

Anthony's face fell at the sharp tone he heard from Thomas. No matter. Thomas had no desire to placate his friend's moods. He would be careful but not suffer fools lightly as it played out.

"No." Anthony shook his head and moved a couple of steps toward them, closing the distance but leaving a few yards between them. "I had no such illusions. You came to try to convince me to free Xavier, which you know I can't do. We all know there's nothing to discuss."

Thomas sneered and shook his head at Anthony. "You're wrong. You're not God. And the Council isn't a panel of gods. You don't have divine authority to issue edicts like you think you do. Not without explanation. Not without sound reason. I won't accept this. Not this time. Not against him," Thomas jabbed his finger toward the fire pit, "who has done nothing but try to help people with his short time on this earth. This punitive measure can't hold up under scrutiny."

Anthony motioned toward the one box hovering over the pit of fire before them. "It's already done. No one claims the stature of a god, but we do enforce the laws that protect all vampires and have for *centuries*. These laws aren't arbitrary or irrational. In becoming a vampire, you enter into this global kingdom whether you know it or not. Whether you want it or not. Xavier admitted he violated the ethic. He accepted his punishment when he bargained for your freedom. There's nothing to discuss. There's nothing I can do."

"He wanted to save lives." Thomas felt his blood boiling and was unable to contain it. "He was on the side of righteousness. He always is. Whether it violates your chance laws or not. He doesn't deserve this punishment." When Thomas stepped toward Anthony, Catherine grabbed him by the arm and pulled him back.

"He made Catherine, against the ethic." Anthony held up a hand and put up his index finger. Then he lifted his middle finger. "Two. He returned to interact with Anne Hébert, against the vampire laws. Three." A third finger lifted into the air. Thomas wanted to snap it off. "He interfered in the human institution of slavery, daring us to find and punish him. Revealing his nature to countless people. That alone should constitute several offenses, not one. His sentence is final."

Anthony dropped his head to the ground. Then he looked up with concern and covered the distance between them. He brushed his hand across Thomas's cheek and spoke in a whisper. "I love you. I love him. And Catherine. You're my family. You know I did everything in my power to protect him, to give him the lightest possible sentence for the severity of his crimes? He's like a little brother to me too."

Thomas fought to maintain his composure, one minute wanting to lash out that no family member would ever allow such a punishment upon a loved one, the next knowing Anthony spoke the truth. He loved them all. He wanted the best for all of them, except his blind sense of duty too often got in the way.

"And what light sentence did you win for our brother?" Thomas detected the hint of sarcasm in Catherine's voice. He knew all too well she resented the inference because she could never punish Xavier, no matter the seriousness of his crime.

"I argued against a death sentence." Anthony turned to address Catherine. "All of our rules. All the Council's guidelines demand execution. I pleaded against it, insisting he didn't deserve such a fate. He didn't. I believe this truth with all my heart. But he also has to learn a lesson because every decade, every century, will bring with it misery humans inflict upon one another. It never stops. They kill each other. They ostracize each other. They declare war against one another. The things that cause Xavier such despair will never end, and he can't interfere as he did every time he sees such injustice. It's too dangerous. The Council and I want to impart to him the seriousness of our concern so we *don't* have to become more stringent. You have to believe me. I orchestrated this for all of us."

"The sentence. How long?" Thomas spat the words at Anthony.

"One hundred years."

Anthony's eyes bulged out, and he cried with shock when he felt Thomas's hands wrap around his neck.

Forty: Battle

18 JUNE 1822
Rocky Mountains

Thomas squeezed as hard as he could, wanting to crush the life out of Anthony for what he did to Xavier. All compassion, all control over his temper, all reason let go of Thomas when he heard the Council in all of its smug glory dared to lock Xavier in the awful place for a century. Thomas could never survive so long without him. He would fight to the death.

In a swift motion, Anthony shot his hands through Thomas's arms and punched out of Thomas's grip. Anthony leaped backward several feet, chanted under his breath, and waved his arms toward Thomas and Catherine.

Having jumped back himself, Thomas saw Anthony freeze Catherine in place. She stood paralyzed, her eyes glancing about the cavern but otherwise unmoving. Thomas realized Anthony expected the same enchantment to work against him, so he stood motionless as if also stilled by the magic.

Anthony rubbed his neck. "Thomas. Don't. You can't win." He walked toward them. "I've already controlled you, with hardly a thought to it. Don't do this to us. To yourself. Please, I'm *begging* you to understand."

When Anthony got close enough, Thomas grabbed a nearby torch and swung it at Anthony, catching him on the side of the head. Stunned, Anthony swatted at the fire in his hair as Thomas raised the torch to again smash it into Anthony's skull.

Anthony reared backward and slapped at the fire on his head at the same time. Thomas charged forward, but Anthony jumped across the pit and landed opposite Thomas, on the ledge surrounding the rest of the fire pit. He smothered the fire out of his hair as Thomas leaped onto the iron casket so he stood above the pit and higher up than Anthony.

Too late, Thomas realized his mistake. Anthony controlled the magic suspending the crate and shook it, causing Thomas to lose his balance. He dropped the torch as he launched himself back to the ledge. He pulled his body up and jumped behind Catherine but lost Anthony in the process.

Thomas yelled in pain when he felt the arms reach around his body and a finger gouge into his eye. Thomas bit Anthony's arm, tasting the blood and making Anthony release him. Thomas ran across the cavern to the other side again, scared.

"Stop! Both of you!" Catherine shouted, able to talk, though she stood frozen.

Thomas disregarded her pleas, too lost in his rage, and ran at Anthony. They locked together around the waist and both fell to the floor. Thomas ripped open Anthony's shirt and tried to force his fingers into Anthony's chest so he could tear out the heart of stone sitting beneath it. Anthony rammed his knee into Thomas's genitals and tried to pin Thomas to the ground.

Thomas kicked up with all his strength and pushed away from Anthony, rolling across the room. He looked up to see Anthony stood but did not move, instead incanting a new spell he hurled across the room at Thomas. Thomas smelled a pungent odor and felt a tingling, but it evaporated without any further effect. He got to his feet, squared his shoulders, and glared at Anthony.

"Your spells won't work." Thomas spat blood out of his mouth but felt everything else inside of him healing.

"You're in league with the devil, then? How will that protect him?" All of Anthony's hair had grown back.

Thomas laughed, loudly. "Leave it to you to try to reduce this to a battle between good and evil so you can take the side of good and feel noble." Thomas shook his head. "Always so simplistic. You're *always* so simplistic. I found a counter potion. This is vampire combat. We don't need gods to do each other in."

Thomas flung himself across the room and collided with Anthony, pushing him back against the wall. Anthony crashed into it with a thud, which reverberated around the room and caused stones to fall from the ceiling on top of them. Anthony righted himself and threw a large rock at Thomas, which hit him on the forehead.

"Will you two listen to me? Please? Before you destroy this place and all of us in it?" They both paused, glancing out of the corner of their eyes at Catherine, but staring at each other. "Think of Xavier. Think of what this argument would do to him. There has to be another way."

"I'm sorry, Catherine." Thomas jumped into the air, grabbed another torch, and thrust it toward Anthony, who charged right at Thomas, pushing him back toward the fire.

Thomas made a grave error. He lost control of his footing, and Anthony's momentum shoved Thomas back toward the edge of the pit. He tried to regain his traction but fell backward into the black hole below. As a fiery death awaited him below, at least he knew he had done everything in his power to save Xavier, despite his failure.

Yet he fell a foot when his entire body lurched to a stop, suspended in midair by the back of his coat. Thomas looked up to see Anthony lifting him to the surface and setting him on the ground.

Thomas sat stunned for several seconds, not knowing how to take Anthony's deed. "Why did you do that? You know I'm going to try to kill you." Thomas lay motionless, assessing the situation and wondering how to continue the fight since Anthony's soft side got the better of him.

"Catherine's right. We should talk."

Thomas frowned at Anthony, then glanced at Catherine.

"Please, Thomas," she said. "Think of Xavier and what he would want. At least, give it a chance."

A twisted mess of emotion raced through Thomas, making him lie on the ground without moving or saying a word. Thomas sought to murder Anthony to save Xavier, to free him from the awful place. He could not imagine any other situation sending him into such a rage against his dearest friend in the world, but it had seemed like the only option. His anger continued to brew beneath the surface. Yet Catherine reminded him of something deeper, more meaningful to him than anything else: Xavier. Thomas was not thinking about having Xavier by his side or even their intimate and personal love. Rather, he was remembering Xavier the being, the vampire who cared about the world and the people in it. The man who would go to almost any length to protect and nurture those he loved. Catherine reminded Thomas of what Xavier would say and do in the circumstance. If Thomas wanted to honor his lover, then he had to take his lover into account. Freeing Xavier but then having to tell him Anthony died to make it happen might destroy Xavier yet again. Not that soon after the revolution, after he lost a brother, a faith, and then put his life back together.

It also hit Thomas hard how Anthony saved him. Locked in mortal combat, what opponent would reach out and pluck their nemesis back from the depths of hell and forego an easy and clear victory? Only Thomas had been fighting to the death, not Anthony. Anthony still loved him. Somehow, Anthony must have believed they could find a solution to the whole mess.

Thomas decided to give Anthony another chance to explain himself and reduce Xavier's sentence through a reasonable conversation. Perhaps since Anthony understood the full extent to which Thomas would go to free Xavier, he would discuss the situation.

"We can talk on two conditions," Thomas said.

Anthony nodded and slumped to the ground next to Thomas, guarded but listening.

"Release Catherine from the spell. You can't harm me, and you know she's the more reasonable of the two of us. Let her take part in this."

Catherine stepped forward, straightened her clothing, and sat herself between Anthony and Thomas. Even in a cavern and after a horrendous fight, she could add a certain decorum and energy to the conversation without saying a word.

"And the second condition?" Anthony asked.

"You tell us everything. No more games. I love you. And you saved me, when given the opportunity I would have allowed you to burn in the fires of that pit. Nonetheless, I expect a complete and open conversation about *everything*."

"That's your anger talking." Anthony smiled at Thomas, a knowing grin of affection.

"Perhaps. But don't forget it hasn't gone away. If I glance at the box in which you locked Xavier, it will flare anew. I'll reignite the battle against you if you don't come clean and explain everything, so we can understand."

Anthony nodded again. "You're right. You both deserve knowledge. But I'm uncertain. And afraid. Where should we begin?"

"By telling us how we can get a reduced sentence for him. What lasting effects of what he did will there be for vampires? If we can undo it, maybe with his help, that could be part of the lesson and reduce the amount of time he has in the box. You could make our argument to the Council. They'll listen to you."

Anthony paused for a long moment, and a blood tear formed at the corner of his eye.

"What is it?" Catherine asked and reached over to hold Anthony's hand.

"I don't know where to begin. I'm on the verge of telling you both so much I should never tell another soul. It could endanger all of us and undo everything the Council fought so hard over the centuries to create. All of the order and protection for vampires instilled in us after the vampire war, when we almost lost everyone, could be undone with but one conversation."

Thomas reached into his pocket and handed a hanky to Anthony, who wiped at the blood tears. "Unless one of us must die, you don't have much of a choice." Once again Thomas disliked his own tone, wishing he had compassion for the obvious angst his friend felt. Yet none existed, despite being saved, despite everything, because he did not know where the conversation would lead them.

"I know." Anthony took in a deep breath and wiped at his eyes. "I'll try my best to avoid that fate, for both of us.

You have to listen, though, and not judge the Council. Thomas, you have to remain rational and in control, or I won't continue with this discussion, regardless of the repercussions."

"I'm doing my best. Start talking."

"To your first point," Anthony said and released Catherine's hand by patting her. "The danger from what Xavier did *has* passed. The villains of the story, if you will, have died. The slaves respect and admire what he and Catherine did, those who figured out his undead nature included. There is no serious concern from them. Yes, his crimes were widespread, but he killed the white people who found out about him. The slaves revere him. Especially Duncan, who is grateful for what Xavier did."

"How do you know all of this?" Thomas asked.

Anthony shrugged. "Part of the investigation. We interviewed a number of people to assess the threat risk and to determine what action we needed to take outside of punishing the vampires who committed the crime. We determined no further action was necessary."

Catherine arched her eyebrow. "Nothing? All of the hunting for us, all of the warnings and chaos because of what Xavier and I did, and with a quick investigation you and the Council decide Xavier needed punishing, and everything else went away? I find it hard to believe."

"That's the whole of it. If we run around trying to conceal everything you two did, it would require killing anyone who witnessed Xavier or you as vampires in the process of freeing slaves." Anthony held his hands up, as if to say the Council had no other choice. "This would either require massive purges, deaths if you will, of too many innocent people, or risk further exposure as we tried to reason with everyone or attempt to take away their memories. We could have tried to change the reality of what they witnessed, but that's the riskiest course of action. Both of those options are either immoral or impossible to enact. Probably both." Anthony paused in reflection, tapping his fingers along his pant leg and peering up from time to time at Catherine and Thomas. Then his face lit with recognition. "There was one thing I had to do. This will prove what I'm saying.

"I don't know how much Xavier told you about this." Anthony looked at Catherine as he spoke. "Xavier visited two free blacks who were plotting to instigate a slave revolt near Charleston. Denmark Vesey and Gullah Jack wanted to arm the slaves and take over, hoping to mimic what happened in Haiti."

"How did you learn about this? From another vampire?" Catherine asked.

"From my investigation. I learned Xavier visited a witch doctor for help in finding Duncan, who made a bargain with Xavier. He would help Xavier find Duncan if Xavier pretended to be a religious vision or God appearing to Vesey in order to inspire him to implement the plot. So Xavier acted the part of a spirit or divine visitor to convince them to do it. He purchased and stockpiled armaments for them. This appeased Malcolm, and Xavier got what he wanted."

"Malcolm?" Thomas interrupted Anthony and shot Catherine a look. "From Charleston?"

"Yes." Anthony nodded and then smiled. "I already figured out who protected you from my magic. It had to be someone smart and powerful, who accepted the presence of vampires. Who else but Harriet's associate?"

"Is Harriet in trouble?" Catherine asked.

"No." Anthony shook his head.

"Is Malcolm in danger?" Thomas worried about the man who had done so much for him. "Did you do something to him?"

"Of course not. He would have the power to stop me, anyway. Besides, his wife told me everything."

"Why would she do that?" Catherine scrunched her brow in confusion.

"She always thought the plot was doomed and stupid. She wanted to protect Malcolm, because he would have died, too, had they discovered his involvement. I protected him but did need to stop the insurrection Xavier helped inspire. It was pretty easy to foil. I bribed the house servant of a slave owner whose slaves were involved in the plot. I convinced the slave to rat out the conspiracy. I gave him the details of it, even though he had not known about it earlier. As his reward, I purchased his children and moved them to freedom in Canada. He pretended he overheard the plans for an insurrection, told his master everything, and vampire interference in slavery ended."

Catherine's eyes grew wide. "Did they kill slaves? What did they do to Vesey? How's that not *your* interfering in human affairs as much as what we did?"

"Anyone found involved in the plot was executed. Listen, it was a distasteful business for me too. You have to believe me. I hate slavery as much as you. But imagine if they succeeded. Picture the stories of an undead God coming to visit Denmark, who inspired his mission. What if they traced the munitions Xavier had stockpiled to him? I had to get rid of them and eliminate this scheme. It was the one significant danger, and we got rid of it."

Catherine started to ask another question, but Thomas held up his hand to stop her. "We won't go into what you did to those people, or what that might mean. I don't have time to debate the finer points of morality the enforcement of your vampire laws tread upon. We're here to talk about how this applies to Xavier. What does this mean for his captivity?"

Catherine nodded and turned her head toward Anthony.

"You're right, of course. We should stop dancing around the true direction of this conversation." Thomas had never seen Anthony speak with such hesitance, almost as if afraid of what he had to say. Anthony always spoke with authority when it came to the Council. What secrets did he conceal? "This has nothing to do with Vesey's plot or anything we did to disguise the presence of vampires."

Thomas agreed with one thing Anthony said. He shook his head. "No. It has to do with Xavier's sentence. I don't give a damn about all this other nonsense, except how it affects Xavier. What do we need to know, what information should we gather, in order to go before the Council and request they reduce Xavier's sentence? That's all we need to discuss."

Anthony put his face in his hands and rubbed hard. When he looked up, he had again smeared his face with blood tears.

"What is it?" Thomas scrunched his brow, unsure how to take these theatrics. "I demand a meeting before the Vampire Council. We can present this evidence to plead with them to reduce Xavier's sentence. I don't believe you anymore that it's impossible. There has to be a way. Tell me how we can meet with them."

"It's not so simple." Anthony took a deep breath.

"Then I'll simplify it more. Either you arrange this meeting for us before the Council, or we fight again. I'm not in a mood for games anymore. I thought you understood."

Anthony sighed. "You won't like what I'm going to tell you about meeting with the Council."

"Why, because you'll refuse to try to get me before them? Or because you think they'll refuse?" Thomas could feel his rage returning.

"No." Anthony shook his head and his shoulders slumped in resignation. "Because you're already meeting with the entire Council."

Forty-One: Anthony's Secret

19 JUNE 1822
Rocky Mountains

Anthony's words hung in the air, almost thick enough to see. What had he meant by saying they already *were* meeting with the entire Council? Did they hide in the shadows, spying on the conversation, watching the battle between he and Anthony and waiting to storm in and take charge? Was it another form of their insipid magic?

Somehow, though, Thomas wished he was right with his theory. For what he feared, what he heard next, ignited his temper anew at the person whom he always considered his dearest friend.

"Already meeting with them?" Catherine furrowed her brow, glancing between Anthony and Thomas, her face bewildered. "I don't understand."

Thomas lowered his head and pursed his lips together. His head tilted downward, and he glared across at Anthony. "You'd better start explaining."

"You're already meeting with the entire Council," Anthony repeated. "How many times have I told you about the vampire wars? Do you remember the stories?"

"Spare me more tales of vampire woes from long ago." Thomas clenched his fists together, ready to pounce. In trying to control himself, he missed the motion as Anthony reached over and slapped Thomas hard across the face.

Thomas readied for another fight but Anthony once again sat immobile, so instead, Thomas swallowed his rising anger for the moment.

"I lost my lover during those vampire 'woes.' You wouldn't be here if the Council hadn't fought the war. Do you understand me? I'll talk to you about all of this. I'm telling you everything. *Every goddamned thing you don't deserve to know.* The least you could do is respect what I lived through. People died to give to you this life."

As Anthony spoke, Catherine scooted over and wrapped an arm around Thomas. With her free hand, she grabbed his wrist and then leaned into him. "Let this play out. He's our friend. We have to hear him. Please?" she whispered in his ear.

Thomas nodded once but still stared daggers at Anthony.

"I was mentioning the vampire battle because it pertains to what I told you. Yes, I've lied to you, sort of."

"Sort of?" Thomas tensed every muscle in his body.

"Thomas, please," Catherine again pleaded with him.

Anthony wiped away more tears. "The war wiped out more vampires than I ever let you, or anyone, know. We almost all died. Everyone, Thomas. Every single vampire except the two or three who supported the demon. My lover. My friends. And everyone on the Council but me. All dead in a matter of a couple of months. Sure, a few stragglers remained here and there who avoided the conflict. But not many. I almost didn't succeed but at last killed the one who fomented all the chaos. Lost and alone, I had to determine what to do going forward. I decided to continue in my sworn duty as part of the Council. First, I made sure none of his associates remained, and no one knew the full extent of what happened. Once I knew the few remaining vampires were safe again, I continued as if the Council won. As if the extreme amount of death was smaller than it was, and as if vampires remained all over the world with a powerful Council in charge.

"The laws to govern vampires existed long before this war. I added a few things to them and continued to enforce them. To anyone who asked, I consulted the Council in all decisions and was chosen to carry out their wishes. In many respects, that *is* the truth. Everyone on the Council knew at times we had to make decisions by ourselves, for the good of everyone, knowing we would have the Council's blessing. The elders trained me to let the ethic guide my decisions. I continued the same process. I made a few more vampires and allowed a slow repopulation of the earth, though I restricted it. Still today, I don't think more than one hundred vampires exist."

"This is all a sorry charade?" Thomas hardly believed his ears. "No Council exists? The laws don't exist?"

"That's not what I said." Anthony pounded his fists into his knees. "It all exists. As it had long before I became a vampire. The rules. The ethic. The Council. It protects us, and it protects humanity. It has and always will."

"But there is no Council," Thomas shot back.

"There *is* a Council. In spirit. In tradition. And in me. That's what I'm trying to tell you. I'm the Council now. I have the burden of continuing its legacy for all of us."

Thomas started to speak but bit his tongue, his mind a whirl of confusion. Of course he was mad as hell, because Anthony hid it for so long, but more because Anthony imprisoned Xavier of his own accord. Why couldn't he have made an exception for a friend if the decision was his alone to make? All the lies about placating the Council were concealing the demon sitting before him. Thomas wanted to strangle Anthony. How many times had he sat and listened to Anthony speak of the Council in the plural, as if a group of vampires sat down to make a decision? He justified what he did to Xavier by hiding behind vampires who no longer existed.

Yet something in his friend's demeanor gave Thomas pause. Thomas had never seen Anthony so distraught, so forlorn. While Thomas did not agree with Anthony and questioned his becoming the Council all alone, Thomas had a strange reverence for the self-deprecation it took Anthony to bear the burden alone. Is that why he never partnered again? What must it have been like all these years to keep such a secret? Despite himself and his deeper angst, Thomas felt his voice quiet and his tone soften. "Why? Why did you keep this responsibility to yourself? Why not find more members of the Council?"

"It must have been awful," Catherine added. She had moved across to Anthony and held him in her arms.

"It was my duty. I was young at the time of the war and had no idea how members of the Council were selected. No one told me why they picked me, so I didn't know the procedure for selecting other members. It wasn't written anywhere. I never knew what to do, except continue as I had for the good of all involved. For example, they trained me in all the magic we use, but I don't know if it happens because one sits on the Council, or if it comes from natural ability."

"This explains so much about what the Council missed. The rogue vampire Xavier and I killed deserved punishment. He violated the ethic as we did, didn't he? Harriet and he explained it away, but perhaps you didn't even know?"

"I had no idea." Anthony agreed. "But not because of any limits by the Council. Our magic is powerful and notifies the Council of almost any transgression. However, he possessed his own form of magic that concealed his deeds from the Council. Xavier and you happened to expose him because I was tracking you. He somehow made himself invisible to me, and I intended to examine how after I dealt with Xavier. I doubt many more, if any, can trump the Council's magic."

Thomas moved to better hear Anthony who whispered. He wanted to ask for clarification about the magic, because it sounded as if Anthony had the means to locate Xavier a lot sooner than he did. But, as Thomas he turned his head, he saw the iron box out of the corner of his eye, hovering over the fire with Xavier locked inside. Whatever sympathy he'd almost mustered for Anthony evaporated in an instant.

"Release him. Now." Thomas got to his feet and pointed at the box. He scowled down at Anthony.

Anthony looked up, remaining in Catherine's arms. "We can discuss it. Now you know I'm the Council, so present your case, and I'll reconsider what we need to do to teach him a lesson."

"No teaching." Thomas ground his teeth together. "No lesson. Release him, and *then* we'll talk."

Anthony hugged Catherine and then stood up, also pulling Catherine to her feet. Thomas assumed he decided to obey, and he realized he could not win the argument after he disclosed the truth.

Instead, Anthony continued to negotiate and, in the process, infuriated Thomas all the more. "It's not so easy. I told you everything because I thought you deserved to know. As my friend, and because of what has happened to Xavier. But it's the law for vampires. The ethic is in effect, regardless of who oversees it or how many vampires sit on the Council. Xavier admitted to violating the ethic. He accepted his punishment, and vampire rules demand he serve his sentence. This will insure he understands the magnitude of his crimes. I wasn't lying about the fact the ethic mandates death for what he did. But I could never have done that to him. This is a good compromise. We know it will teach him a vital lesson."

"There is no *we*," Thomas shouted at Anthony. "Just *you*." He jabbed his finger into Anthony's chest.

"Then negotiate with me. Present your case to the Council. I gave Xavier the lightest sentence possible. Do you understand if the full Council existed, they would have put him to death? That much is very laid out. Death, Thomas. Executed. I love him too much for execution and respect him too much to give him the full jail time even a lesser crime would demand. A century was the minimum. I'm not going to reverse it because you and I are friends, or because of my love for him."

Catherine walked over to Thomas's side as Anthony spoke, the crease on her brow giving away her anger. "There has to be a way to make an exception. We can rethink this whole thing. It's just you, and you don't have to do this alone anymore. Perhaps the laws are outdated and need to be revisited."

"I'm sorry." Anthony bowed his head. "I don't see how."

"I'll tell you how," Thomas spat back. "Here's your negotiation: your magic won't work against me. I know the truth about the Council, so the game is up. You release him, and we'll talk about all of this and what to do from here. But if you persist with this charade of law and order and inflict this sentence upon him, I'll fly out of here and tell the truth to every vampire I can find."

Anthony's body went limp. "You wouldn't. You can't."

Thomas stood inches from Anthony's face. "I'll do anything for Xavier, and you know it. *Anything*. I'll go make a thousand rogue vampires and bring your little kingdom to a screeching halt. I'll massacre humans and make sure they all know the truth of the vampire's existence. Your world, so carefully crafted, will come tumbling down."

"If I let him go, we'll talk? You won't expose the truth of the Council?" Anthony spoke in a defeated whisper.

"I may be brash and angry, but I hope you know I keep my end of a bargain. You have a much better chance with Xavier by my side speaking reason to me, than if you try to discuss this further with me in my angry state with him in that hellhole." Thomas pointed at the iron box in anger.

"And don't think I'm on your side, at all." Catherine folded her arms over her chest.

"Are you sure this will work?" Anthony shook as he spoke.

Thomas laughed mockingly. "I've no idea. I'm sure you have no other choice. Free him, or I go."

To emphasize his point, Thomas walked toward the cave entrance with an intent to leave unless Anthony released Xavier before he said anything else. He had just gotten to the tunnel when he turned around to gauge the situation.

"I love all of you," Anthony said in a hushed tone as he lifted his arms into the air. He whispered an enchantment, and the iron box moved through the air toward them.

Thomas stepped back into the cavern. Xavier...at long last, he would be reunited with Xavier. The impenetrable prison rested on the ground in front of them, and Anthony raised its lid with his magic.

Part Ten

A New Council

Forty-Two: Liberation

19 JUNE 1822
Rocky Mountains

Xavier sat in the pitch black, wondering how long he'd already been in prison. He had no idea. He'd learned the very first day his body went to sleep during the daylight hours, the same as if he lived outside the box. At least sleep offered respite from the confines imprisoning him. Yet he awoke each evening, too, and then spent a night of contemplation about his life, his crimes, and what the world would look like when he emerged one hundred years later.

Most of all, he worried Thomas would have forgotten him. What would keep his lover waiting for so long? Beautiful, confident Thomas would most likely find someone else in the interim. After all, Thomas's rage at Xavier's subterfuge must already have disenchanted his lover with their relationship. Did Xavier even want to live to see that happen?

More troublesome, Xavier thought he may very well go insane. Completely and utterly mad from the solitude and darkness. Too much time to himself. Too many insecurities and fears to take hold of his mind with no relief or other person to bring him back to reality. Xavier determined to lose track of the days so he would never know for sure how long he remained inside the iron box. He realized it had not been long yet, but clouding reality and not counting down the days until Anthony freed him might keep a semblance of his sanity.

Oh God, what if Anthony died? What if Xavier was imprisoned for eternity? Did the other members of the Vampire Council know he was here? Or would he wither away because of the lack of blood? Anthony assured him no such thing would happen during his century of imprisonment because of the magic involved in jailing a vampire, but what if it went longer?

Xavier turned to prayer, the long involved prayers he used to pray at the seminary and then when alone in his church before Thomas seduced him. Prayer soothed him for a while but also made him angry. He followed St. Michel's instructions. He did everything in the name of God since fleeing Paris, thinking he obeyed a higher calling. But since his capture, he heard nothing from the supernatural. Where was St. Michel when Xavier most needed him? Xavier's conviction in following his faith did not guarantee protection from earthbound laws started to anger him. He clutched at his brother's medal, which was in his pocket when he got inside the coffin. He had gotten it out as a comfort, but it led to more questions. In his other hand, he held the cross he always wore around his neck. Why had these supernatural forces Xavier had been so convinced came from God abandoned him in his hour of need?

Still, he remembered to pray for those outside the crypt—that they may find peace and happiness. He prayed for Anthony, who felt such a burden in sentencing Xavier and bringing him here. Dear Anthony, who performed his job. He prayed Denmark Vesey may succeed in his plot, and for Malcolm and all of the other free blacks and slaves Xavier met in the last months. He prayed for Duncan to remain free, and for all slaves to soon find their freedom. He prayed for Catherine's safety, so he could see her again when they released him. He knew if anyone, Catherine would wait out the century and love him as she had from the day he was born.

When he could remain calm and logical, he thought the same of Thomas. His lover could not abandon their love, which was so intense and complete, could he? Yet one hundred years was such a long time. Longer than Xavier had walked the earth. Truth be told, *Xavier* first forsook Thomas when he launched his quest by sending Thomas away. Xavier started to pray for Thomas when he heard muffled voices outside his box.

He had wondered if the iron box was soundproof. But he could make out people talking, though not their words or voices. Had Anthony returned with another prisoner?

After some time, Xavier's trunk swayed back and forth, the sounds of someone having jumped upon it alarming him. It shook violently, and just as fast, the intruder disappeared, though the sounds of scuffling and shouting continued to reverberate outside his crate. Once his prison stopped shaking, he appreciated the momentary diversion. But it stunned Xavier when his box began to move—he assumed back across the pit to the ledge. To safety?

Had Xavier already served his one hundred years? If so, he had become catatonic for most of them, having almost no memory of being trapped inside the iron vault for so long. He felt the casket lower to the ground and come to a rest. When the hinges creaked and the lid moved upward, Xavier was relieved to see light again.

As the top opened, Xavier leaned up on one elbow to look out. The sight of Thomas, his black hair flowing over his shoulder, his stern brown eyes gazing down, his strong chest heaving up and down, caused Xavier to collapse. He fell back into the crate and wept.

Thomas leaned into the coffin, hovering over him. He reached down and took Xavier in his arms, lifting Xavier out of the iron cell and then kicking it closed before he carried Xavier several feet away and lay him on the ground. But Xavier would not let Thomas go. He clung to him and buried his face into Thomas's chest. Whatever the length of time, whatever the reason for his going free, Thomas had waited. Thomas was there to get him.

"Shh," Thomas said. "You're safe. You're out. It's fine now." Thomas petted his head and rocked back and forth with Xavier in his arms, hugging him. A couple of times he kissed the top of Xavier's head, then his forehead, always comforting him with soothing words and gentle caresses.

At last able to speak, Xavier looked into Thomas's eyes and smiled. "You waited?" The last syllable caught in his throat. He held his breath, waiting for the answer, but knew it before Thomas said a word from the way Thomas snorted a laugh and tossed his head back.

Thomas hugged him tighter and leaned over to kiss Xavier's cheek. "Waited? I suppose you could call it that. More like hunted for you and fought to get you out of there. Did you think I'd sit around for a century and let them do this to you? Never." Thomas then bent and kissed Xavier hard on the lips.

"How long was I in there?"

"You don't know?" Thomas wiped at the blood tears trickling down Xavier's face. "Could you think in there? Did you know when the days passed?"

Xavier explained his state of mind in the box. Then he repeated his question.

"I'm not sure," Thomas answered. "About a week, I'd guess."

Xavier slumped over and cried again. A week. He had missed about a week inside the iron prison. It felt much longer because of the time that lapsed since last he saw Thomas. "Are you mad at me?"

Again Thomas laughed at Xavier, as tears streamed down his own face. He picked Xavier off the ground and clutched him, burying his head in Xavier's neck. "Could I kill you for what you did? Yes. But no, I'm not angry with you. Never with you." Then Thomas held Xavier a slight distance away and frowned down at him. "But promise you will never, ever, do that again under *any* circumstances. I don't care who visits you in your sleep. Christ Himself could come down, and you had better tell him you'd rather visit Satan than inflict such a punishment on me. Do you promise?"

"I promise." Xavier reached up and pulled Thomas closer, content to be held for several more minutes, back in his lover's arms. Only when Xavier felt assured of their connection did he wonder how Thomas managed to free him. How did Thomas find him? How did he overcome the magic? Xavier looked around and saw no one else.

"Are you here alone?" Xavier asked.

"Kind of." Thomas nodded. They moved to sitting upright but were entwined in one another's arms.

"What kind of an answer was that?" Xavier laughed.

"Catherine and Anthony are waiting in the tunnel. They stepped out to give us privacy."

That meant Catherine was safe. And, unlike Xavier feared, Thomas had not battled Anthony or gone around him and the Council to free him. Or worse. "How did you get them to free me?" was all he asked.

"Shall we have them join us, so we can explain everything? In fact, Anthony has a bit more explaining to do himself."

Forty-Three: Explanations

21 JUNE 1822
New York City

Xavier looked around the luxurious surroundings of Anthony's flat in New York City and smiled. He'd grown up surrounded by luxury, and during his years as a priest never wanted for comfort, but he had a new sense of appreciation for it after he escaped from vampire jail.

Waiting for tonight's summit between the vampires involved in the last few months of chaos put Xavier in a reflective mood. He came into the parlor before everyone else to give himself time for peace and quiet before the storm. He leaned back, took a deep breath, and ran his hand over the marble statue of a naked god sitting on the table next to him. Then he remembered everything he'd learned once Anthony and Catherine came into the cavern-cum-prison two nights ago.

After a heartfelt reunion with Catherine and a pleasant greeting from Anthony, Xavier turned his attention to the hostility between Anthony and Thomas. Thomas clenched his jaw so tightly a vein on his forehead popped out, a sure sign he struggled to keep his anger under control. Xavier had grabbed his hand and squeezed to rein him in, which served to keep Thomas quiet, though it did nothing to relax his demeanor. Before anyone said another word, Catherine announced Anthony and she agreed everyone needed to avoid "unpleasant topics" until they explained everything to Xavier. Thomas nodded to indicate his approval, though Xavier could sense his continued stiffness.

Through a combination of Thomas speaking and the other two interjecting when necessary, Xavier learned about what happened since he surrendered to Anthony. He heard about Catherine and Thomas reuniting, the spell Malcolm placed on Thomas to protect him from vampire magic, and the ultimate confrontation in the vampire prison between Thomas and Anthony. Anthony's revelation about the Vampire Council stunned Xavier, who then understood Thomas's anger, though Xavier sympathized with Anthony and wanted to hear more about it. Unlike Thomas, Xavier harbored no ill will for Anthony doing his duty and having imprisoned him. Even Anthony's subterfuge and white lies about the truth made sense to Xavier. Regardless of whom and how many issued the verdict against him, he deserved a penalty for so defying the ethic. He accepted his punishment.

When the friction between Anthony and Thomas threatened to ignite anew toward the end of the story, Xavier begged his lover to calm down and let things simmer for a while before he made any judgments. Catherine negotiated they should all return to New York City, where they could mingle away from each other for a night before returning, more level-headed, to further discuss the entire mess—from Xavier's imprisonment to Anthony and the Vampire Council, or lack thereof.

On their rapid journey through the American West and during the previous night here in New York, between bouts of passionate sex and Thomas scolding Xavier again and again for having left like he did, Thomas filled Xavier in on more of the details about the Council, the war that destroyed it centuries ago, and all of the little things leading to freeing Xavier.

Xavier apologized to Thomas a million times, insisting God commanded his actions but promising never again to abandon him. They reconnected in an intense and intimate way almost at once. Though Xavier had loved being in Thomas's arms since the day he gave into his desire years ago, they'd never felt more reassuring and safe.

Which brought Xavier to the current moment—the called-for discussion. Xavier arrived first because the time alone focused his energy on what he thought should be his primary task during the summit: peacekeeper. A short time later, Thomas bounced into the room, smiling. "You'd better still be here," he said and pecked Xavier on the forehead. He hid one hand behind his back and brought it out to give Xavier a bouquet of flowers. Xavier smiled and reached up to kiss Thomas on the lips. Before anything else started, however, Catherine barged into the room, grinning and greeting everyone. She had Harriet in tow, whom she found after they left the mountains and before coming to New York. Harriet was pleasant toward everyone but stood rigid, Xavier guessed, because of the proceedings about to occur. When Anthony arrived, Xavier tapped Thomas on the leg to remind him he promised to hear their friend out.

When everyone else took a seat, Catherine remained standing. She'd revealed her plan to Xavier the night before, one he approved of, which started with her wanting to take control of the meeting before Thomas attacked Anthony or became angry. She planned to give him time to vent, but not until the meeting moved in the right direction. Also, she did not want Anthony seizing control as if he alone commanded the proceedings. If anything, she and Xavier thought they needed the exact opposite.

"I'd like to begin with a proposal." Catherine paced back and forth, running her finger over each person's shoulder to get their attention. Xavier had seen her act a hundred times back in Paris, when she commanded a room full of male financiers or instructed the servants about her desires, yet Xavier marveled at her powers of persuasion.

She turned to Anthony. "I admire you. I don't know how you kept your secret for so long. It doesn't do any good for us to debate the merits or problems inherent in it. What's done is done. That you did it for the good of all vampires is admirable. The Council's code *is* important." When Thomas grunted behind her, Catherine whipped around and frowned at him. He put his hands in the air in surrender and snuggled back against Xavier. "Because of this reality"—Catherine turned around the room, looking at each of them—"the ethic must remain in force."

Xavier glanced at Anthony. He sat upright but smiled and nodded.

"However," Catherine continued, "we must make adjustments." She spun around and cupped Thomas's chin with her hand and then tapped him on the nose. "Thomas has a point. There was too much intrigue and mystery to the Council. I understand you had little choice. But a change is in order to take away your burden of having to decide everything. Therefore, henceforth, I propose the vampires in this room make up the Vampire Council to enforce its laws and pass judgment."

Though part of Xavier hated the idea of the obligation, he'd thought long and hard about it after Catherine suggested it to him. They had no other choice, for the good of each other and for the protection of humanity and vampires. It was a burden he would accept. Xavier peered at Thomas, with a smirk on his face, and felt him chuckle.

"Yes," Anthony said and clapped his hands. "Yes, wonderful!"

"I'm not finished." Catherine tilted her head at him and held up her hand. Anthony sat back again but smiled as Catherine continued. "We must institute certain changes. The Council was made at a different time. Before the Enlightenment. We have to adapt our laws to the passage of time, as we change our personal habits and mindsets with each passing era. Xavier?"

Catherine walked over and placed her hand on Xavier's shoulder. She squeezed it and then sat, waiting for him to take over the part he promised to lead.

Xavier stood, intimidated by the nature of the meeting. The magnitude of today weighed heavily upon him because of the high stakes. He believed in Catherine's plan. What if the others rejected it? He worried most of all about Anthony because his knowledge and magical gifts made his cooperation essential. He fretted less about Thomas, knowing he could persuade his lover to go along, even if it took time.

"Go on," Catherine whispered behind him. She had taken his place next to Thomas.

"First, I understand what I did was careless and wrong. I pledge not to do such things anymore, especially if I'm to sit on the Council. You have my word. However, part of the ethic also requires we protect humanity. It necessitates it, in the way it dictates whom we may kill. So we need a guideline within the laws to allow for individuals or groups to petition the Council for exceptions to the rule. The Council will then determine the risk and approve or disapprove of the proposal." Xavier's voice rose with excitement as he continued. His nervousness slipped away. "Let me give you an example. With slavery, I suggest we fund abolitionist societies throughout America. In exchange for my behaving and not using our powers against the peculiar institution, I expect we'll release a large amount of money to those organizations run by humans."

Xavier whirled around, looking at each of his friends to gauge their reaction. Catherine beamed at him, Thomas winked, and Harriet sat with her usual proper posture but nodded an assent his way. Which left Anthony, who would have shot down the entire notion under the old rules.

Instead, Anthony sat with a grin and also nodded. "May I?" Anthony asked Catherine. She laughed at his submission and urged him on. "I think this is wonderful. Yes, it makes sense. Of course. Let's do it! The entire plan. I think it's a wonderful idea."

"There are a few more things," Xavier continued. "I'm not sure how, but the practice of imprisoning vampires in the god-awful mountain chamber inside iron boxes has to stop. Or at least it needs to be a last resort for the worst of offenses. It's a relic from a past long gone. We have to do something else." Xavier turned again to Anthony, already knowing the others agreed with him.

Anthony nodded again. "Of course. I'll take your counsel on this issue."

Xavier detailed a few more minor things to change in the ethic and then explained how he and Catherine proposed to communicate much of it to the vampire world.

"Anthony," Catherine said and stood back up. "You indicated the Council's magic could communicate to all vampires. Does it still exist or was it another myth designed to scare us all into submission?"

Anthony chuckled. "No myth. It exists. The Council can get a message through magic to every vampire in mere seconds. For example, it sends out the ethic as a rule book to remind everyone of our laws."

"I hate when that thing appears," Thomas frowned.

"But I limited how often I sent it. I worried the more I exposed the work of the Council, the more I risked people figuring out my solo nature. It's also why I pretended we had to catch people in the act of defying the ethic, when in reality the magic informs the entire Council the moment someone violates it, and where."

Thomas shot Anthony a look of fierce anger but clenched his jaw without a word. Xavier, too, found that revelation stunning. It meant Anthony knew of Xavier's actions from the moment he converted Catherine, not because of a drawn-out investigation, and he could have located Xavier at any time."

As if sensing the questions, Anthony held his hand in the air. "I know what you're thinking. It was just... I didn't know how to handle it. I was buying time, because I loved and trusted you, Xavier. Because I had no issue with bringing Catherine over, despite your not seeking approval first. I'd never experienced such conflicting emotion."

Catherine pushed them past the awkward moment. "It's good to know. And thank you for the honesty." She smiled at Anthony, then clapped her hands together. "We'll send the revised ethic, including a way to contact the Council, in case anyone wants a hearing with us. Open communication is essential. No more mystery. The victims have the right to face us."

Anthony next shocked Xavier by announcing he would teach each of them the vampire magic in order for it to work, even insisting they begin the lessons very soon. He joined their plan with enthusiasm, offering his own recommendations for improvement, applauding their suggestions, and transforming from a one-man Council to the full Council with ease.

After they exhausted the proposed changes and Anthony employed the magic to revise a mystical copy of the ethic, the room grew quiet when Anthony bent over in front of them, convulsing in tears and inconsolable. Xavier leaned next to him and placed his hand on Anthony's back. Catherine, too, knelt beside him. When Harriet joined, Thomas alone remained in his seat.

Anthony released his emotion for a while before sitting up and looking at each of them. They sat in a circle on the floor, except for Thomas who hovered above them on the couch.

Forty-Four: Healing

21 JUNE 1822
New York City

After waiting for Anthony to recover, they gathered in a circle, with Thomas remaining on the couch, though Catherine scooted to the side to bring him into their midst. Xavier glanced up to measure Thomas's mood; his lover peered down and smiled but otherwise sat motionless, his lips pressed together, his brow furrowed. Xavier thought it best to wait for Anthony to speak first, and the others' silence indicated their agreement. Anthony straightened his posture, combed his hair back, and dried the blood tears that had streamed down his face. He smiled, as if embarrassed, and then took a deep breath.

"I'm sorry for my display." Anthony looked at the floor, his face turning sorrowful, his voice sounding sad.

Xavier reached over and touched Anthony on the arm. "Please, the members of the Council will need open and honest communication with one another. You always present yourself as so aloof and unemotional. Maybe it was time for you to open up."

Anthony nodded. "I suppose it was time. I have something to say to all of you."

Catherine urged Anthony on with a motion of her hand.

Though Anthony's commanding demeanor returned, his hands trembled as he began. "After the war, when I defeated the bastard, but he killed the entire Council, it took me weeks to recover. Actually months. Years. I went into hiding. I didn't speak with anyone, vampire or human, and mourned. I emerged to enforce the ethic for those who remained but for nothing else. I grieved for my lost lover and then for all the friends I lost. The ache is with me. Still powerful and harsh.

"But something else concerned me too. I told you I determined to maintain the illusion of the Council for the good of the vampires. I tried to think of something else to do, but nothing came to mind. I didn't trust anyone else, though those remaining either helped me in the end or had no idea about the conspiracy. I didn't trust anyone. Instead, I brooded. To feed, I chose the vilest of creatures and tortured them to release my rage."

As Anthony spoke, Xavier went over to join Thomas on the couch. Xavier could feel the eruption about to burst forth. Maybe he could stop it or at least soften the blow when it came.

Anthony lost himself in the story and either ignored Thomas or failed to notice. "I'm crying in relief. A little more mourning too. But mostly relief. That's all." He tossed his arms in the air and smiled as tears reappeared at the corners of his eyes. "It's been such a burden. I can't tell you how alone I've felt all these years. We're talking of *centuries* of doing this alone. Every decision, the weight of the world pressing down on my verdicts and actions. At times, I wanted to end it all and burn myself in the sun. But my sense of obligation wouldn't allow me that release."

Tears trickled down his cheeks. Catherine got up and handed Anthony a hanky and wiped at her own eyes before he continued.

"I can't thank you all enough. For doing this, agreeing to become a new Council. I'm humbled more than ever before."

Xavier slapped Thomas on the knee when he *humphed* next to him.

"I know." Anthony whipped his head around and stared at Thomas. "I know. I deserve much worse. The lies. The deceit. Each of you has to know I never wanted to deceive you. I never meant to hurt any of you. I didn't know what else to do. If anything, each of you saved me. My befriending of you, my love for each of you was always genuine. Always." Anthony stood and walked over to Thomas, sitting on the opposite side as Xavier but not touching Thomas. "You most of all. You're my dearest friend. Hurting you makes it all the worse to me. Anytime I thought of telling you, I was too afraid you'd reject me. Better to keep it to myself and maintain our friendship, I thought. I love you, Thomas." Anthony looked around the room at each of them. "I love you all. Can you forgive me?"

The room fell silent. Harriet got up, pulled Catherine with her, and went to Anthony. She leaned over and kissed him on the forehead, then grabbed his hand. "I understand. It's not easy for me, but I think I appreciate what you did, and why. I love you too." Then she reached down and hugged him.

When Harriet finished, Catherine said much the same thing, followed by Xavier.

"What about my imprisoning of you?" Anthony asked.

Xavier shook his head. "Perhaps it was God's will to bring about this transformation in the Council. I detested every minute of being in the box but never blamed you, even after I learned you were the entire Council. I did it to myself. I forgive you, though I'm not sure it's mine to give. You did what you thought was right, which is all any of us can ask of one another."

The room became quiet again as everyone waited for Thomas. The vein in his forehead pulsed with tension.

"Thomas?" Xavier asked. He squeezed Thomas's hand and wrinkled his forehead, a silent communication they often used when Xavier wanted him to keep his temper under control.

"This was a lovely little scene." Thomas sounded terse. "I wish I could join the festivities. But you were my best friend. I trusted you. All these years, all the experiences we shared together, and you never thought you could tell me?" Xavier thanked God for his vampiric strength, knowing it kept his hand from breaking as Thomas clutched it tighter and tighter. "I suppose that would hurt enough, but these last months—" Thomas shook his head. "You knew what I was going through as we looked for Xavier. You knew I'd do anything to help him. Why did you disregard me if you love me so much?"

"Because I thought it was my obligation." Anthony sounded more distraught and confused than Xavier had ever heard him. "I thought I had to, and because you always got so angry with the Council, I didn't think there was a chance you'd accept the truth and allow the Council to exist. I almost told you. I never knew how to approach it. When I took you to the prison, I wanted to tell you then. That's why I took you there. I thought you'd ask a million questions about why the Council allowed me to take you and reveal their secret. I thought you wouldn't rest about it and would force me to tell you the entire story. I would tell you all about Xavier. Where he was. What he was doing. That we could protect him. But then I figured you'd denounce any punishment, and I didn't have the courage to come out with the truth."

Anthony stopped, took a deep breath, and then snatched Thomas's hand out of his lap.

With Thomas's other hand in his, Xavier spoke before Thomas could say anything he might regret. "You haven't always been the easiest friend either. How many times did you trick Anthony? From the time he made you and you pretended to submit, to all the years he helped you with your anger, and then with finding me. We wouldn't be together without Anthony. Regardless of how you hurt, isn't it obvious he loves us? He loves you most of all? Forgive him. You don't ever have to agree with anything he did. Just find it in your heart to forgive him. He makes mistakes like the rest of us."

As Xavier spoke, he felt Thomas loosen his grip more and more. Blood tears appeared in Thomas's eyes. First, he stared at Xavier. "I was going to kill him. Do you understand? To save you."

Xavier engulfed Thomas in a hug. "It's over."

"Would you have let me kill you?" Thomas asked Anthony when he released Xavier but held him next to his side.

"I never thought about that. I'm sure you'll accuse me of more arrogance, but I assumed I would always win. And I'd never have let you die. I could have when you toppled into the pit, because a magic fire burns deep below. I doubt the spell from Malcolm could have protected you against that. I had no idea how our battle would end in there, but I wasn't going to let you die."

Thomas leaned back. "The lies hurt. I'm trying to heal and learning. About my anger, about how to control it. I mean, I'll never become 'Mister Stoic' like you."

Xavier smiled and then heard Catherine laugh from across the room. Even Anthony managed a weak grin.

"I get maddest when I'm hurt. To protect my feelings." Thomas surprised Xavier with his open communication in front of everyone. "Xavier taught me about myself during the revolution. These last couple of months, I was so infuriated about Xavier running off and the fact you were hunting for him in order to punish him. It was because I wanted to protect him. And now?" Thomas tossed his hands in the air. "Now? I'm angry because it feels like you betrayed our friendship for all these years. I love you so much."

Anthony leaned into Thomas and put his head on his shoulder. "You said it in the present tense."

"Yes, I love you. You're a complete ass at times. And self-righteous. I understand everything you said about obligation and all, but it also was a sort of divine behavior. Like you thought you were God. You have to promise to tone the act down, at least around us."

Xavier felt the tension drain out of his body. Anthony and Thomas continued to speak to one another. They talked about when they hurt each other, discussed why they never brought it up afterward, and in general mended their relationship.

Then Harriet and Catherine took their leave to hunt. When the conversation digressed into Anthony and Thomas once again bantering with one another, Xavier knew they had forgiven each other. He expected to still get an earful from Thomas when they were alone and knew the two had more nights ahead of processing their relationship. But they returned to being friends, which was more than Xavier expected when he first saw Thomas's anger earlier.

Forty-Five: The Council Formed

22 JUNE 1822
New York City

"We have time to talk." Thomas pulled Xavier away from everybody to an abandoned farm on the outskirts of New York. They each loved to hide in the hay of a barn and remember the time Thomas took Xavier out of Paris so Xavier could tell him he was ready to become a vampire.

"I figured that's why you brought me out here," Xavier answered. "What do you need to talk about?"

"Classic Xavier." Thomas chuckled and pulled Xavier into a tight embrace. "Always worried about everyone else, always ready to help us out with our problems, but never wanting to discuss his own."

Xavier smiled but kept up the game. "What do you mean?"

"What do I mean? I can't imagine." Thomas yanked him into the hay and started tickling him until Xavier screamed for him to stop. "Let's see, we woke up, and you made me talk about my feelings for Anthony. Once you were convinced I was coping, you had us go check on Anthony, and when he was fine, you checked on Catherine and Harriet. I suppose you were about to take us out to save the world when I brought you here instead. But you can't imagine what I might be alluding to?"

Xavier lay his head against Thomas's chest and laughed. "Maybe I know a little."

"A little?" Thomas kissed the top of Xavier's head and patted him. "I can feel the tension in your shoulders. I can sense the reserve in your actions, in even how you approach me. We didn't all go through hell over the last three months for you to come out the other side like nothing happened."

"I told you I was traumatized by the prison. I admitted it was much worse than what I would ever tell Anthony. But it *was* only a week. And I felt complete relief from it once I knew it would never happen to anyone ever again. It's like I had to suffer a small amount of time to make it better for everyone else."

"How about if you tell me what else is bothering you?"

Xavier played with a button on Thomas's coat. "I got all of those people killed in South Carolina. For every slave I managed to save while I was on the run, I killed another one because I urged Vesey and Gullah Jack into their insurrection."

"That's not true." Thomas held Xavier. "They may have succeeded or gotten to freedom had Anthony not interfered. He's just as guilty. And you didn't come here to free all the slaves. Freeing them was a residual effect, brought about by your feeling the guilt of all humanity. You came here to help your friend, Anne. And you did that. Everything you did with Malcolm and the slave plot was to help Anne by saving Duncan."

"That's what convinced me to join the Council and make the rules I did. Because there was nothing I could do. I could save one person, but as I did, another one in a different location was beaten to death. All the running around and trying to help people did little. You're right. I have to have *something* to feel guilty about."

Thomas laughed, and so did Xavier—at himself. Xavier sat in Thomas's arms for several minutes before his lover spoke again.

"Maybe you need to take all of those lessons about forgiveness and apply them to yourself. You made me forgive Anthony. And you helped Anthony forgive me. You're good at healing other people. Turn that sharp instinct onto yourself. You can't save the world, but you make the part of the world you touch a much brighter, happier place. Forgive yourself."

Xavier felt the weight of the world lift off his shoulders. The guilt still hovered at the back of his mind, but it didn't sting as much. They talked a while longer before making love.

"I'm hungry," Thomas said as he lay next to Xavier.

Xavier laughed hard. "You always want to feed after sex."

Thomas laughed, too. "Can we go hunt?"

"One more thing." Xavier took Thomas's hand in his and traced a finger along it. "You did a good job last night of controlling your temper. I'm proud of you."

Thomas chuckled. "Proud? I'm not sure you should be proud of my doing what normal people can handle on a daily basis."

"Stop it. We both know what happens when you feel hurt. And we both know how much you've changed. I think there's reason to celebrate any time you do such a good job."

"I tried." Thomas took a deep breath. "The entire time you were gone, I kept reminding myself what you would've said to calm me down, or of what you would want me to do."

Xavier clenched his teeth as his stomach churned in knots, one more thing on his mind. "Can you forgive me for running away? It was a terrible thing to do to you."

"It was terrible, I agree, but you aren't alone in having done awful things to one another."

Xavier looked up at Thomas, puzzled.

Thomas brushed a strand of hair out of Xavier's eye. "You're not the one who pummeled the other one and smashed his face into oblivion. I did that to you, during the French Revolution. I know you don't like to talk about that moment. It's the most unpleasant memory of my life. You found the means in yourself to forgive me, when I never deserved it. You never should have forgiven me. But you did. And because you did, I got better and we got together. So now you need my forgiveness? I don't agree.

"But if you need it, I'll grant it. I know what happened to you in your dreams. I know you see things, experience things, feel things, whatever you want to call it. Whether I believe it's happening or in your head doesn't matter. I trust you, and I trust your instinct. You were right. I never would have let you go on your fool quest if I had anything to say about it. I would never let you put yourself in harm's way. So I'll forgive you for your peace of mind on one condition."

"Which is?"

"That you never, ever do it again. I'll trust you from here on out. But never abandon me again."

"I already promised I wouldn't."

Their light mood turned heavy when Thomas grabbed hold of Xavier and nuzzled his face in Xavier's hair. Xavier could hear Thomas crying. "I don't want to live without you. I can't. Speaking of forgiveness, I would *never* forgive myself if you ran away again because you couldn't trust me and then something happened to you. *Never*."

Xavier turned over and pulled Thomas into a deep and passionate kiss.

"We've never talked about that night in Paris during the revolution."

Thomas grinned. "Because you still can't say it. I hit you."

"You won't admit it wasn't all your fault."

"And I never will. This is one argument you'll never win. Regardless of what you do or how angry I become, there's never an excuse for violence. Your forgiveness means the world to me. That I can live with what I did is a relief. But I will never forget what I did because it reminds me every day to be a better lover and vampire."

"Your insecurity prompted the anger." Xavier twisted a strand of Thomas's long, black hair in his fingers. "I had to find the ability to nurture you out of it after I healed myself. I wasn't ready soon enough."

"It's interesting we've never talked about this before," Thomas said. "It means a lot we've come this far."

Xavier could think of no response, so he pulled Thomas back into a passionate kiss. They made love in the hay, again. Thomas's fingers lingered over every inch of Xavier, and when he turned Xavier on his side and entered him, it felt like the first time all over.

Finished, they headed back toward the city and their coffin hidden in the house Anthony had purchased. Along the way, they fed on a couple of vagrants and left their bodies for the rats to eat. Xavier fell asleep in Thomas's arms, feeling safer than he ever had in his entire life.

Forty-Six: The Council's Book

23 JUNE 1822
New York City

"We need to hurry, or we'll be late." Xavier tugged at Thomas, who stood amused as he watched two young men have anal sex in the alley, oblivious to the vampire voyeurs.

"Doesn't that make you want to join them?" Thomas reached over and grabbed Xavier's crotch. "Apparently it does."

Xavier slapped Thomas's hand away. "We don't have time for this. Come on. We were supposed to meet Anthony, Catherine, and Harriet an hour ago."

"You could call them the Council. It'd be easier." Thomas started to follow Xavier.

"I'm getting used to it."

They got to the house and found everyone assembled in the living room.

"We almost thought you'd backed out," Anthony said when they got inside. "Especially you." He pointed his finger at Thomas. "All your talk for all those years about the aloof and hidden Council and how impossible it was to meet with them. But here we have our first declared meeting, and who doesn't show up on time? The aloof and hidden Thomas."

Thomas rolled his eyes and kept from grinning, though it was difficult with Catherine and Harriet sitting across the room, laughing at Anthony's antics.

"You shouldn't encourage him," Thomas told them. "He isn't as funny as he thinks. And it will make him believe he's still in charge."

Anthony held up his hands. "No one is in charge. That's one of the things I love about our creation. I don't have to be responsible for you, because Xavier accepted that duty."

"Someone will need to reign him in when he goes on a rant about the Council. He'll no doubt forget from time to time he's on it." Xavier grinned at Thomas as he spoke.

"Well, you bring up one thing I think the Council should consider." Thomas stood next to Anthony. "Are all of you serious about having *me* on the Council? Me? I'm happy to oblige. I just think you're forgetting what I've said about the Council over the years and how I've felt about it."

"Well, you *are* a hypocrite, but we already knew that," Anthony shot at Thomas.

Thomas failed to contain himself and laughed. "You think I was kidding, I know. Maybe to an extent. But seriously. Think about how I've felt about these rules and this body for all those years. And now I'm supposed to parade onto it as if it's normal. It's ludicrous!"

Anthony placed both hands on Thomas's shoulders and became serious. "It's not. Yours is the voice we need. The cynic. The one who thought the Council went too far. The one who wanted it to open up. We need leadership from you."

"So you won't mind when I refer to you as an asshole at the meetings?"

Xavier laughed out loud, followed by everyone else.

"As much as I'm enjoying the show," Harriet stood and addressed them, "I believe we have official business for tonight?"

"Right. Let's get to it." Catherine pulled out a bound book and held it out to everyone. "Here it is."

Anthony took it from her and went to the center of the room. "We're ready then. Everyone is in agreement with the new ethic? The Council is unanimous?"

All agreed, and then the room fell silent as Anthony began chanting in his mystical language Xavier had only heard him use a couple of times. The book levitated off the floor and encased itself in an orange ball glowing before them. With a few more words, the book spun around and disappeared, to reappear a few moments later, hovering in front of each of them. As they took hold of it, the orange orb disappeared and the volume remained in their hands.

"There," Anthony said. "We each have our own copy. And every vampire on earth now has one as well."

"Just like that?" Catherine asked.

Anthony nodded. "Just like that."

"Then our work is done for the night. We're free to go." Thomas started toward the door. "I was watching a scene I hope is continuing when I get back."

Xavier shot Thomas a look and smirked.

"One more thing." Anthony stopped them and looked at everyone. "Tomorrow night we begin the lessons about vampire magic. We can't be a Council unless all of you know how to do it. The alerts about ethic breakers may start coming to you tonight. You'll need to learn everything, in particular the capturing and incapacitating of other vampires. It will take at least a week."

Thomas turned and bowed before Anthony. "Yes, Your Majesty. We already agreed. You can still be in charge until we finish those lessons. Then I'm going to incapacitate *you!*"

Anthony shooed him out the door, Xavier following Thomas.

Thomas did head back to the alley but the men had gone. Instead, Thomas grabbed Xavier from behind and kissed his ear. His hands ran down the front of Xavier's chest to his pants and then started unbuttoning them.

"Not here!" Xavier was hard but embarrassed at the same time.

"Yes, here." Thomas kissed him harder, and before Xavier knew it, they were making love right in the alley. He came all over the brick wall and then yanked his pants up. "You're unbelievable."

"But you liked it." Thomas tapped Xavier on the nose.

"That's beside the point."

Forty-Seven: Ghostly Visitors

23 JUNE 1822
New York City

Xavier snuggled next to Thomas as he drifted to sleep, content. He started to adjust to the idea of being on the Council, though the weight of the responsibility hit him full force earlier when they sent the revised ethic out to all vampires.

At first, he wondered if he had fallen asleep. He could feel Thomas lying next to him, his arms wrapped around Thomas's rock solid chest. Yet he thought his eyes were open and knew the sun shined outside.

Without seeming to move, he stood in their room, looking around. The room swirled and then transformed into a cloud of white all around him as the walls, furniture, and the entire building disappeared. Xavier stepped forward and felt solid ground beneath him, though everything else looked surreal.

Michel stepped before him, laughing when Xavier jumped in fright. "My little brother, always the jumpy one. Even as a vampire?"

"This isn't a normal situation." Xavier reached out to touch Michel to reassure himself once again he stood before his long dead brother.

"I'm real." Michel reached out and pulled Xavier into a hug. "You did well. You always do. And one day I hope you'll forgive yourself and trust in your goodness."

Though less assured than Michel about his goodness, Xavier smiled. "I have something for you." Xavier held up Michel's medal. "Thank you. It gave me strength. And a bit of your courage." He attached it to Michel's uniform and then patted his chest.

Michel nodded. "Say hello to Catherine. I'm watching over you both."

Before Xavier could respond, Michel disappeared and out of the cloud came an enormous figure. Gigantic wings spread from behind his back as St. Michel charged into the white space with a golden ray of blinding light surrounding him. As always, he held his sword high in the air. A stern countenance on his face masked the beauty of his body, the muscles strong and enticing.

Xavier bowed before him, afraid.

"Stand, loyal one."

Xavier obeyed.

"You have done well, and I am pleased." Michel extended his hand and tapped Xavier on the top of the head with his sword. Xavier tried to ask him a question, but everything went black and then he felt his entire body shaking.

"Xavier, get up. You're dreaming. The sun's been down for a while. You're safe."

When Xavier's eyes opened, he saw Thomas staring down at him from outside the coffin with concern.

"Another dream?" Thomas asked.

"Perhaps."

"Meaning?" Thomas yanked Xavier out of the coffin and hugged him. "Talk to me."

Xavier rubbed his face in his hands and then ran his fingers through his hair, trying to gain a better perspective on reality. He stopped and felt the top of his head again. "It's gone."

"What's gone?" Thomas grabbed him by the shoulders, looking at Xavier as if he had gone insane. "Are you going to explain this to me? What's gone?"

"The bald spot. Remember? From St. Michel? It's gone. He healed it."

"What are you talking about?"

Xavier grabbed Thomas's hand and took his finger, then reached on top of his head and rubbed it where the bald spot used to be. "Remember? After he came to me in my dream with the fire? And burned my head?"

Thomas nodded. "Yes."

"Well, it's gone."

Thomas reached up and felt all over Xavier's head. "How?"

"My brother came to me last night. Followed by St. Michel, who healed my head and said he was pleased with me."

Thomas frowned at Xavier. "He didn't send you on another quest, did he?"

Xavier laughed. "No. Just back to you."

About the Author

Damian Serbu lives in the Chicago area with his husband and two dogs, Akasha and Chewbacca. The dogs control his life, tell him what to write, and threaten to eat him in the middle of the night if he disobeys. He has published The Vampire's Angel, The Vampire's Protégé, Santa's Kinky Elf, Simon and Santa is a Vampire with NineStar Press. Keep up to date with him on Facebook, Twitter, or at www.DamianSerbu.com.

Facebook: www.facebook.com/Damian-Serbu

Twitter: @damianserbu

Website: www.damianserbu.com

Other books by this author

The Vampire's Angel
The Vampire's Protégé

"Professor Ghost" within *Teacher's Pet, Volume One*

Santa's Kinky Elf Simon
Santa is a Vampire

Also Available from NineStar Press

Connect with NineStar Press

Website: NineStarPress.com

Facebook: NineStarPress

Facebook Reader Group: NineStarNiche

Twitter: @ninestarpress

Tumblr: NineStarPress